HaPPY reading!

Dania Voss

DANIA VOSS

EVERNIGHT PUBLISHING ®

www.evernightpublishing.com

Copyright© 2018

Dania Voss

Editor: Audrey Bobak

Cover Artist: Jay Aheer

ISBN: 978-1-77339-670-5

ALL RIGHTS RESERVED

DANIA VOSS

DEDICATION

I want to thank Stacey and everyone at Evernight Publishing for taking a chance on me. It's quite an amazing feeling to have my dream of becoming a published author come true. I'm incredibly proud to be a member of the Evernight family.

I'd also like to thank my husband for his encouragement, support, and occasional well-meaning nagging in getting On the Ropes written at long last. Mr. Voss is my biggest fan and I'm so lucky to have him in my corner.

Many thanks to all of the readers for taking a chance on me as well. Luke and Abbey's story was truly a labor of love for me. I hope you decide to stay with me for future escapades featuring the Windy City Nights crew, the cast from Envy and Rapture Texas and the sexy exploits at Club Envidious and the Twisted Tea Society.

Here's to living naughtily ever after...

Dania

DANIA VOSS

ON THE ROPES

Windy City Nights, prequel

Dania Voss

Copyright © 2018

Chapter One

Luke "Strike 'em Out" Stryker sat quietly in the back of the stretch limousine in the Grace of God Lutheran Church parking lot in Elmhurst, Illinois, with his good friend and part-time bodyguard Rocco Moretti, his "summons" in hand. Even with the shit storm that had just become his life, he couldn't help but smile as he reread the top secret note.

Top Secret
June 24, 2017
Mission: Tyler Project
Agent: Luke "Strike 'Em Out" Stryker
You have been selected due to your very particular set of skills: skills that you have acquired over the years.
If you accept this mission now, that will be the end of it. I will not look for you, I will not pursue you. But if you don't, I will look for you, I will find you, and you will be taken.
Will you be my best man?
Job Description: Remind me again why I love my

Bridezilla; make sure my in-laws behave; keep our childhood stories to yourself (I mean it, Luke); last and most importantly, hand me a beer before, during, and after the ceremony.

Luke tucked the mission note in his jeans pocket and scanned the parking lot. "You think we were followed?" he asked Rocco.

Rocco did a visual sweep of the parking lot, the former Marine not missing a thing. "Doesn't look like it."

Luke put on his sunglasses, grabbed his black garment bag, and a cooler with his best friend's favorite beer, and made to exit the limo. He glanced over his shoulder to Rocco before stepping out. "You sure you won't go up in flames, this being a Lutheran church and all?" he asked and chuckled.

"I guess we'll find out, asshole." Rocco scanned the parking lot one more time. "Looks like the paparazzi found you after all, dude."

Luke felt his blood pressure rise. He turned and looked out the back window only to see a couple of florist vans pull up and he sighed in relief. "Dick. I don't want any bullshit today. Today is about Jake and Cassie." The last thing any of them needed was the damn paparazzi fucking up what should be the happiest day of their lives. Luke had hired an entire security detail to make sure of it, with Rocco in charge.

Due to his game schedule with the Chicago Cobras, Luke hadn't been able to carry out his best man duties as he would have liked. He knew Jake understood. Luke had been pitching for the Chicago Cobras, which his Uncle Darren owned, for the past ten years. The one thing Luke could and would do was make sure his notoriety didn't ruin the day.

"That's what you get for Catholic jokes." Rocco motioned for Luke to get out of the limo as he followed close behind.

Luke stepped out into the warm June afternoon, the limo driver taking the cooler from him. "Beautiful day for a wedding, sir," he commented.

Luke raised his face to the sun, warmth filling him for the first time since his life took a U-turn two days ago. His right shoulder, his pitching shoulder, ached and throbbed, another not-so-subtle reminder of the major changes that lie ahead.

"It sure is, Ernie. A perfect day." Luke smiled at his uncle's long-time driver and friend of the family. He'd known Ernie nearly all his life. He was more like an uncle than an employee. In his mid-sixties now, Ernie was still as friendly, helpful, and loyal as he'd ever been. The years had been kind to him. "It wasn't so long ago you were walking your little girl down the aisle, was it?"

Ernie beamed. His only child Michelle had gotten married less than two years ago. Luke had been in Houston pitching against the Astros and wasn't able to attend. Michelle's wedding had been one of many events he'd missed over the years due to his baseball schedule.

That's not going to be an issue anymore. I'm going to have a lot of time on my hands now.

Ernie leaned in close like he had a secret to share with Luke. "I'm gonna be a grandpa soon," he whispered.

Luke smiled and whispered back. "That's wonderful, Ernie, congratulations. Why are whispering?"

Ernie waved a hand dismissively. "Just me being silly. It's not really a secret anymore. Michelle just finished her first trimester. We didn't want to say anything since she miscarried eight months ago. Her doctor says she and the baby are doing great though.

What a relief."

Luke stilled. Michelle miscarried? Shit, he hadn't heard. Michelle was as kind as her father. It must have been heartbreaking for her. Hell, for the entire family. He'd call her after the wedding weekend was over, and after what he assumed would be the upcoming press conference, which would take place Monday or Tuesday of the following week.

"Congratulations again, Ernie. I'm sure you're thrilled. First grandchild, huh?" Luke one-armed hugged the man with his shoulder aching like hell. Time for more pain meds. The over-the-counter kind. He took no chances with anything stronger than absolutely necessary. There was too much going on to worry about his shoulder right now.

"Yes, sir. First of hopefully a few!" Ernie laughed and gave Luke the beer cooler. The weight of the cooler didn't bother his shoulder too much. Thank God. He needed to get through the day without calling too much attention to himself, more specifically to his shoulder.

He and Ernie turned to see Rocco a few feet away on his cell phone, waving his free hand around as his spoke, a serious expression on his face. "Must be that Italian thing," Luke joked. He and Ernie laughed and Rocco gave them both the finger.

"Security detail is here." Rocco ended his call and did another quick scan of the church parking lot. "Go on inside, Luke, and we'll take care of everything out here."

"Great, thanks, man. Ernie, you'll take care of decorating the limo for Jake and Cassie?"

"Of course! I've got everything in the trunk ready to go. Don't you worry about that. Go on, get inside and get ready. Tell Jake I said good luck. I'll see you later in church." Ernie shut the limo passenger door, got in the driver's side door, and drove to the front of the church to decorate the car.

Rocco was already gone when Luke turned to him after Ernie drove off.

Guess that's my cue. Time to get this show on the road.

Luke made his way inside one of the back church entrance doors, not sure where to go. He'd missed the wedding rehearsal because of, well—everything that was going down. Fuck! Was it supposed to be so quiet back here? He looked down the hall to his right and then heard the click clack of heels to his left.

Coming toward him at a brisk pace was a pretty, dark-haired woman. If he had to guess, she was in her mid-thirties, wearing a navy-blue pantsuit, with a clipboard in one hand and large black travel bag in the other. She touched her ear and nodded. "Are you Luke Stryker?"

Not wanting to be unkind to a fan he smiled his famous dimpled smile. "Yes, that's me." It was then he noticed her earpiece.

"Okay, I've got him," she said into her earpiece. She looked at him, disapproval in her dark-brown eyes. "They thought you might get lost. Thanks for being on time at least." She shoved the travel bag strap to her elbow, grabbed the beer cooler, and began power walking down the hallway to Luke's right.

"Hey! That's for the groom! It's part of my mission! Give that back!" Luke chased after the pantsuit woman and Jake's beer, unable to take his time and admire the beautiful stained-glass windows that graced the walls of what he assumed was the office area of the church building.

Pantsuit woman stopped at a doorway and turned toward him. "I know, Luke, I'm taking you to Jake." She opened a door and Luke walked through to a large room with a dark mahogany desk and matching bookcases with a variety of what looked like religious and philosophical texts. A cross was on one wall, along with religious paintings arranged on most of the other walls in the room. An eight-foot folding table had been placed against one wall, a small box with flowers set on top. Boutonnieres, Luke guessed. Two black garment bags, like his, also lay on top of the table. There was a full-length mirror hanging on another door at the back of the room. What Luke didn't see were Jake or his other good friend and groomsman Heath Jackson.

Luke was about to ask about Jake and Heath when they entered the room through the mirrored door, both in jeans and t-shirts. They saw him and smiled.

Luke laid his garment bag on the table with the others and went to greet his friends. God, it was good to see them.

I'll be able to see them any time I want from now on. Everything's going to be all right.

Jake hugged Luke tight, clapping him on the back a little too close to his aching shoulder, and he winced. Jake stood back, concern in his dark-brown gaze. Heath stepped up, raising his hand to Luke's shoulder, then seeming to change his mind, pulled it away. Pantsuit woman who had been talking on her earpiece frowned and walked over.

"What's wrong, Luke?" She placed her hand lightly on his aching, throbbing shoulder.

"Yeah, man, what's wrong?" Jake asked.

Luke wasn't ready for this. He wasn't ready for everything to change. And he didn't want to burden his friend on his wedding day. He was so stupid to think he could keep it all under wraps until after the wedding.

"You don't have to worry about Hannah. She signed an NDA," Heath informed him.

"Actually, our company has a standing NDA with the Chicago Cobras and since you're a player, that NDA applies as well," Hannah added.

Luke was confused, who *was* pantsuit woman—Hannah? "Should I know you?"

Hannah chuckled. "You should, but you probably know or have seen my mother Patty Hailey. She owns Hailey's Events. Her company, with my help of course, has organized all the team's events for the last fifteen years. I take after my father's side of the family. Mom and I look little alike."

He knew Patty Hailey and Hannah was right, they didn't look very much alike. Patty was taller with dark-blonde hair and blue eyes, and Hannah was shorter with dark-brown hair and eyes. Hailey's Events was *the* event planner in Chicago and why his Uncle Darren had booked them for Jake and Cassie's wedding as soon as they had set their wedding date a year ago. Events planned by Hailey's always went off without a hitch, or so they made it seem. Luke beat his uncle to it and booked the honeymoon suite at the Fairchild Hotel in Oak Brook for the happy couple and a block of rooms for the family.

Luke removed his sunglasses and tossed them on the table. He rubbed his eyes and sighed. "Just promise me you won't let this interfere with your day, okay?" The day had to be about Jake and Cassie, not Luke's issues. He wouldn't settle for anything less.

"I promise, Luke. I know it's my wedding day, but that doesn't mean I don't care about anything or anyone else. Just tell us what the hell is going on. Obviously you're hurt. Your pitching arm for fuck's sake. Oh, um … sorry, Hannah." Jake turned to Hannah, apparently embarrassed for cursing in front of her.

Hannah, in all her professional glory, waved Jake

off. "Please, working with the Chicago Cobras all these years, you don't think I've heard my fair share of swearing?"

Heath chimed in. "Don't I know it. The Cobras have some mouths on them and that's saying something as a former Marine."

Luke sighed. *Just get it over with.* "Wednesday night I got into a motorcycle accident. That's why I didn't make it Thursday to rehearsal, dinner, and your combined bachelor slash bachelorette party. I was in the hospital."

Jake threw his hands up in frustration. "What the hell, Luke? Why didn't you tell me that when you called to say you couldn't make it?"

"Because, dammit, I was trying to keep the focus on you and Cassie."

Heath shook his head, a confused expression on his face. "I don't understand. You're always so careful. Were you wearing a helmet?"

Luke nodded. "Of course. It was late, I was going down 294 South. I was distracted. I didn't see the dead—whatever it was until it was too late and I wasn't able to veer around it like I should have, and shit, I sailed through the air and landed hard on my shoulder."

"Distracted by what?" Jake and Hannah asked.

Luke smiled because his other mission, long overdue, was the most important of his life. "My other mission."

Now Hannah looked confused, but it didn't matter. Luke shared a knowing glance with Jake and Heath. It was on. Fuck his shoulder.

"Abbey," the three of them said.

"It's about fucking time," Jake and Heath added.

Chapter Two

Abigail Jayne, or Abbey as her friends called her, looked out the window of the honeymoon suite of the Fairchild Hotel, courtesy of Luke Stryker. The room faced the Oak Brook Mall but she wasn't paying much attention. Her attention was on other things. Too many other things. Like having to face Luke after ten years, for starters. Shit. What a nightmare this day would be.

Abbey sighed, tightened the belt of her fluffy white hotel robe, also courtesy of Luke, and turned to see her sister Cassie, seated in one of the suite's luxurious, stuffed, beige chairs as her hair was being styled in an elegant up 'do by the Bennett sisters Vanessa and Angela, or Angel as everyone called her.

Beautiful blondes like Cassie, Vanessa and Angel effortlessly worked on her sister's hair. Their friends, Madison Roth, a stylish brunette, and Roxanna Gibbons, a sexy redhead with the most stunning green eyes Abbey had ever seen, would do her and Jake's sister Leah's hair and makeup.

Abbey managed a smile. Angel was a member of the Kiss Army, proudly wearing a Kiss t-shirt as she worked on Cassie's hair. She had asked if it was all right to play some Kiss songs while the got ready. Abbey had thought it would be weird, but it turned out weird was actually fun. Kiss playing in the background was just the distraction she needed.

Roxanna and Madison each set up a chair next to the long dining room table, along with their makeup and hair supplies, and motioned to her and Leah. Leah and Abbey both took their seats.

"Thank you guys for getting us ready today, we

really appreciate it," Cassie said as Angel and Vanessa finished up with her hair and started on her makeup.

"Yes, thank you so much. I'm not much of a makeup girl," Abbey admitted.

"It's our pleasure." Angel answered for the four stylists. "You and Cassie have been hair clients of mine for what—seven years now?"

"Wow, it has been that long." Abbey couldn't believe it. The years just rolled on, whether or not she wanted them to. Whether she was happy or sad. In love or heartbroken.

Don't think about Luke. He betrayed you. He's moved on and so should you. Get over him already.

"Speaking of being clients for so long, what about that salon you wanted to open? I have no problem going to Essential Beauty for appointments, but I thought the four of you were looking to branch out on your own," Cassie said and took a long sip of orange juice.

That was odd. The rest of the group had been sipping on mimosas and snacking on delectable pastries, but Cassie had stuck with straight orange juice. And come to think of it, she hadn't seen Cassie drink any alcohol during rehearsal dinner and the combined bachelor slash bachelorette party Thursday night. Not that Cassie was a big drinker, but she and Luke indulged in their favorite—Samuel Adams Boston Lager. Abbey chalked it up to wedding jitters. Lord knew she was jittery, although for different reasons. Luke wasn't the only thing she needed distraction from.

Vanessa, Roxanna, and Madison turned to Angel. Angel took a brush to Cassie's eyebrow. "Actually, I'll be finishing up my MBA soon and I've got our business plan completed. So after graduation I think we'll be ready to make something happen. Right, guys?" Angel turned back to Vanessa, Roxanna, and Madison for confirmation.

"We're ready when you are," Madison said, and Roxanna nodded her head in agreement, with Vanessa not nearly as enthusiastic, but nodding as well.

"You're still going with that beautiful name, Ullustra Salon and Day Spa?" Abbey asked.

"Yes, that's the one. I just love it! And I can't wait. This salon has been a dream of mine, well, of ours, for a long time," Angel said as she and Vanessa started on Cassie's makeup.

Abbey turned to Roxanna, lifting her chin and closing her eyes. "I'm ready. I decided I'm going to wear my hair down." And that had nothing to do with Luke liking her hair down. No, she preferred her hair down. Screw Luke and what he preferred. He was probably bringing his girlfriend, Hollywood It girl and chestnut-haired bombshell Brenna Sinclair. He wouldn't notice if Abbey's hair were on fire so her hair and makeup for the day were for her and no one else. That was what she told herself, anyway.

"Brenna Sinclair's not attending, Abbey," Cassie said. Had she said Brenna's name out loud? Damn.

Roxanna stopped working on her makeup for a second. "*The* Brenna Sinclair? She's dating Luke Stryker from the Cobras, isn't she?"

No, no, no. Abbey didn't want to get into this right now, or ever. Brenna not attending Cassie's wedding meant nothing. She was probably on location somewhere across the world and couldn't be bothered with some commoner's wedding. Luke was undoubtedly with her Thursday night instead of taking his best man responsibilities seriously and attending the rehearsal, dinner, and Cassie and Jake's bachelor slash bachelorette party.

"Yes, but Abbey had him first, and he's the best

man," Cassie teased.

Abbey needed to put a stop to this conversation. "First of all, I didn't *have* him. We dated when we were younger. I was eighteen, and he was twenty when he won his first World Series championship. How did he want to celebrate? By cheating on me with some bleached-out blonde, fake-boobed bimbo, that's how. Secondly, he's been dating Brenna Sinclair for the last three years. We ended things ten years ago. He's moved on. I've moved on. End of story and no big deal." There, that should shut everyone up. Except now she felt sick to her stomach. When would she get over him? Wasn't ten years enough time?

Leah and the four stylists remained quiet, but Cassie wouldn't let it go. "I call bullshit. I know Luke. He'd never cheat on you. He adored you, Abbs. He still does."

Abbey's hands clenched in her lap, her anger boiling over. "Well, you didn't walk in on him and that skank naked and drunk in their hotel room, I did. So, so … bullshit back at you!" Her ears rung. She was lightheaded and panting.

Roxanna kneeled down and took Abbey's hands in hers, unclenching them. "Slow breaths Abbey, it's all right."

Cassie came rushing over and Roxanna moved aside, allowing Cassie to take her place. Cassie rubbed Abbey's arms, trying to calm her down. Abbey took deep breaths, slowly regaining her composure. She was ruining everything. This was Cassie's special day and she was having a meltdown. She felt a tear run down her cheek. She was hopeless.

"I'm so sorry, Abbs. If you say he cheated on you, that's that. If you say it's over, it's over. I won't bring it up again."

Abbey looked up at her sister, so beautiful and composed. She was actually glowing. Jake would be floored when Cassie made her way down the aisle to him later that afternoon. "I'm sorry, too. I didn't mean to overreact, but I don't need to relive that horrible day, all right? I thought Luke and I had what you and Jake do, but I was wrong."

Abbey continued before Cassie could respond. "And that's okay. We were young, his major league career was just getting started. It was wishful thinking on my part to believe we had a future together. He went on to become an MLB superstar and I didn't do too shabby myself, right? A BS in Computer Science and an MBA. A ten-year stint at Office Supply Galaxy. I'm pretty awesome, I'd say."

Abbey made sure she didn't mention she'd gotten laid off on Wednesday, just as she was getting ready to leave the office for the day. She had put in for vacation time on Thursday and Friday for the wedding. She had been asked by her new manager, who she couldn't stand, to a small conference room where a HR representative was sitting at the conference table with a stack of termination paperwork waiting for her.

She had been taken completely by surprise, although she should haven't been. Her manager Tim Webber was an arrogant, know-it-all blow hard. He'd only been with Office Supply Galaxy for three months but he acted as if owned the place, or at least the IT department. He hired a couple of guys from his previous company two weeks after starting, so Abbey suspected he wanted to bring on another one of *his* people and needed to get her out of the way and use her vacant position to do it.

Abbey was shown a document indicating over fifty additional people were being let go and that her responsibilities and skill set were no longer needed. She had almost laughed at Tim when he told her that since she was the only person at the company who administered and engineered the software system she managed.

When Tim finally shut the hell up and left the conference room, the HR rep had reviewed the termination paperwork with her. At least she was given six-month severance and three months of paid health insurance. That took some pressure off. Abbey hadn't been allowed back to her desk. A company security guard brought her purse and escorted her to her car, like she was a criminal. She was due back at the office Monday evening to meet with the HR rep and collect her personal belongings from her cubicle so it wouldn't be a distraction to the other employees.

Cassie stood up, holding Abbey's hands. She looked at other women in the room with pride on her face. "I'd say you rock, Abbey. Not only did my little sister get her BS in Computer Science and her MBA but she did it on OSG's dime, fully paid for through their tuition reimbursement program, no student loan debt. And she did it while working full time."

"Good for you!"

"That's amazing!"

"I agree, you rock, Abbey!"

Abbey felt herself blush. "All right, everyone, yes, I'm amazing. But today's about you Cassie, not me." She giggled and hugged her sister tight. "Thanks. I love you."

Abbey stood back, looking Cassie over. She was absolutely radiant. She couldn't wait to see her in her wedding dress. "Angel, Vanessa, you did a great job with Cassie's hair and makeup. She looks like a princess."

Vanessa came forward and looked Cassie over.

"We didn't really do very much with the makeup, not that we're heavy handed with it. Cassie just has a natural glow."

Cassie squeezed Abbey's hands, a huge grin on her lovely face. Cassie looked in the eyes and whispered, "I'm pregnant. That might have something to do with my natural glow."

The room erupted into squeals. Leah rushed to their side and the three of them ended up in a group hug. "Oh my God, we're going to be aunties!" Leah exclaimed.

"Shhh, you're the only ones I've told other than Jake. I told him he could tell the guys as long as no one says anything."

Abbey noticed Vanessa and Roxanna had concerned expressions on their faces. They both came closer and both said, "How far along are you?"

Cassie beamed. "Eight weeks."

Vanessa and Roxanna shared a knowing look and Roxanna spoke up. "You really shouldn't say anything until you reach the third trimester, you know."

"I don't mean to be a downer, but I miscarried twice. Once at six weeks and then again at ten," Vanessa added.

Angel and Madison came over to the group. Angel put a supportive arm around her sister Vanessa's shoulder. "Yes, and now you have two amazing little boys, don't you?"

Vanessa smiled at her sister. "I sure do."

"I know I shouldn't have said anything, but I'm so excited. And the wedding is today. I just couldn't keep the news to myself. And I know there's a risk, but Jake and I will handle it. It'll be all right, regardless. Just promise you won't say anything, please?" Cassie looked to the group of women around her, a pleading expression on her lovely face.

Abbey gave Cassie a quick hug. "We won't say a word. Right, ladies?"

"Right!"

"Okay then, that's settled. Now for some raspberry pastry before I get dressed." Cassie scanned the dining room table for a savory raspberry treat and filled a glass with orange juice. "We better finish getting ready. Patty Hailey, the photographer, and videographer will be here soon."

That got everyone's attention. Patty Hailey owned *the* premiere Chicago event planning company Hailey's Events. Luke's Uncle Darren had booked them for Cassie and Jake immediately after they chose their wedding date.

Abbey and Leah quickly took their seats with Roxanna and Madison at the ready. "Cass, would you mind if Madison did an up 'do for me? I really want to impress today," Leah said.

Cassie swallowed a mouthful of pastry and dabbed her lips with a napkin. "Of course not. I want you and Abbey to feel beautiful today too."

Abbey smiled, knowing who Leah wanted to impress. Poor Leah. She'd been in love with Heath Jackson all her life. The sexy, blond-haired, hazel-eyed mountain of man and former Marine was one of Jake's closest friends and a groomsman. Heath had been Leah's second next-door neighbor growing up. Unfortunately for Leah, Heath was ten years older than she was and regarded her as more of a pesky little sister than a potential love match. At twenty-five, Leah wasn't a child, but Heath hadn't seemed to notice. Maybe today Leah would make sure he did. Abbey didn't envy Heath. When Leah put her mind to something, she went after it with gusto.

"This need to impress wouldn't have anything to do with a certain sexy, blond-haired, tattooed Marine, who's also a groomsman, would it?" Abbey teased.

"Oh, do tell," Madison said as she worked on Leah's hair.

"Absolutely. I want to hear this," Roxanna added.

Leah sighed and seemed to take a minute to organize her thoughts. "Well, the short version is he's one of Jake's good friends, and his family lived in the next house over to us in Elmhurst. I've known him all my life. Loved him all my life, actually. He's ten years older than I am, not that it should make a difference, and it doesn't to me. But to Heath, I'm just his friend's annoying little sister. And yes, when I was younger, I probably was annoying. But I'm twenty-five now, a grown woman, most definitely *not annoying*. Hell, I even work for the Cobras in the finance department with him although he's not my direct manager. We're perfect for each other. He's just a stubborn jerk and won't give us a chance."

Cassie returned to her seat so Angel and Vanessa could touch up her makeup before she got dressed. "Jake says he's changed a little since returning from Afghanistan. And I don't mean from his hearing loss."

Heath had returned from Afghanistan six years ago, injured after IEDs, improvised explosive devices, exploded during one of their missions. He'd lost two men in his unit with several others sustaining severe injuries, including Heath who had lost seventy percent of his hearing as a result of being so close to the blasts.

Physically, Heath had healed from his injuries, with Luke replacing the clunky, outdated hearing aids the VA provided him with a state-of-the-art tiny pair that were barely visible and provided much better sound. Emotionally though, Abbey suspected Heath still suffered. Maybe Leah could help her wounded warrior. Abbey hoped so because she agreed with Leah. If Heath was willing to give them a chance, he and Leah could be happy together.

Leah frowned, nodding her head in agreement. "I know that. I know war changes you. But that doesn't mean you can't be happy. Once Luke replaced Heath's hearing aids, he went to college using his VA education benefits and got his finance degree and MBA, and now he manages the Finance department for the Cobras. He turned a bad situation around. He should be proud of himself. I am."

Madison finished up with Leah's hair, adjusting wisps on each side of her face. "Leah, if he lost members of his unit, he's probably feeling survivor's guilt. I know how that feels. My husband passed away a year ago. And although I know in my head I should move on and not feel guilty for being alive and try to be happy like I know my late husband would want me to, my heart says something different. Don't be so hard on Heath is all I'm saying."

Leah nodded and took a hold of Madison's hands, squeezing tight. "I'm so sorry, Madison. And I'll try to go easy on Heath, but I will not take no for an answer. I believe my love can help him if he would just give me a chance."

Madison smiled back at Leah. "I think all the women in this room know the love of a good woman can make even the most stubborn, jerky men come around. You, my dear, are ready to get dressed." Madison handed a Leah a hand mirror to show off her wonderful work.

"Madison, wow. Thank you so much! This is perfect. Not overdone at all." Leah admired herself in the mirror before making her way to one of the suite's bedrooms that had her and Abbey's clothes. "Hurry up,

Abbey, let's get ready."

Abbey looked up at Roxanna and she smiled. Roxanna handed her a hand mirror and she couldn't believe what she saw. Leah was right. The makeup was flawless but not overdone. "Thank you, Roxanna, Leah was right." She looked up to see Cassie smiling over at her. Even though her life was a total mess at the moment, Abbey felt beautiful. For the first time in a long time.

Abbey could do this. She could put her personal issues aside and be there for her sister's big day. She would be the best maid of honor a bride could ask for, and she wouldn't let Cassie down. She'd be calm and collected. She'd be gracious and considerate for Cassie and for herself.

Time to put on her big girl panties and suck it up. It had been ten years since she'd broken up with Luke. That was long enough to pine after someone who didn't want her. Abbey had gone to great lengths over the last ten years to steer clear of Luke and could now admit that might have been a bit drastic. Weddings were a time of new beginnings. Maybe she could begin again with Luke as friends. In actuality, Abbey didn't have much of a choice. He was dating someone else and from everything she's seen and heard about Luke and Brenna as a couple, they seemed happy. And she would do her best to be happy for them. That knot in her stomach over the thought of Luke with someone else would eventually go away. Maybe if she put an effort into dating, she wouldn't feel so preoccupied with Luke's love life. Maybe.

As Abbey padded to the bedroom to get dressed, Angel called out to her. "Don't forget, we made up bags for the three of you with everything we used today so you can recreate your looks whenever you want. I'm a rep with the cosmetic company so you can order the exact items anytime you need them."

Abbey liked that idea. She normally didn't wear much makeup, but if she was going to start dating again, she'd take more time on her appearance. "Thanks, that's really thoughtful of you and so helpful for me."

Leah had just finished putting on a delicate white lace bra and panty set when Abbey walked into the bedroom to get dressed. Heath was in trouble if he got the chance to see what Leah was wearing under her bridesmaid dress. The bra and panty set complemented her sexy curves just right. "What do you think?" Leah did a quick spin as she giggled.

"I think you're gorgeous and Heath's not going to know what hit him if he gets a chance to see what you're wearing," Abbey said.

Leah pointed to the lingerie set Abbey purchased for the wedding, the cornflower-blue matching her dress perfectly. "Looks like you got something special too."

Abbey felt herself blush. She had never bought lingerie so fancy before. "I just wanted something pretty to go with my dress. I didn't have a specific someone in mind to model it for." Although she couldn't help wondering what Luke would think.

Stop that. It doesn't matter what Luke would think.

Leah slipped into her hose and a long slip. Abbey held open the unzipped bridesmaid dress so Leah could step into it without ruining her hair and makeup. Once it was comfortably in place, Abbey zipped it up and Leah turned to face her.

The lace and illusion mesh bodice of the bridesmaid's dresses was delicate and feminine. The cornflower-blue color flattering on both Abbey and Leah. And with elbow-length lace and mesh sleeves, and a floor-length skirt, it was the perfect. "God, Leah, you're stunning, really."

"You think so?" Leah asked, a huge smile on her face.

"Absolutely." Now Abbey was excited to get dressed herself.

"Okay, now get that sexy lingerie on and I'll help you too."

Leah admired herself in the dresser mirror while Abbey put her new lingerie set, hose, and slip on. When she was ready, Leah helped her into her own dress and pulled up the zipper. Leah fluffed up Abbey's hair, laying it just so around her shoulders.

"Wow, Abbey, just—wow. You were right to leave that gorgeous blonde hair down." Leah turned Abbey to face the dresser mirror

Abbey looked at herself in the mirror, shocked. She almost didn't recognize herself. A little makeup and hair styling made such a difference. She would definitely order makeup from Angel after the weekend was over. "I *feel* wow."

"Jake's invited a few of his single lawyer friends and college buddies. You never know who might get a peek at *your* lingerie tonight." Leah waggled her eyebrows and took her dyed-to-match, much too high heeled for Abbey's safety, pumps and went back to the dining room.

Abbey wasn't so sure she wanted anyone else taking a peek at her lingerie tonight, but for the first time in a long time, she felt amazing. She grabbed her own dyed-to-match, safe one-and-half-inch heels and followed Leah out to the dining room.

Cassie rushed over to them both, giving Abbey and Leah quick hugs. "You both look wonderful. I knew this dress would be perfect for you guys." Cassie teared up.

"Don't cry, Cassie, your makeup! Look up and blink. It will stop the tears from falling," Vanessa suggested.

Cassie laughed at herself and did as Vanessa suggested. It worked, no tears fell.

Abbey looked around the room and found Roxanna and Madison missing. Had they already gone on to the church? All four stylists agreed to stay through the ceremony to help with hair and makeup touch ups if needed for pictures.

"I sent Roxanna and Madison to help Mom and Jake's mom real quick. Let me take a couple of quick pictures before I get into my dress. Patty Hailey and friends should be here in fifteen."

Abbey and Leah posed while Cassie took a few shots with her smart phone.

Where the bridesmaids' dresses had a touch of the lace and illusion mesh, Cassie's wedding gown took the mesh and lace effect to the next level. The entire bodice of her gown had the appearance of a strapless dress with what looked like lace dripping down her sleeves and up her back. Intricate lace appliques dotted a cathedral-length train to finish her fairy tale look. A delicate, lace-trimmed, elbow-length veil complemented the dress rather than detracting from it. "Let's wait until the photographer and videographer get here before putting the veil on," Cassie suggested.

Everyone agreed and Abbey and Leah snapped a few photos of their own while they waited. "So, Jake and I tried that new steak house down the street here on Butterfield Road, Golden Horns." Cassie held her arms out, admiring the sleeves of her gown.

Abbey was confused. She'd seen their sign, but she didn't think they were open for business yet. "I didn't they were open for business."

"They're not officially. They're doing a *select* soft open right now. Luke contacted the owner, Kyle Asher, and got us a table for dinner this past Tuesday night. We got our steak on, just like their sign says."

Abbey chuckled. The restaurant signage actually said *Get Your Steak On*. It was unusual and fun. She wasn't sure what to make of it though. Chicago and the surrounding suburbs had quite a few quality steak houses. And leave it to Luke and his connections to get Jake and Cassie in on the restaurant's *select* soft open.

"Lucky you. Was it any good?" Leah turned when she heard the suite door opening. Madison and Roxanna were back.

"Was what any good?" Madison and Roxanna asked.

"I was just telling everyone that Luke got me and Jake into Golden Horn's select soft opening this past Tuesday. And yes, it was fantastic. The filet I had cut like butter and was so flavorful, and Jake's porterhouse was cooked exactly the way he likes it. And their desserts. Wow, they were amazing. I had the best carrot cake I've ever had and Jake tried their triple layer strawberry cake. It's hard to describe, it was so good. The best part, though, was getting to chat with the owner Kyle Asher himself and his younger sister." Cassie shot Abbey a playful look.

"Oh no, Cassie, what did you do?" Abbey would lose it if her sister had something up her sleeve. Since she and Jake got engaged, Cassie wanted everyone around her to be happy and in love. Abbey knew from personal experience everyone didn't get their happy ending.

Relax. Luke isn't the only man in the world. I can still have my own happy ending with someone else.

Abbey's heart wasn't completely on board with

29

that thought yet, but she was confident it would get there.

"Relax, Abbey. I didn't give him your number or anything. Although you could do a lot worse than Kyle Asher. Kyle and his sister gave us a tour of the restaurant and kitchen and told us about their expansion plans."

"Where are they from, then? Are they a part of some restaurant group like Lettuce Entertain You or Landry's?" Madison asked and took a seat the dining room table with Roxanna joining her.

"Not exactly. They're from a small town south of Dallas called Envy. And they don't just have restaurants. Their group is called Envy Entertainment," Cassie explained.

"What sort of entertainment?" Abbey was curious. It was an unusual combination to her, restaurants and entertainment. Although she supposed it didn't need to be. Restaurants could be considered a form of entrainment.

"I don't know if you can handle it. Are you sure you really want to know?" Cassie had everyone's attention now.

Abbey rolled her eyes. "Yes, Cassie, of course we all want to know. Dramatic much?"

"It's my wedding day, I can be dramatic if I want."

Abbey took Cassie's hand in hers. "Of course you can." She didn't want to detract from Cassie's day, but the suspense was killing her. She had to know what Envy Entertainment was into. And maybe get a little more information about Kyle Asher? Why not, she told herself. What would it hurt, right? There was no harm in a date or two. Maybe.

"You all know Heather Bellatoni, right? The semi-retired super model?"

Who didn't know Heather Bellatoni? Abbey

sighed. Heather's father Enzo was half of the design genius behind one of Italy's premiere couture design houses, House of Bellatoni. He and his older brother Paolo built a clothing empire from the ground up, starting with nothing but Heather's mother Stacey, who they'd literally plucked from her family's dairy farm in Ohio.

Heather Bellatoni inherited her mother's good looks, blonde hair, and blue eyes. She also inherited her father's Mediterranean skin tone, giving her a more exotic appearance than her mother Stacey's girl-next-door look. Heather had been thrust onto the runway at age ten.

"Kyle met Enzo, Jr., Michael, and Heather in New York a couple years ago. Apparently EJ, as Kyle calls him, and Michael are amazing tattoo artists and Kyle wanted them to do his ink. Kyle had his dress shirt sleeves rolled up a bit when we met him on Tuesday and I got to see some of his incredible ink. From what I was able to tell, he's got arm sleeves of exotic animal tattoos. It was sexy as hell. And that southern accent." Cassie actually fanned herself. "So hot, guys."

"Hey! You're getting married in a couple of hours. You're drooling over some Texas dude?" Abbey had to admit, so far Kyle Asher sounded pretty hot. She might have to seriously consider getting herself invited to the select soft opening. *I wonder if I should ask Luke to get me on the soft open list like he did for Cassie and Jake.*

Angel pointed to Madison who promptly shook her head. "Tell us more about hunky Kyle Asher."

Madison quickly jumped in. "Not on my account. Rox?"

Roxanna just shrugged, not appearing very interested.

"Kyle's probably about six and a half feet tall, broad-shouldered, with sandy blond hair, sexy blue eyes, and dimples. He's well-built and has a dreamy southern accent." Cassie looked around the room for everyone's reaction.

"I think he sounds amazing, don't you think, Abbey?" Leah turned to her and winked.

She rolled her eyes. Although Kyle sounded amazing, she would not let on about her possible interest to anyone else. "Cassie, just continue without all the Kyle commentary, okay?"

Cassie stuck her tongue out at Abbey and continued. "So when Kyle was in New York getting his ink done, he met Heather. She was considering retiring from modeling. It turns out she was more of a small-town farm girl than her mother. All the traveling just got to be too much for her. She wanted to do something else and Kyle helped her come up with a business idea and plan for a shop that sells lingerie, adult toys, costumes, etcetera. It's called Impulse. They opened their first shop in Envy and her brothers moved their place to Envy too. It's called Envied Body Art. Impulse is a part of the Envy Entertainment group or family of businesses. Kyle used the word 'family' a lot when describing how he wants to build their brand and company."

"Cassie, that's not so scandalous." Abbey didn't understand what the big deal was. There were adult shops all over Chicago and online.

"Oh, but a lot of Impulse's customers are from Envy Entertainment's *other* business." Cassie smiled and everyone waited to hear about this other business.

After what seemed liked forever, Cassie continued. "It's a kinky sex club called Club Envidious!"

"No way, like BDSM?" Vanessa asked.

"Red room of pain-type stuff?" Madison

speculated.

"Never say that to Kyle. Real life differs from books, but it's not a room, it's more like a complex. The original Club Envidious is in Envy. Kyle's older sister Lauren lives there and manages it and the Golden Horns there. Kyle is behind their expansion plans."

Abbey hadn't expected a sex club. She might have to reconsider Kyle Asher after all. She wasn't into the BDSM scene. At least she didn't think she was. She had never tried anything very kinky. After she and Luke split up, she hadn't dated very much. She had focused on her job at OSG and night school.

Cassie had everyone's attention now. "They're putting their Chicago site in Oak Brook, down 22nd Street here at Camden Court."

"That's just some vacant office building," Angel said.

"Envy Entertainment bought it and it's been completely renovated. It has a lounge and bar, a huge dungeon, themed play rooms, and executive apartments on the top floor." Cassie looked so excited and Abbey was surprised. Were her sister and her soon-to-be brother-in-law into BDSM? Was Luke?

It doesn't matter what Luke's into now. You're moving on, remember?

Leah seemed uncomfortable but looked at Cassie with a serious expression on her face. "I don't want details, but are you and Jake into that stuff?" That was what Abbey wanted to know but was too embarrassed to ask. From the looks on Angel's, Vanessa's, Madison's, and Roxanna's faces, they were curious too.

"No, not really. I mean, aren't we all maybe a little curious though?"

All the women in the room looked intrigued. Roxanna spoke up first. "Curious, sure. I don't think I could ever actually *go* to BDSM club though." Everyone in the room nodded in agreement.

"Me either. But there's another section of the building that's separate from Club Envidious where the Twisted Tea Society meets twice a month."

Madison spoke up this time. "And what's that?"

"You can read all about how it started on their website, but it's a kinky erotic book and social club for women. There's a membership process similar to Club Envidious, but there's no sex, whips, Doms, or anything like that. And the twisted part is that naked male servers serve the members tea and refreshments, and give them footbaths, foot and shoulder massages. And did I mention, the male servers are naked?" Cassie smiled brightly, proud of herself for knowing something the rest of the group didn't.

Abbey couldn't help herself. "Liar. They are not naked."

Cassie nodded. "You're right. They're not completely naked. They wear bow ties."

Roxanna typed furiously on her smart phone. Her mouth dropped open and she looked up. "Cassie's right, it says that on their website. Beverages and refreshments served to you by *naked male servers* wearing bow ties. It says it's a safe, discreet place to indulge your *kinky curiosity*, or the Clothed Female Naked Male fetish."

Abbey could admit she liked the sound of the Twisted Tea Society. It was probably as daring as she'd ever be. What the hell? It could be fun. Another part of her plan to move on with her life post-Luke. Maybe Kyle wasn't so bad after all if he cared enough to make something like the Twisted Tea Society available to ladies like them.

Madison typed away on her smart phone. "Oh, I like the sound of this. One of the benefits of membership is a break from your hectic life where you can just be for a few hours, twice a month, in a relaxing, comfortable environment. Oh! And a fifteen percent discount at Heather Bellatoni's Impulse store. Great!"

This Twisted Tea Society was sounding better and better.

"They're looking at potential Impulse locations here in Oak Brook and Elmhurst. Heather will be here for the grand opening," Cassie said.

"That sounds really amazing." Angel went to answer the door.

"Angel, just a second before you answer the door. Kyle's looking for a salon to bring into the Envy Entertainment family of businesses. They use a salon in Rapture, Texas. It's Envy's sister city the next town over. The salon's owner is a small-town girl. She doesn't want to expand. Kyle's looking to expand the businesses to New York, Chicago, Nevada, Los Angeles, and Florida, to name a few. It could be an exciting opportunity for you. For all four of you." Cassie looked at all four stylists, seeming to hope they were interested. Vanessa, Roxanna, and Madison all turned to Angel, waiting for her feedback.

Angel smiled at Cassie and nodded. "Thanks, Cassie. It's something to consider. I want to finish my MBA program before I tackle the next step. Are you all ready for me to open the door?"

Cassie took a deep breath and nodded her head. Abbey took a couple of deep breaths herself. Now wasn't the time to think about Kyle Asher or naked male servers at the Twisted Tea Society.

Abbey had to be at her best today for Cassie. She was going to be the maid of honor Cassie needed and deserved. And she would deal with seeing Luke for the first time in ten years. Calmly and confidently—she hoped.

Chapter Three

Hannah shook her head. "Abbey? No, you're dating Brenna Sinclair, aren't you?"

Luke frowned. He didn't want to get into any of this. He needed to keep the focus on Jake and Cassie, for shit's sake. The timing of the clusterfuck that had just become his life couldn't have been worse. "Well, let's just say not anymore, but that's not public knowledge at the moment."

Jake laughed and pointed to Heath. "I knew it! Pay up, Heath."

What? Jake and Heath were betting on his breakup with Brenna? Did that mean they knew? No, he and Brenna had been careful. They'd played the part of a doting couple well. He knew they did. If you believed the tabloids, they had been secretly married weeks ago and were waiting until her newest film premiered in three weeks to announce it and Brenna's pregnancy. Luke shuddered at the thought of what the tabloids would do to them both once the truth, more specifically their version of the truth, actually came out.

Heath took out his wallet and handed Jake some bills. He shook his head and frowned at Luke. "Thanks a lot, man."

Jake happily took the bills from Heath with a huge smile on his face. "I should have bet Heath more than a hundred bucks. I knew your *relationship* with Brenna was bullshit. You both put on a great act, but I knew it wasn't real. Oscar-worthy performance, though."

Hannah and Heath both shook their heads, not seeming to believe Jake's suspicions. Jake was right of course, but now wasn't the time to get into it.

"I have no comment on the matter, other than to say—don't say anything. I'll give you your hundred back, Heath, don't worry about it."

Heath shook his head. "You don't need to do that. I lost fair and square. Damn, Jake, how did you know?"

Jake smiled like an idiot. "Because I've known Luke since he was two years old."

Heath rolled his eyes. "I've known Luke since he was two years old, too, ass. We were all next-door neighbors, remember?"

That was true. Luke and his folks, God rest their souls, had moved to Elmhurst when he was two years old, buying the house in between Jake's and Heath's families. Jake had been four and Heath had been seven. Despite Luke being just a toddler, he, Jake, and Heath formed a fast and deep friendship that lasted to this day. Heath probably felt in charge as the oldest of the three. Jake and Heath were not just his closest friends, they were his brothers. There was nothing he wouldn't do for them. He only wished they would let him do more. He was now a wealthy man, and who better to share his money with than Jake and Heath? Unfortunately, they were not receptive to what they perceived as "grand gestures" or "handouts".

When Luke's parents had been taken from him when he was ten years old due to a drunk driver, his Uncle Darren, a confirmed bachelor, real estate mogul, and owner of the Chicago Cobras MLB and Windy City Rattlers MILB teams, immediately moved him from his family home in Elmhurst to Chicago's Gold Coast to be closer to Stryker Stadium and their corporate offices.

Darren had become his father, mother, and everything else overnight. Luke was grateful for his uncle's love, support, and understanding. To his credit, Darren had made sure that Luke maintained his close friendship with Jake and Heath. Thanks to Darren's efforts, the three of them remained close, surviving the pressures of Luke's baseball career, Heath's military service, and Jake attending Stanford to study law.

This time, Jake rolled his eyes. "Yes, of course I remember, but I spent more time with him than you did. Especially after you joined the Marines."

"That doesn't mean I don't know him as well as you. After I was discharged, we spent a lot more time together, especially when we were trying to figure out the best thing to do about my hearing loss after those fucking IEDs practically exploded in my face."

Hannah gasped. "Oh my God, Heath, I'm so sorry. Saying thank you for your service seems so trite." Hannah gave a Heath a strong hug. "Thank you anyway for your service and sacrifice. No matter what you think, we all appreciate everyone who serves."

"Thank you, Hannah. It was an honor."

Hannah turned to Jake, curious. "Real quick, because we have to get you three dressed for pictures before the ladies get here. How did you know Luke and Brenna's relationship was bullshit as you said?"

"Abbey," Jake replied.

Hannah lightly punched Jake in the arm and Luke winced. Damn, but his shoulder was aching.

Jake chuckled and explained. "Abbey was, or should I say is, Luke's soulmate. Luke did and said all the right things publicly with Brenna Sinclair to make it seem like they were this happy couple. But he never looked at her like he did Abbey. Sure, he smiled for the cameras and did the whole PDA shtick with Brenna, but only someone who had known Luke and Abbey together would have been able to tell he and Brenna weren't the real deal."

Hannah nodded. "I agree with you there. It all

looked *very* real to me."

Heath appeared to be deep in thought, perhaps contemplating Jake's assessment. "Jake's right. I should have paid closer attention to the media on you two. I would have seen what Jake did. And you're not telling your two best friends in the world, guys who are more like brothers than friends, what the hell was really going on with Brenna?"

Luke laughed at Heath. Heath was laying it on thick. It wouldn't work. "Nope. Can't. Sorry." Jake and Heath would have to wait like everyone else as the events of the weekend unfolded. He prayed the tabloids didn't skewer him when it was all over.

In his rush to get everything ready to bring to the church, Luke had forgotten to bring something for pain. He needed a little something to take the edge off. "Do any of you have any kind of pain reliever with you?"

"Didn't the hospital prescribe you something?" Hannah asked.

"Anything stronger than extra strength Tylenol and Darren would shit," Jake replied. Darren kept a close eye on him. He didn't mind, not really. Some might have found his Uncle Darren to be overbearing when it came with Luke, but he saw his uncle's behavior as concern and love, and he didn't want to ever let him down by doing something as reckless as tempting his fate with drugs.

Hannah dug through her travel bag and produced a pill bottle. "This will help. It's over-the-counter all-day pain reliever." She shook a couple of pills into her palm and offered them to him.

Jake went to the mini fridge near the desk, retrieved a bottle of water, and handed it to Luke. He popped the pain pills in his mouth and drank half the bottle of water. He hoped he'd feel relief soon.

A knock at the door had everyone turning to look. "Hey, it's Rocco. Can I come in?"

Hannah let Rocco in and Jake and Heath greeted him with man hugs. "Guys, you've got to get dressed. Time to get serious, all right?" Hannah put her hand to her ear piece. "Thank you. I'll be right there to take a look. All right, I'm going to take a look at the flower arrangements while you all get dressed."

Luke didn't want to risk it. "I think I need help getting my t-shirt off."

Rocco raised a brow. "What's going on?"

Hannah quickly filled Rocco in on Luke's accident and subsequent shoulder injury. She stood by while Jake and Heath helped Luke take his t-shirt off. Luke was relieved somewhat. His shoulder didn't hurt too badly. He knew it didn't look good though.

Hannah was first to comment. "Oh my God, Luke, that looks awful. Do you need a sling? I don't think anyone on my team has one. There's a Walgreens nearby, I'll have someone get one for you."

"You don't have to do that," Luke said. "I brought a shoulder support. It's in my garment bag. No way am I wearing a sling for everyone to see. No one is supposed to know about this injury."

"When did this happen?" Rocco asked.

Jake seemed upset. "Wednesday night. Luke, this doesn't look good. Do you need surgery?"

Heath frowned, shaking his head. "It's still pretty early in the season. If you get surgery after the wedding, you should be finished with rehab fairly quick, right?"

Theoretically, Heath was right. Luke didn't need surgery though. He hadn't dislocated his shoulder or broken any bones. He was badly bruised, and his shoulder looked much worse than it was. He'd just hit the ground really hard.

Luke would need time to heal before he could return to play. During his brief hospital stay, his uncle had shared news so devastating and unexpected, he still couldn't quite believe it. Hadn't fully processed it yet. And it was that news that had Luke reconsidering returning to play at all.

Luke was thirty. For a pitcher, he was getting old. Although he was still one of the fastest pitchers in the MLB, over the last couple of years, his fast ball had slowed. He needed more recovery time between games compared to three or four years ago. In a year or two, he would probably be traded to another team if it weren't for the fact that his uncle owned the Cobras and would never let him go.

The truth of the matter was Luke was tired. Ten years of non-stop Major League Baseball, coupled with going to college online to get his business degree then MBA, and everything else that being a professional athlete entailed—Luke had no more to give. The farce that had been Luke and Brenna for the last three years didn't help either. Thankfully that was coming to an end this weekend.

It was time to focus on what mattered most, getting Jake and Cassie married. And Abbey. Luke's sweet, beautiful Abbey. Just thinking of her made his cock twitch. God, how he missed her. Her soft silky hair, the feel of her warm skin against his, and that body that fit so perfectly with his.

Luke should have fought harder to convince her to stay with him after she walked in on him in his hotel room with that groupie his former manager and all-around asshole gave him to celebrate his first World Series win. Other than his teammates, there were only two people he had wanted to celebrate with, his Uncle Darren and his girl Abbey.

Christ, he'd never forget the look on her face when she walked in on him and whatever the hell her name was. He'd been drunk for the first in his life. The groupie was naked and had gotten Luke's shirt off. He had been drunk, sure, but he'd had enough sense to know he didn't want some random chick with bleached-out hair, fake tits, and who smelled like cigarettes anywhere near him or his dick. Luke had been trying to push the groupie off of him when Abbey had walked in. It must have looked like he was encouraging her rather than trying to fight her off. She'd taken one look at them, hurt and betrayal in her bright blue eyes, cried, and ran off.

That was it. That was the last time Luke had seen Abbey. She'd effectively frozen him out. For ten years. She told him over the phone the following day that it was better if they weren't together. She was letting him go so he could focus on his career and whatever else he wanted without her getting in his way.

Luke wanted Abbey by his side while he focused on his pitching career and everything that went along with it. But she wouldn't hear of it. She refused to listen to anything he had to say. Refused to believe that he hadn't cheated on her. He assumed Abbey needed time to calm down before he could make her see reason. Months went by and she never allowed him to explain what happened the night she walked in on him and never forgave him.

That was then, and this was now. Luke would not allow her to push him away any longer. No. This weekend he'd have his say and he'd prove to her that they belonged together. Always had. Mission Abbey was on.

Luke watched Hannah dig through that magic travel bag of hers. "Okay, no more shoulder talk, all right? It's crunch time."

Hannah held up a white jar in her hand, smiling brightly. "I think this will help, too. Let me put a little of this on your shoulder before you get dressed. You can keep the jar in case you need to apply more." Hannah scooped some cream onto her fingertips and touched his shoulder.

Luke hissed when the cream made contact with his skin. Rocco grabbed Hannah's wrist so fast he startled everyone. "You're hurting him," he growled.

"No, she's not, Rocco. Stand down. The cream is cold, that's all. I wasn't expecting that. What's in this?" Luke wasn't interested in some crazy potion or tricks. He just needed to get through the weekend before meeting with his orthopedic doctor and surgeon.

Hannah pulled her arm away from Rocco. Both of them stared at each other a little too long. All right, *that* was interesting. Rocco and the lovely Hannah Hailey. Yeah, Luke could see them together. Rocco needed someone tough like Hannah. Someone who wouldn't put up with any shit. Someone who was their own person. Who might soften the tough Italian guy up a little. Smooth out some of the man's rough edges.

Hannah gently rubbed the cream all around Luke's shoulder. It warmed up as she did. It had a light pleasant smell. Not medicinal. "It's natural, don't worry. It has healing botanicals and emu oil in it. It'll help with the soreness and the bruising. If you need relief later in the day, I'll apply more."

Luke had to admit, she was right. As she continued to work his shoulder, he was feeling better. Add in the fact that the pain reliever started kicking in, and he was confident he could get through the wedding and the reception with little trouble.

"Thanks, Hannah. It's helping. We'll get ourselves ready. You go and do whatever you need to do.

We're good here." Luke moved his arm up to the side, thankful there wasn't much soreness at all. It would be all right.

Hannah put the lid back on the jar and shoved it in Rocco's chest. A little blush stained her cheeks. "Think you can hold on to this for Luke?"

Rocco seemed a little dumbstruck. He nodded and took the jar from her.

"Good." And with that, Hannah left, closing the door quietly behind her.

Jake smiled at Heath and Luke, then turned to Rocco. "That sure was interesting. I think maybe Rocco's got a thing for little event planner Hannah," Jake teased.

Rocco's mouth fell open and he quickly closed it. "Bullshit, no, I don't. She's bossy. I'm not used to that."

It was Luke's turn to take a little dig. "Uh huh. When you grabbed her, I didn't know if you wanted to hurt her or fuck her, man."

"And the way you watched that ass as she walked out the door. Yup, I agree with Jake and Luke, you want her. She's got some nice curves under that little pantsuit of hers. Can't say I blame you," Heath added and chuckled.

Rocco put the jar of wonder cream on the table, shaking his head, just as Luke felt his cell phone vibrate in his pocket. He pulled it out and read the text he just received.

Brenna: **Are we still "a go" for Mission Abbey?**

The guys looked over Luke's shoulder as he typed his response. So much for privacy. The guys would have to wait out the weekend. Luke wasn't planning on telling them shit. They would have to wait for events to unfold this weekend like everyone else.

Luke: **Yes, we're still "a go", I'll keep you posted.**

Brenna: **Excellent. I'll enjoy my down time in the Windy City** ☺

Luke: **Thank you Bren, appreciate you.**

Brenna: **Thank YOU, it's the least I can do.**

Luke: **Talk later, assholes not giving me privacy.**

Brenna: ☹ **later…**

"Fuck you, man." Heath smirked. "Now we're assholes?"

"No, not now. You've guys have *always* been assholes," Luke answered.

Jake was visibly upset. "I'm tired of all the secrets, Luke. What the hell was that?"

"Yeah," Rocco and Heath added.

"Look, guys, you need to trust me on this. I'm sorry I can't tell you. I'm not trying to keep secrets, but you know how crazy it's been for me these last ten years. Living in the public eye isn't easy. Please, let's focus on the wedding." Luke looked at Jake, Heath, and Rocco, hoping they could trust him and let things go.

Jake sighed. He raised his hands in surrender. "Fine, Luke. You win. But I don't like it. Shit, you said you weren't together anymore and clearly Brenna's in town. And she knows about Mission Abbey."

Luke would not divulge any more. He took Jake's mission note out of his pocket and held it up. "Let's continue with the Tyler Project mission, okay?"

Everyone nodded their heads in agreement. Luke jerked his head toward the cooler he brought that Hannah placed under the table. "A beer before the ceremony, right?"

"Let's get your shoulder support on first. Then we'll continue with the Tyler Project." Jake said.

Rocco removed the white shoulder support from Luke's garment bag and held it up. Luke slid his right arm in the half sleeve portion of the brace, which was more of a compression support garment than a brace or sling. The sleeve went over Luke's entire shoulder, ending under his neckline. The Velcro fastening strap ran around his back and underneath his left arm. Once Rocco and Heath secured the strap, Luke breathed a sigh of relief. His shoulder felt secure without being too confined. Not much soreness at all.

Jake helped him put a white t-shirt on, stood back, and looked Luke over. "Looks good. You can barely see it underneath the t-shirt. How's the shoulder feel?"

Luke rolled his shoulder and felt only a twinge of discomfort. "It feels good. That emu oil cream and pain reliever made a big difference. I'll be fine. Stop worrying. Let's get back to the Tyler Project."

Jake and Heath went to the cooler while Rocco removed Luke's tuxedo shirt from his garment bag. Rocco made to help him put it on, but he took the shirt from him. "I got this, it's all right, relax."

"You sure?" Rocco asked, looking skeptical.

"Positive." Luke put his crisp white tuxedo shirt on, not having any difficulties with the buttons. The fit was comfortable, even with the shoulder support and t-shirt. He waited for Jake to blow a gasket once he got a good look inside the beer cooler.

"Holy shit, Luke, you're kidding me right now!" Jake turned to Luke with a shocked expression on his face.

Rocco raced over to the cooler, looking to see what the matter was. Luke smiled and shrugged. Luke had secured six bottles of Samuel Adams Utopia, their most renowned and sought-after, extreme barrel-aged beer. They wouldn't be released until later in the year but he was able to get Jake this special gift in exchange for doing some commercial spots for the brewer. Luke had also promised to get a few shots of himself and Jake in their tuxedos holding the specialty beer bottle.

"Luke, this is too much. There are six bottles in here and two of the special Riedel glasses."

Rocco turned back to Luke, seeming confused. "I don't understand. What are these?"

"They're Samuel Adams Utopias. And I can't believe he got six. They're only producing fifteen thousand this time around. I didn't think they were available yet though," Heath said.

Jake frowned at Luke and shook his head. "They're only releasing thirteen thousand bottles, not fifteen. And they aren't due out until later this year. This is too much, Luke."

Rocco shrugged, not seeming to understand what the big deal was. "It's just beer. There's Boston Lager in the cooler too."

Jake took out four bottles of the Boston Lager and closed the cooler lid. He handed everyone a bottle, keeping one for himself. "It's not just beer, Roc. The Utopias are only produced every two years, this being the tenth release. And those bottles are two hundred dollars each."

Rocco chocked on a sip of his beer. "What?"

Jake continued. "Yeah, two hundred bucks a bottle. The blending, brewing, and aging process of the Utopias is time consuming and complex. It's sort of like a vintage Port, old Cognac, or fine Sherry. It has a twenty-eight percent alcohol content, and is illegal in twelve states."

Rocco took another pull of his beer. "No shit."

"Samuel Adams recommends only drinking an

ounce or two at the most at one time since it's so strong." Jake took a long pull of his own beer. "This is twelve hundred dollars' worth of beer plus the cost of the two Riedel glasses. Plus the honeymoon suite at the Fairchild Hotel for two nights, plus Darren paying for the event planner. It's all too much."

Luke didn't see it that way. He wanted to share his good fortune with his friends. Some beer, a hotel room, and event planning fees were a drop in the bucket to Luke. He would have paid for Jake and Cassie's honeymoon in Aruba but it hadn't been worth the argument with Jake. "Look, Jake, I know it seems like a lot, but shit, did you expect me to go to Nordstrom's and get you a pair of candle stick holders from your bridal registry? This was something special just for you and Cass. I would have done so much more if you had let me, so let me have *this*, all right?"

Heath put a hand on Jake's shoulder. "I'm with Luke on this one. It's something special no one else would have considered or been able to get for you and Cassie. Be gracious and enjoy it. I think Cassie will be touched by the gesture."

Luke agreed. Jake and Cassie weren't heavy drinkers, but they both enjoyed their Boston Lager and the six Utopia bottles would last them a long, long time. He hoped Jake would accept his gift without feeling bad about it. Everyone took a few more pulls from their beers, waiting on Jake to answer.

Jake went to his garment bag, pulled out his tuxedo, and began getting dressed. Heath and Luke looked at each other, shrugged, and got dressed too.

Cassie had wanted something old school and traditional for the men. Once they were all decked out in their black tails, Luke couldn't take Jake's silence any longer. "Jake, tell me you're not that upset over some beer and a hotel room. Come on, man." Luke couldn't have Jake upset on his wedding day. He'd take the Utopias back if he had to.

Jake shook his head and stared at his feet. "You're right. I think Cassie will be excited by the Utopias. It's just she won't even be able to enjoy them for a long time…"

"What? Why," Luke pressed.

"I really shouldn't say anything." Jake looked at both doors to make sure they were still closed. He switched to ASL, or American Sign Language. After Heath's injury in Afghanistan, the three of them learned to sign in case Heath's hearing deteriorated to the point where even the most state-of-the-art hearing aids couldn't provide him with adequate hearing. Rocco had picked up enough to converse pretty well in sign too.

Jake: *Because Cass is eight weeks pregnant.*

Luke: *Couldn't wait until the honeymoon, huh?*

Jake*: Well, she went off the pill three months ago and since then we haven't been as careful as we should have been, I guess.*

Heath*: Even so, congratulations.*

Rocco: *Heath's right, this is great news, a blessing.*

Luke: *You two can enjoy the Utopias after the baby's born. It's not a big deal. They'll keep.*

Jake: *Oh, I know, just don't say anything. We're waiting until after she's past the first trimester before we tell everyone.*

Luke was thrilled but also couldn't help but feel envious of his friend. If things had worked out how they should have ten years ago, he and Abbey would probably have a few kids by now. All boys, of course. Future Chicago Cobras. Just thinking of Abbey swollen with his baby had his cock hardening. Soon enough, he'd have his blonde-haired princess pregnant with their first child. He grinned, excited for the future.

Luke grabbed his beer bottle and held it up in salute. Heath, Jake, and Rocco did the same with their bottles. "The first toast of the day. To Jake and Cassie," Luke began. Then he whispered, "And little baby Tyler." All four men clinked their bottles and took long pulls.

"Hey Rocco, why don't you go find the lovely Miss Hannah and she if she has any mints in that magic bag of hers? I don't want us smelling like a distillery during the ceremony." Jake waggled his eyebrows at Rocco and he frowned back at him, shaking his head.

"She said she was coming back after she checked on the flowers and whatever else. I don't need to look for her," Rocco replied, looking flustered.

Heath laughed and joined in on the teasing. "Damn, Roc, you've got it that bad? A little event planner's got you all rattled?"

"Fuck you, Heath, I'm not rattled. And you're one to talk. What you gonna do when Leah gets here in a little while, huh?"

It was Heath's turn to look flustered and rattled. Luke knew that Leah, Jake's younger sister, had always had a crush on Heath. It had been cute when she was a little girl, vying for Heath's attention. Heath, for his part, had just treated Leah like his own little sister. With a ten-year age difference between them, what else could he do? Jake had been good natured about the whole thing. Getting digs in when he could, which pissed Heath off. As if he expected Jake to protect him from his baby sister. Luke found the whole thing rather funny.

But Leah wasn't a little girl anymore. Far from it. She was twenty-five now and that ten-year age difference between her and Heath wasn't an issue anymore. No, Leah Tyler had grown into a gorgeous chestnut-haired, deep brown-eyed, curves-in-all-the-right-places siren.

Not only was Leah a beautiful woman, but she was smart too, graduating from Northwestern University with honors and a degree in Finance. She was a Financial Analyst for the Cobras but didn't report to Heath directly. Heath had recently been promoted to Finance Director and Leah reported to one of Heath's direct reports. The Cobras' finance department wasn't large so Leah and Heath saw each other every day.

Luke suspected Heath wanted Leah, but he'd fended her off so far. How Heath kept his hands off her while being tempted every day, Luke had no idea. If Luke saw Abbey every day at work, they would have been reprimanded or fired for fucking in the supply closet, or the copy room, or anywhere else they could find.

Luke believed part of the reason that Heath didn't make a move on Leah was loyalty to his friendship with Jake. You just didn't fuck your buddy's little sister. Period. End of story. Luke didn't think that Jake would actually mind if Heath and Leah got together. Heath was a good man, and he'd never intentionally hurt Leah.

To Luke's amusement, Heath played dumb. "Leah who?"

Jake just laughed and winked at Luke. "Leah Remini. You know, from *King of Queens* and now *Kevin Can Wait*."

Heath's eyes grew wide. "Was Luke able to get her to attend?" Was Heath kidding?

Rocco, Jake, and Luke laughed. Jake threw his hands up. "No, idiot. I meant my sister Leah. Like you didn't know who I meant. Leah Remini, right." Jake sighed and shook his head. Obviously Heath was going to fight this thing with Leah until the bitter end.

"What about your sister? What are saying? That

I've got a thing for her or something?"

Rocco grunted and chimed in. "Or something."

Heath looked panicked. "Well, I don't. She's your kid sister, Jake. I'd never do that to you. She's like a sister to me and is my employee." Heath looked to Luke for support.

Luke wasn't having any of it. "You're not fooling anyone with this denial shit, Heath. Man up for fuck's sake. *Marine.*"

Rocco stepped up to Luke, a scowl on his face, eyes narrowed. "Got a problem with the Marines, *civilian?*"

Luke had no issue with the Marines or any service branch. In fact, it had been Luke's idea for the Chicago Cobras to partner with the Veterans Ticket Foundation and donate three hundred fifty free game tickets to veterans and active duty military and their families for every home game. Once a year, the Cobras hosted a Military Appreciation Night, providing twenty-five hundred free tickets and performed a special ceremony honoring the men and women in uniform. Luke's own father had been in the Army.

Jake stepped in, pushing Rocco back. "Relax, man. No one's insulting the Marines, all right?"

Rocco and Heath nodded. Luke blew out a breath, relieved.

Jake turned to Heath, a serious expression on his face. "Look, I know Leah's my kid sister and you've always treated like she was yours too, but she's never been shy about her feelings toward you."

"No, that's not true." Heath shook his head. "She had a little crush when she was younger, that's it."

"Heath, come on. Get real. Little girl crush time is over. She's a grown woman. Do I really need to tell you what you already know?" Jake looked to Luke and

Rocco. "What we *all* know?"

Heath rolled his eyes, in full denial mode. "And what is it that we all know, Jake? Enlighten me, please."

"Stop playing dumb. We all know Leah's in love with you. Has been for a long time." Jake turned and went to the mirrored door and checked his appearance. He brushed some lint from his shoulders, adjusted his white bow tie, and turned back around to face Heath.

Heath shook his head. "No, she's not. Even if she was, I wouldn't never act on it or encourage her. I would never do that to you. Friends don't touch their friend's sisters. We all know that. I can't believe you think I'd do something like that to you."

Jake walked back over to Heath and looked over to Luke. Luke nodded slightly to Jake.

"What if I said I didn't mind if you did do something about it?"

Heath's mouth fell open. Before he could answer Jake, there was a knock at the main office door. "Boys, it's Darren and Hannah. Can we come in?"

Chapter Four

Abbey and Leah watched their mothers fuss over Cassie as they waited for the wedding ceremony to begin. They were all tucked away in a conference room left of Grace of God's main entrance. Angel and Vanessa calmly listened as Abbey's mother made suggestions for Cassie's hair and makeup. Cassie looked perfect and Abbey was impressed at how Cassie kept her cool despite all the fussing around her.

Madison and Roxanna were seated at the conference room table, chatting and busy on their cell phones. Madison looked over at Cassie and nudged Roxanna with her elbow. They both stood up, gesturing to their chairs. "Moms, how about we do a quick touch up on your makeup before the ceremony starts?"

"Good idea, Mad. You ladies have been so teary-eyed, with good reason of course. But let's make sure you two look perfect before you're escorted down the aisle." Roxanna winked at Abbey and Leah with a smile on her face. Nice save.

Jake's and Abbey's moms stopped fussing. "You'll both make sure Cassie's ready, right?" Abbey's mother asked Angel and Vanessa before she and Jake's mother took Madison's and Roxanna's seats at the table for their touch up.

"Don't worry, Mom, we've got everything under control." Cassie mouthed a *thank you* to Madison and Roxanna.

Leah snickered next to her while she typed on her cell phone. Abbey's own cell phone chimed and vibrated with a text message as it lay on the table. Her heart skipped a beat, thinking it might be Luke. The guys were in an office somewhere on the other side of the church getting ready themselves. She knew she shouldn't care if the text was from Luke or not, but she couldn't help it. Luke had been her first love. Today would be the first time she saw him face-to-face in ten years. It wasn't all that surprising she was a little nervous to see him again.

Tom Murphy: **Hey how are things going? Ready to walk down the aisle with Luke?**

Abbey chided herself for being disappointed it wasn't Luke who texted her, but instead, one of her co-workers, the Support Desk Manager at OSG. Abbey had confided in him and a few others at the office about Cassie's wedding and her nervousness about seeing Luke again after ten years.

The women she told were excited for her, going on about how Abbey should strut her stuff and consider hooking up with Luke for old time's sake. What happened at a wedding stayed at the wedding and all that.

The men couldn't have cared less about how Abbey felt and only wanted details about "Strike 'em Out" Stryker's workout regimen, eating plan, etcetera. They wanted to know if Abbey could score them tickets to Cobras games, team gear, and so on.

Being the masochist Abbey was when it came to Luke, she knew a lot details about Luke's professional life, in part from her own research and from what Cassie and Jake shared with her. Cassie worked for the Cobras as a Manager for Season Ticket Services. She'd been with the Cobras for seven years. Jake joined the organization a year ago as a corporate attorney.

But Tom Murphy hadn't cared about Luke's personal information, tickets, or gear. No. Tom had offered to be Abbey's date to the wedding, her plus one. Why? To make Luke jealous.

Leah peeked over Abbey's shoulder to look at her

phone. "Oh, who's Tom Murphy?" she whispered. Abbey looked up to find her mother and Jake's mom still busy with Madison and Roxanna.

Abbey whispered back, "No one."

Abbey: **Ha, ha. Ceremony starts soon.**

Tom Murphy: **You sure you don't need me to be your date tonight? Make Luke squirm a little?**

Leah giggled beside Abbey. "What an awesome idea. Make Luke jealous. Good plan. So who's this Tom guy?"

"Shush. Tom's just someone I work with."

Abbey *had* worked with him, up until Wednesday afternoon. She wouldn't dare mention she'd been laid off now. She had enough to deal with as it was.

Tom Murphy was thirty-one years old and OSG's resident IT bad boy. He had thick, wavy, light-brown hair kept a little too long, was six-feet-two of solid muscle, had tattoos running down both arms, and rode a Harley. Abbey saw the appeal Tom presented, but the guy was an enormous man-whore. No two ways about it. So much so that OSG's HR department had to step in, demanding he not "date" anyone from their IT department because his playboy antics resulted in three very upset female employees leaving the company after discovering he was seeing them all at the same time.

Tom's manager had gone to great lengths to ensure he wasn't fired because even though he had no couth when it came to women personally, he had an amazing technical mind and was an exemplary employee otherwise. He ran their Support Desk like a well-oiled machine.

Abbey: **What? No hot date tonight?**

Tom Murphy: **Nah, left my day wide open for you.** ☺

What was wrong with him? Although Abbey had

no romantic feelings for Tom, why would he risk his job even pretending to be her date? She had been careful to never encourage him personally. She'd always kept her interactions with Tom professional but friendly.

They worked rather closely as the Support Desk employees were power users of the software system Abbey managed. She and Tom had redesigned processes that improved efficiencies and significantly reduced call resolution times. A few weeks before being laid off, they had worked with their retail store support vendor to integrate OSG's help ticketing systems, allowing both companies to create and pass ticket information back and forth between both systems. It was a huge accomplishment and a significant process improvement.

At least it's something I can add to my résumé.

"Tell him you accept, Abbey," Leah whispered, acting much too nosey.

"No. I don't want to play those kinds of games, especially at Cassie's wedding."

"Fine, be a spoiled sport." Leah went back to her phone and left her alone.

Abbey: **I hope that's not true. Thanks, but I'll be fine.**

Tom Murphy: **You sure? I look amazing in my suit.**

Abbey: **Positive, I'm good.**

Tom Murphy: **Yes, you are. But I'll check back later, just in case.**

Abbey: **You don't have to, I'll be fine.**

Tom Murphy: **Yes, you're very fine but I'll check with you later anyway.**

Abbey: **Whatever. Bye.**

Tom Murphy: **There's always the after wedding brunch tomorrow at the Fairchild Hotel. I LOVE brunch!**

Abbey: **Just stop, don't worry. See you Monday at the office.**

Tom Murphy: **We'll see...**

Come on, Tom, give it a rest. It's never gonna happen between us.

She hoped Tom would get the hint when she texted she'd see him on Monday at the office. No one probably knew she had been laid off, other than her asshole manager and his two minions, since everyone knew she was taking Thursday and Friday as vacation days to prepare for the wedding. At least she was being paid for all her unused vacation time in addition to her severance.

The extra money would help as she embarked on her job search next week. With her severance and vacation pay, Abbey was in decent shape financially. She wouldn't need to dip into her savings for quite a while. And she always had the option of taking contract or consulting positions if she had to and continue to look for something permanent that offered paid vacation time, health benefits, and paid holidays. Her education and experience would warrant a decent hourly contract rate. It would be all right.

Leah leaned over and whispered in Abbey's ear. "So, no Tom, then?"

She nudged Leah away, smiling at her soon-to-be sister-in-law. "No Tom, and let it go."

Just then, Patty Hailey breezed into the room wearing an elegant blonde up 'do and a powder-blue power suit. She turned to Abbey's and Jake's mothers. "All right, moms. You two are up. Ready to be escorted down the aisle?"

"Oh! Is it time already?" Abbey's mother stood up. Her eye's glistened with unshed tears. Same for Jake's mother.

"Don't ruin your makeup again, just look up and blink," Abbey told them. They both did and went to Cassie one last time before leaving.

Cassie, her mother, and Jake's mother all held hands for a moment. "Welcome to the family, Cassie."

"Thanks, Mom. Welcome to ours." All three women laughed.

Jake's mother turned to Abbey's. "I'll meet you at the entrance doors."

Angel, Vanessa, Madison, and Roxanna collected their supplies. "We'll take our seats too. Good luck, Cassie," Angel said for the stylists as they left conference room.

Patty Hailey put a hand on Abbey's mother and Cassie's shoulder. "I'll give you both a minute. I looked in on the men. Great choice going traditional with black tails. They all look *very* handsome. I'll send your father in once the mothers are seated." Patty left the room and closed the door.

Abbey's heart raced at the thought of seeing Luke all decked out in his tuxedo. She needed to get a grip and fast.

Get over it, Abbey. It's just Luke, no big deal.

Leah leaned over. "I can't wait to see Heath in his tux. And then maybe later, out of it."

Abbey giggled and nudged Leah. Poor Heath. He didn't stand a chance. She knew eventually Heath and Leah would get together. Leah wouldn't allow for any other option. Abbey hoped it worked out for the two of them. Everyone knew Leah had been in love with the man her entire life. It would be a real shame if they didn't end up together.

Abbey's mother held on to both of Cassie's hands. "This is it, my little girl is *finally* getting married. I had my doubts Jake was serious about you, you know."

Abbey felt Leah stiffen beside her and Abbey took a hold of her hand. She spoke up before Cassie or Leah could. Jake didn't deserve to be shit on, especially on his wedding day. "Mom, Jake just wanted to be sure he was able to take care of Cassie and their future family. He wanted to finish law school, pass the bar, and establish his career first. That's a good thing."

Her mother turned to her and Leah, a sympathetic look in her blue eyes. "I know and I wasn't trying to insult your brother, Leah. I just meant a seven-year engagement is unusual."

Cassie squeezed her mother's hand tight. "I know it is. But I never doubted Jake. He's a little old fashioned in that regard. He knows I want to keep working after we start a family and he's fine with that. He just wanted to put himself in the position to comfortably support us if I wanted to stay home. That's all. It took him a little while, but I can't fault him for it. The minute he accepted his position with the Cobras, we set our wedding date, remember?"

Abbey's mother nodded. "Of course, and you're right. You're only twenty-nine, and there's plenty of time to start of family. But don't wait seven years, all right?"

Abbey and Leah laughed and Cassie glared at them. "No worries, Mom. We *definitely* won't wait seven years."

Abbey's mother air-kissed Cassie's cheek. "I'd better get out there. I'll see you all in a few minutes. I love you, Cassie."

"Love you too, Mom."

Before leaving, Abbey's mother turned to her and Leah. "I love you too, Abbey, very much. And you too, Leah, welcome to our family."

Abbey turned to Leah and saw her get misty eyed. "Look up and blink!"

"I'm okay, don't worry. And thank you, Mrs. Jayne."

"Leah, we're family now. Please call me Monica."

"Thank you, Monica."

Abbey and Leah went to Cassie after Abbey's mother left the room. "Oh my God, I thought you two would spill the beans when Mom went on and on about starting a family and not waiting seven years."

"You know they're all eager for grandchildren now since you and Jake have been engaged for so long," Leah commented.

"Yes, I know. They'll only need to wait about seven months." Cassie held their hands tight. "Thank you both for all your help planning this day and standing up with me. Oh no!"

Cassie looked up and blinked her tears away.

Abbey and Leah laughed and did the same. "Okay, there's no time for a touch up, let's keep it together, ladies," Abbey joked.

Leah squeezed Abbey's and Cassie's hands, a serious expression on her lovely face. "All kidding aside, though. I'm really glad we're going to be sisters."

Cassie air-kissed Leah's cheek, careful not to get too close and ruin their makeup. "We are too."

After a full round of air-kisses between them, they ended up in a fit of giggles. "Think we can convince everyone to air-kiss us so we don't ruin our makeup?" Abbey asked.

Cassie frowned and shook her head. "Probably not, but at least we have the makeup bags Angel made up for us. We'll be able to look amazing for the entire day."

"That's true," Leah agreed.

Someone knocked on the conference room, startling them. "It's Dad. We're ready for you."

"Okay, Dad, one minute. Leah, can Abbey and I have a minute?"

Leah nodded and headed to the door. "Of course." The door clicked softly behind her as she left.

"Abbey, can you do me a favor today and this weekend?"

"I'm sorry I overreacted at the hotel about Luke. It's just…"

Cassie squeezed both of Abbey's hands tight. Her warmth seeped into Abbey. "I don't really mean Luke. I can tell something's bothering you. Something other than Luke."

Abbey desperately wanted to tell Cassie about losing her job. About her nervousness of the future, and yes, of seeing Luke, but she held back. Although Cassie seemed calm and collected, she wondered if Cassie had her own anxieties too. After all, Cassie was getting married, was pregnant, and keeping her pregnancy a secret for now. She didn't want to add to Cassie's own worries. Especially today.

"I know you probably don't want to say anything, especially today and that's all right. I understand. It's not necessary, but I understand. Just promise me you'll give that overactive brain of yours a break this weekend. Have fun. Don't overthink anything. Just relax and go with the day. Can you do that?"

Abbey scoffed. "I don't have an overactive brain."

"Oh, really? You've spent the last ten years at OSG working your ass off while going to night school. Your brain needs a reboot—for the weekend at least."

Cassie was right to a certain degree. The last ten years had been hectic for her. She'd worked hard at OSG, initially being hired as an entry level Support Desk Analyst and working her way up to a Senior Systems

Engineer, responsible for the IT Service Management system they used to manage the support desk, computer assets, and IT change management process. All the while attending night school to first earn her BS in Computer Science and then her MBA six months ago. Maybe Cassie had a point—a weekend brain reboot might be what she needed.

"Maybe you're right."

Cassie smiled brightly at her, her sparkling blue eyes filled with love and understanding. "I know I'm right. So just go with the flow this weekend and have fun. Whatever fun means to you. Regardless of what happens today and over the weekend, know in your heart you'll be all right. That everything will be all right. Can you do that?"

"Cassie, we really need to take our places," their father said through the door.

"Okay, Dad, one second," Cassie called out to him.

Abbey smiled back at her sister. She felt the stress of the last couple of days slowly drift way. She would do her best to do as Cassie asked. To go with the flow and have fun. She could pick up the pieces of her life on Monday.

"I will, Cass, I'll relax and have fun this weekend. I promise. And I'll be fine come Monday. Now enough about me, let's get you married."

****

All the men looked at the door. Heath looked visibly relieved, assuming the conversation about Leah had ended. Luke didn't think Jake would be so easily deterred.

"Come on in," Jake called out. "We're not finished talking about this," Jake told Heath.

Hannah and Luke's Uncle Darren stepped inside

the office. "Darren," Jake, Heath, and Rocco called out.

Luke stood back while the guys greeted his uncle. His stomach tightened as he looked at the strong, vibrant man before him. In his mid-sixties, Darren Stryker was still a force to be reckoned with. Six-feet-two with a full head of mostly gray and blond hair, he had the outward appearance of a healthy and successful businessman.

And at the moment, Darren Stryker was exactly that. He had inherited ownership of the Chicago Cobras from Luke's grandfather Bradford twelve years ago, along with all real estate amassed by Stryker Real Estate Holdings. Stryker Real Estate Holdings owned and managed a significant number of commercial and residential properties throughout Chicago and the surrounding suburbs, as well as properties in Nevada where the Cobras' Triple A minor league team, the Windy City Rattlers, was located. Darren had grown the company's real estate portfolio several times over since inheriting it. The success of the Cobras, Rattlers, and his real estate holdings had made his uncle a billionaire. Darren had never married, making Luke his uncle's sole heir.

Luke felt a boulder-sized lump form in his throat and his eyes burned. Shit, he was going to lose it in front of everyone. His shoulder problem was nothing compared to the news his uncle had shared while he was in the hospital Wednesday night and Thursday. Darren turned to Luke and shook his head slightly.

Luke stood up straight, cleared his throat, and took a deep breath. Then another. He nodded at his uncle.

Keep it together. It's not over yet. Uncle Darren, Dad, is the toughest man you know. Just relax and enjoy the weekend. Darren's counting on you.

Luke looked around the room. Darren's long-time companion wasn't here. "Where's Maureen?" Maureen

Taylor, a lovely woman in her early fifties, had been with his uncle since the day she interviewed with the Cobras Children's Foundation five years ago. She made his uncle happy, and he loved her for it.

"I already escorted her to her seat. I'll join her in a minute. I wanted to see you boys first," Darren replied.

Jake shook Darren's hand and clapped him on the back. "Thank you for everything, Darren. Everyone with Hailey's has been amazing. They've made preparing for today a lot less stressful. Cassie's been thrilled rather than stressed out and we have *you* to thank for that. We wouldn't have been able to book Hailey's otherwise."

Darren waved a hand dismissively. "No need to thank me. You've been like a brother to my boy and so has Heath. Anything you two need, just say the word."

Luke was touched by Darren's sentiment. It couldn't have been easy for him when Luke's parents died and Darren became an insta-daddy to a devastated ten-year-old boy. Luke's father James, a former Army veteran and a member of the All Army Sports Program for softball, was Darren's younger brother by two years.

The brothers had been close and Darren hadn't hesitated in becoming Luke's guardian after his parents' death. Although a confirmed bachelor with no children of his own, Darren did all he could to fill the void that losing Luke's parents had created in his heart. He would be forever grateful for his uncle's guidance and support the last twenty years. Luke was the man he was today because of Darren's guiding hand, sound advice, and influence.

"Thank you, sir," Jake and Heath both said.

Darren turned to Hannah, who had been sneaking glances at Rocco. An adorable blush stained her cheeks. "They all cleaned up pretty well, wouldn't you say?"

Darren looked at Luke with a brow raised. Luke

grinned and shrugged.

"Um … well yes they did. The tuxedos fit perfectly. But what about the boutonnieres?"

Jake grabbed his out of the box on the table and handed it to Hannah, looking embarrassed. "Yeah, no way any of us would have been able to pin these on. Can you give us a hand?"

Hannah made quick work on pinning Jake's boutonniere to his tuxedo lapel. The groom's boutonniere was comprised of a white and cornflower-blue dyed rose with some additional frilly flowery stuff attached to it. Luke's and Heath's boutonnieres were only a single cornflower-dyed rose with the same frilly flowery stuff attached. Hannah pinned Luke's and Heath's with quick care and stood back, admiring her work.

"Perfect. I think you three are all set. The ladies are here and they look absolutely beautiful. Wait until you see Cassie, Jake. She's stunning." Hannah smiled at Jake as he tried to make his way out the door. She grabbed him by the shoulders, doing her best to stop him.

Luke ran to the door, standing in front of it, blocking Jake's escape. "Whoa, you can't see her now, Jake, you know that."

Jake fisted his hands. "Why not? We've been together for years. What difference does it make if I see her for a minute before we start the ceremony?"

"Tradition," everyone in the room except for Jake exclaimed.

Luke laughed when Jake crossed his arms over his chest and pouted. "Fine. It's a stupid tradition, don't you think? It's 2017, not 1817."

"Maybe so," Hannah said, "but it is what it is. I've got to finish up with a few last-minute arrangements. I'll come back when we're ready for you to take your places."

Luke backed away from the door entrance, giving Hannah enough room to walk out.

"Hannah, wait," Rocco called out.

Hannah turned to Rocco, blushing. Luke chuckled to himself. Whatever this thing was between the Italian Marine and the little event planner, it would be fun to watch play out.

"Do you have any mints in that magic bag of your for the guys?"

Hannah stared at Rocco for a beat, not saying anything, and then rummaged through her bag. She retrieved a small clear plastic container and shook out a couple tiny white mints into Jake's, Heath's, and Luke's hands.

Rocco walked up to Hannah with a smirk on his face. He held out his hand out, palm up. "Don't I get some too?"

Hannah looked at Rocco with wide eyes and nodded. Luke saw her hand shake slightly as she shook three mints into Rocco's palm.

Rocco popped them in his mouth. "Mmmm."

Hannah gasped, blushing even harder and turned to leave. "I'll be back soon to get you all," she said and dashed out the door.

"Damn, Roc. Get a room, why don't you?" Luke laughed and winked at his uncle.

"What are you talking about?" Rocco crunched his mints with gusto.

Darren rolled his eyes. "Come on, Rocco, you're obviously interested in the woman. From what I saw, Hannah appears interested in you as well."

Rocco shook his head. "No sir, not interested."

Darren grunted. "You should be. Hannah's an amazing young woman. She's bright, educated, a hard worker, and as lovely as can be. I happen to know she's not seeing anyone seriously at the moment. There were sparks between you, don't deny it."

"No, sir, there most definitely were not. I was just giving her a hard time is all. She's a bit bossy." Rocco pulled out a bottle of water from the beer cooler and chugged half of it down in two gulps. He wiped his mouth with the back of his hand. "Heath's not seeing anyone, maybe *he* should ask her out."

Jake took the bottle from Rocco and chugged down the rest. He shook his head. "No, Heath is interested in Leah."

Darren clapped Heath on the shoulder, smiling. "That's wonderful. The girl adores you. Always has. Good for you."

"No, not back to this. I'm not interested in Leah like that. I told you. And even if I were, and I'm *not*, I wouldn't do that to you." Heath looked to Luke for support. He just smiled back at him and shook his head.

"And I told *you* that I wouldn't stand in your way if you wanted to pursue Leah. I know somewhere along the way your feelings for her changed. You stopped thinking of her as an annoying little sister and started thinking about her as a woman."

Heath frowned and looked down at his shoes, seeming embarrassed. "Jake, Leah and I together isn't a good idea and I won't do anything that could ruin our friendship."

Darren stood in front of Heath and placed his hands on his shoulders. "Look at me, Heath. That girl has loved you all her life. Before she knew or understood what love was."

Heath blew out a breath and raised his head. "I don't think I'd be good for her. She can do a lot better than me. And what if things didn't work out? I don't want to ruin a lifelong friendship."

It hurt Luke to know Heath thought so little of himself. As far as he was concerned, any woman would be lucky to have him. He was a good man.

"Bullshit," Rocco said. "You're more than good enough for Leah."

"She deserves someone whole," Heath whispered.

Jake motioned to Darren, and he stepped aside. Jake looked Heath in the eyes. "None of us are perfect, Heath. A good woman will love us flaws and all. Mine does. She trusted me enough to wait until I felt confident I could provide for us. I knew there were people who tried to convince her to leave me. Tried to convince her I was just stringing her along. But she loves me and stuck with me."

"What if my hearing deteriorates and hearing aids don't work for me anymore?"

Jake laughed and shook his head. "Dude, Leah knows how to sign better than we do."

Luke had no idea Leah could sign. She'd never mentioned it. Heath was a lucky man. She had prepared herself for that possibility all long, just like he, Jake, and Heath had.

Heath looked shocked at that. "Really?"

Jake nodded. "Yeah, I saw her at mom's one day. The news on and she was translating the newscast. She was really good. She doesn't know I saw her."

Heath frowned. "Don't you see? She shouldn't have to deal with something like that."

"But she chose to learn without anyone saying anything. That means something," Rocco stated.

"Relationships are hard even under good circumstances. If things didn't work out between us, what about our friendship? She's your sister, not some random woman."

This time Darren spoke up. "As I see it, as long as

you approach a relationship with Leah honestly and make a sincere effort, and if it doesn't work out, then I'm sure you and Jake will be just fine. Isn't that right, Jake?"

"Darren's right. If you both make an honest effort and things don't work out, you won't have any issues from me. You have my word on that. I know you wouldn't intentionally hurt her." Jake stuck his hand out to Heath. Heath hesitated a moment and shook it.

"I'm still not sure it's a good idea, but I'll think about it, okay? That's the best I can do for now."

"That's a start," Darren said. "Now that that's settled, I'm going to join Maureen. Good luck, Jake." Jake and Darren shook hands and Darren left the room.

"How about you guys give me a break and we talk about Mission Abbey," Heath suggested.

Luke was good with that. "Unlike other people, I'm ready to go after my girl," Luke said, grinning. Heath flipped him off and everyone laughed.

With a determined look in his eyes, Jake said, "There are too many secrets being kept today, but what can we do to help?"

"I know I missed rehearsal, but tell me how the ceremony is supposed to go."

Luke listened intently as Jake explained how the ceremony would proceed. He hoped Cassie wouldn't mind the small changes he intended to make to the processional. It would be the first step in his mission to make Abbey his for good. Luke had been on the ropes for far too long. That ended today.

"All right, I think we have a workable plan for Mission Abbey. Thanks for having my back." Luke couldn't have asked for better or more loyal friends than Jake, Heath, and Rocco.

"No problem, you have ours," Jake said.

Rocco snickered. "Heath, this plan puts you in the

line of fire with a certain someone. Think you're going to be able to handle that?"

"I'll be just fine, asshole," Heath snapped back.

Jake laughed and said, "Laugh it up, Roc. You're seated at Hannah's table."

Heath smirked at Rocco. "Think *you're* going to be able to handle *that*?"

Rocco grunted and shook his head. "I'll be just fine, asshole. I told you I'm not interested in her."

Luke wasn't convinced. "Whatever you say, buddy."

Rocco glared at them all and checked his watch. "I'm going to check on the security detail and take my seat. From what I've seen so far, we're in good shape." Rocco shook Jake's hand and clapped him on the back. "Good luck, Jake."

"Thanks, Roc, for everything."

Rocco nodded curtly and left the room. Luke was eager to get the events of the day and the weekend started. Too much was riding on this mission. His future happiness depended on a successful outcome.

Shortly after Rocco left the room, the pastor performing the ceremony, Pastor Jenkins, stepped in. He was a tall, thin man with a receding hairline, salt and pepper hair that had more pepper than salt, wire-rimmed glasses, and kind eyes. Pastor Jenkins looked solemn in his black suit and white collar. Exactly what Luke expected from a man of the cloth.

Pastor Jenkins shook all of their hands. "So Jake, we're almost ready to get started. Your bride is a vision to behold."

Jake scowled at Heath and Luke. "I wanted to see Cassie for a minute before we got started, but they wouldn't let me." Jake nudged his head toward Luke and Heath.

Pastor Jenkins chuckled. "Good things come to those who wait, Jake. And with a seven-year engagement under your belt, a few more minutes won't make much difference, will it?"

"I know it took us a while to get here, but I wanted to be sure I had everything in place to do right by Cassie. The way she deserves."

Pastor Jenkins placed a gentle hand on Jake's shoulder. "I know that, Jake. And that's commendable. If more people took the time to better prepare before they got married, fewer would have problems down the road and get divorced. It took me a while before I felt ready to marry my wife, but we're all the better for it now."

Luke was so proud of Jake. Jake hadn't succumbed to all the pressure from everyone around him over the years to get married before he felt ready. He wanted to do right by his bride and he couldn't fault the man for that. And Pastor Jenkins was right, Cassie and Jake would be all the better for it.

Jake smiled. "Thanks, Pastor, I appreciate that."

"Why don't we pray before things get started?" Pastor Jenkins reached out and Jake and Luke each took one of his hands and one of Heath's. With their heads bowed, Pastor Jenkins prayed over them, offering God's blessings for a joyful day and holy union. Luke smiled when Pastor prayed for continued pleasant weather. What bride wanted rain on her wedding day? Although Luke vaguely recalled Rocco mentioning something about Italians considering rain on your wedding day to be good luck.

Just as the men finished their amens, Hannah stepped in. "Okay, we're ready for you to take your places."

"All right, gentlemen, I'll see you up front. Before I go though, Luke, I was hoping I could ask you a favor."

"Sure, Pastor." Luke speculated on what Pastor Jenkins was going to ask. And he had no problems with it.

"I was hoping after the ceremony is over if you wouldn't mind just saying a quick hello to my boys? It would mean so much to them. They're—we're huge fans." Pastor Jenkins looked at Luke with pleading eyes.

That was it? Luke would do them one or two better. "I'd be happy to, Pastor. In fact, my uncle keeps team gear and pictures in his trunk. Good thing because I was in a rush today and didn't bring anything myself. I can sign a few things for them too."

Pastor Jenkins's mouth fell open. "Luke, that's so kind of you. My boys will love that! Thank you."

"It's my pleasure, I'm happy to do it." Luke would do anything for his young fans. He got a lot of satisfaction from working with the Cobras Children's Foundation too. He could relate to a lot of the kids in need, losing his parents so young.

Pastor Jenkins nodded with a huge smile on his face and left, leaving Hannah waiting on them.

Jake went to his garment bag and produced a black top hat, grinning like an idiot. "Luke, you're not the only one who wants to changes things up."

"I thought Cassie didn't think a top hat was necessary," Heath commented.

"I know, I just wanted to have a little fun," Jake replied as he put the top hat on.

Hannah froze in place, a panicked expression on her face. "Changes? Other than the top hat, which doesn't look half bad, by the way, what changes?"

Luke led Hannah out the door with Jake and Heath in tow. "Nothing too crazy, Hannah. No need to worry."

Chapter Five

Abbey waited in the church vestibule with Leah, Cassie, her father Phil, and Leah's five-year-old cousin Amy who was the flower girl. She smiled over at Amy. The little dark-haired girl wore her hair down in loose waves. Her little white lace dress was accented with a cornflower-blue sash around her waist. The white lace-trimmed basket Amy held was filled with white and cornflower-blue rose petals.

Leah gently stroked Amy's hair. "You know, Miss Amy, it's not right to look more beautiful than the bride."

Amy giggled and blushed sweetly. "I'm not more beautiful than Cassie."

Cassie acted as if she was giving Amy a thorough once over. "I don't know, you look like a much cuter little bride. I sure hope Jake still wants to marry me after he sees you drop your rose petals down the aisle."

Amy didn't miss a beat and rolled her eyes. "Jake's my cousin, silly, *plus* I'm not getting married 'til after I'm an astronaut."

"I think that's very smart thinking, Amy," Abbey's father added.

The calming sound of classical music wafted through the vestibule doors. Abbey took a few deeps breaths to calm the butterflies fluttering around in her stomach.

It's going to be all right. It's your reboot weekend. Go with the flow and have fun.

Two more deep breaths and she felt some of her stress drift away. She smiled to herself. It would be fine. Her sister was getting married, she was going to be an aunt soon, and she'd find another job. A better job. OSG would regret letting her go.

Abbey turned at the sound of heels clicking on the slate vestibule flooring, Hannah rushing toward them.

Hannah came to a stop in front of Cassie. "I hope you don't mind, but there's a little last-minute change in the procession."

Before Cassie could ask what the *little* change was, Abbey saw Heath and Luke striding toward them. The butterflies in her stomach took flight and her heart raced.

Ten years. It had been ten long years since she'd seen Luke Stryker. He looked exactly the same but different. Gone was the young twenty-year-old boy she'd lost her heart to, and in front of her stood a tall, blond Viking. Luke stood at six-foot-four, compared to the six-foot-two when they last saw each other. His shoulders were broader and his body had filled out and strengthened into the hunk of a man she was now looking at. Thick, wavy, blond hair, sparkling baby blue eyes, and that smirky dimpled grin made her weak in the knees every time. God, he looked delectable in his tuxedo. She could feel her nipples tighten and her pussy get wet. This was not good.

All those old feelings resurfaced as if they'd been in hibernation for the last ten years, waiting patiently to be set free again. Feelings of love, betrayal, and sorrow filled her, nearly overwhelming her right where she stood.

How the heck did she think she would be to handle a reunion with Luke with calm, cool, and confidence when all she wanted to do was screw his brains out and scream at him for breaking her heart so many years ago? She stared at him, dumbstruck.

Snap out of it! Get it together. You're calm and

confident. Seeing Luke again is no big deal. Weekend reboot, remember?

Abbey stood there silently and watched as Luke and Heath shook her father's hand.

"Good to see you, Luke. We missed you at rehearsal." Abbey's father had always been fond of Luke. Abbey hadn't told her parents the real reason they had broken up ten years ago and made Cassie promise her she wouldn't either. For some stupid reason, she hadn't wanted to her parents to think any less of him.

Luke had the decency to look embarrassed. "I know, Mr. Jayne, I'm sorry. It couldn't be helped. But don't worry, you've got me for the entire weekend—at least."

That surprised Abbey as she assumed Luke would be on a red-eye tonight or an early flight Sunday morning, off to another city to pitch another game.

Abbey's father smiled, looking pleased. "That's great. So you'll be joining everyone for brunch tomorrow morning at the Fairchild?"

Luke smiled wide, his sexy dimples on full display, and nodded. "I'll be there. Wouldn't miss it."

Luke was staying the entire weekend? At *least*? What did *that* mean? What was going on? "What's the little change in the procession, Hannah?" Abbey asked before Cassie could.

Luke turned to Cassie, smiling brightly. "We thought it might be nice for Heath and me to walk the bridesmaids down the aisle rather than have them walk down alone. What do you think?"

Cassie smiled back at Luke and nodded. Before Abbey could object to Luke stepping in and taking over, Cassie said, "I like that idea." Cassie turned to Abbey and Leah. "What do you two think? Wouldn't it be nice to walk down the aisle with these two handsome men?"

"I think that's a great idea!" Leah looked over and Heath and flashed him an enthusiastic smile.

Just great. If Abbey refused, she'd seem like a total bitch. She would not be that petty, not on Cassie's wedding day. And not in front of Luke after seeing him for the first time in ten years. "Sure, Cassie. That's a great idea. Very traditional."

Cassie shot Abbey a knowing smile and winked at her. She rolled her eyes. Obvious much?

Abbey's father clapped Luke on the shoulder. It was slight but she could have sworn Luke winced.

No, you imagined it. Luke's fine and he's not your problem. He's got Brenna Sinclair to take care of him now. Reboot weekend.

"Great idea, Luke. I like it," Abbey's father said.

Luke beamed back at her father and she wanted to roll her eyes again at her brown-nosing ex. "Thank you, sir. I thought since the men are in traditional black tails today, escorting the ladies down the aisle would gel with the classy vibe Cassie and Jake put together for the wedding."

Abbey's father, God love him, wholeheartedly agreed. Two peas in pod, those two. Always had been. "I agree completely."

Luke kneeled down in front of little Amy and kissed her cheek. The sweet little girl giggled. Was Luke laying it on thick or what? "Look at you, Amy. You're even prettier than the bride."

"Yeah, well, she's not getting married until after she becomes an astronaut," Abbey blurted out. She needed to pull herself together. Fast. Was she jealous of a five-year-old getting Luke's attention?

Luke tilted his head to the side and frowned at Amy. "Is that true, Amy? You're going to make me wait until you're in the space program to marry me?"

Amy giggled and blushed back at Luke. Abbey had to admit, their interaction was adorable. Luke was really dialing up the charm. "Yes. You'll have to wait."

Luke kissed the little girl's forehead. "I can respect that. You're a smart girl to want to want to get your career all set up before you marry me. I'll try real hard and be patient and wait for you."

Amy thought a moment before answering Luke. "You don't have to wait for me, Luke. Maybe I should marry another astronaut so we could go to Mars together one day."

Abbey snickered. Take *that* Mr. Charm. If the tabloids were right, not that Abbey cared, not really, Luke and Brenna Sinclair had recently gotten married in secret and would announce their marriage and Brenna's pregnancy at the premiere of her upcoming film in the next few weeks.

She needed to get over the sting of Luke not loving her enough or of her not being enough to be the one he wanted to marry. She needed to get over not having the fairy tale wedding with the designer Bellatoni couture gown that Luke would drool over her wearing. Yes, there had been a time where Abbey had been foolish enough to believe she and Luke would go all the way. She had secretly put together ideas, clippings and the like to prepare for what she *knew* would be their amazing wedding day.

Look how well that turned out.

With renewed resolve and determination, Abbey stood up straight and pulled her shoulders back. She promised Cassie she would reboot this weekend and she would do her best to do that. Her interaction with Luke would not deter her from going with the flow and having her fun. There would be plenty of single men at this wedding. Abbey would take her fun where she could.

With whomever she wanted. And if it felt right, she might take someone back to her hotel room tonight too.

So what if Luke was gorgeous? Abbey could still look her fill like all the other ladies attending the wedding would. It didn't have to mean anything.

Luke rubbed his jaw, seeming to contemplate Amy's suggestion of marrying another astronaut rather than him. "You know, I think you might be right, even though you're breaking my heart right now."

Poor Amy believed Luke and started tearing up. "Um … well, you could marry Leah or Abbey?"

Leah, who been openly drooling over Heath, chimed in. "Sorry, Luke. No offense, but I've got someone else in mind." She winked at Abbey and Heath blushed, shaking his head slightly. Apparently it was on.

Good luck, Heath. You're going to need it.

Luke stood and turned to Abbey, those baby blues nearly able to see into her soul. He regarded her briefly and turned back to Amy. "That's a wonderful idea, Amy. Thank you so much for helping me heal my broken heart. Maybe you could be mine and Abbey's flower girl when *we* get married?"

Amy's eyes widened in excitement. "Okay! It's a deal. Thanks, Luke."

Abbey felt herself blush. The thought of marrying Luke had her skin feeling tight, her nipples pebbling, and her pussy getting slick. She would need to change into a new pair of panties if this kept up. She chided herself for getting excited. Luke was full of it. It would be easier on her emotionally to be angry at him this weekend. It wasn't like she didn't have good reasons to be.

Before Abbey could speak up and inform Amy and Luke she wouldn't marry him even though this was all a ruse, Hannah stepped up and addressed them all.

"All right everyone, we're just about ready. Let's

get you all in your places. Leah and Heath are first."
Leah eagerly led Heath by the hand to their place in front
of the vestibule doors and hooked her arm around his.
Huh… Heath shot a heated glance Leah's way before he
turned his head to face front.

"Next we have the best man and maid of honor."

Luke took a hold of Abbey's hand, his hand so
big and warm, and led her behind Leah and Heath.
Holding onto his strong hand brought back too many
memories and had Abbey getting aroused all over again.
She pulled her hand out of Luke's and scowled at him.
The jerk had the nerve to smirk at her.

Hannah placed Amy behind her and Luke. "Okay,
Amy, after Abbey and Luke take their place up front with
Leah, Jake, and Heath, you'll walk down the aisle slowly
and sprinkle your rose petals along the way. Just like we
practiced at rehearsal, remember?"

Amy nodded her head. "Yes, I remember. And
when I get to the end the aisle, I'll go sit with Mommy
and Daddy."

Hannah nodded to Amy and proceeded to Cassie
and her father. "All right, Cassie, Phil. After Amy takes
her seat with her parents, that's the cue for the bridal
march to start. When it begins playing, then you both
start down the aisle. I'll be behind you to make sure your
train looks beautiful, just like you do. Then after you're
in place up front, I'll poof it up."

Cassie and her father both nodded. Hannah and
her assistant each took their places by the vestibule
doors, waiting for their cue to open them.

"You know that was a real asshole move to
change up the procession on Cassie like that," Abbey
whispered to Luke. "And what was that shit about asking
Amy to be *our* flower girl? You can't say those kinds of
things to kids if you don't mean them." Luke hooked

their arms. The heat emanating from his body seeped into hers.

He shrugged. "Tsk, tsk, princess. You shouldn't swear in church, you know."

Abbey's heart ached a little at hearing Luke's term of endearment for her. When they had been together, she felt like a princess. What the heck was wrong with her? He was probably married to Brenna Sinclair and was calling her a princess? Abbey grew angry all over again.

Luke continued, "First, the procession changes weren't a big deal to Cassie, your father, or Leah. Second, who says I didn't mean what I said to Amy about being our flower girl?"

"Oh really? Don't you think your wife Brenna might have something to say about that?" Abbey countered. She felt Luke stiffen beside her. Ah ha! She *knew* it! Luke was married and flirting with her. Did he think she'd be his little piece on the side or something? What nerve!

Luke glared at her. "Don't believe everything you read, princess. You should know better."

So if Luke and Brenna weren't married, they were still dating at least. That meant to Luke, Abbey was nothing more than some easy piece of ass. Nope, she wasn't going along with his two-timing plans. He'd have to find someone else to cheat on Brenna with. It didn't matter that the thought of Luke hooking up with someone else made Abbey's stomach clench up in knots.

"Whatever, Luke. Whatever game you're trying to play, I'm not interested." Abbey saw Hannah and her assistant touch their earpieces and nod to each other.

Pachabel's Canon in D started to play and the vestibule doors opened. This was it. No time to argue now.

Abbey watched as Leah and Heath walked down the aisle. She and Luke stepped up, waiting for their turn. Abbey's heart swelled with love at the sight of the church pews filled to capacity with friends and family sharing in Cassie and Jake's special day.

"Smile pretty for the cameras, princess," Luke whispered.

"Shut up, jerk," Abbey snapped.

Abbey elbowed Luke in the ribs and Hannah indicated they should begin down the aisle. Abbey did her best to *smile pretty* as she and Luke made their way down the aisle. Luke, being used the spotlight, had no problem flashing his sexy dimpled grin and nodding to several ceremony attendees, acting as if he owned the place. Jerk.

Abbey smiled at Jake and Heath as she and Luke arrived at the front of the aisle. Jake was wearing a black top hat?

Luke held on to her arm a little too long. "You can't get away from me, princess. Don't even try it." Luke let go of her and took his place beside Jake. Abbey stood there, stunned for a moment before taking her place beside Leah.

Leah leaned in close to Abbey with an amused look on her face. "What was that? And oh my God does Luke look *hot* in his tux. Not as hot as Heath of course, but still."

Abbey glared at her. She didn't want to think Luke looked hot in his tux. Her body had other ideas, though. Stupid traitorous body. "It's nothing. Luke's just being a jerk. I don't care how he looks or what he does. I'm going to enjoy this weekend and he can go suck it for all I care."

Leah giggled and glanced at Heath, who was staring right back at her with lust in his eyes. "I'd like to suck a few things on Heath, that's for sure."

Abbey chuckled quietly. "Shhh … we're in a church"

"Makes no difference to me. I'd suck Heath in a church, near a church…"

Abbey turned her attention to the open vestibule doors. Little Amy had begun her ascent down the aisle, smiling brightly and sprinkling white and cornflower-blue rose petals along the way. Folks ahhed and oohed over Amy and chuckled as she waved and said hi to some people she knew in the church pews as she walked past them.

When Amy reached the end of her journey, she turned to Luke. "See, Luke? I'll be a good flower girl for you and Abbey."

Luke winked at Amy and nodded his head. Abbey wanted to throttle him for putting that idea in her head. She prayed only the few people close to Amy heard. Amy took her seat with her parents, beaming with pride.

Abbey glared at Luke. He had a smug expression on his handsome face and had the nerve to mouth the word *smile* at her.

She was about to stick her tongue out at Luke when the music changed to the bridal march. Everyone stood and Abbey focused on Cassie and their father at the end of the aisle, ready to take their place up front. She smiled, but not because Luke told her to. Because she loved her sister, and because she would be an auntie soon, and because she wished all the love and happiness in the world for Cassie and Jake.

****

Luke watched Abbey shoot daggers at him and plaster a smile on her face as the music changed to the bridal march. He was transfixed by the look of sheer love and affection that crossed her beautiful face as she looked at Cassie and her father make their way to the altar.

Luke was saddened by her hostility toward him. He had hoped that after ten years she would be more even tempered. Softened a bit. But she was still angry. Very angry. And that smart mouth of hers. It had shocked the hell out him *and* turned him on. When they were younger, Abbey was sweet and gentle and kind. Never losing her temper even when she was upset and certainly never cursing.

Luke couldn't help but smile. He liked the woman she had become. She was angry, sure, but Luke knew his Abbey. His princess was still the kind, giving, intelligent, and loyal person he'd fallen in love with years ago.

When he first came upon her in the church vestibule, he wanted to carry her off on his non-injured shoulder and fuck her senseless until she was too exhausted to argue with him so he could make her understand he'd never been unfaithful to her and he never would. He'd felt his cock get hard in front of her father and he couldn't have that, so Luke made himself think of boring baseball stats, the weather—anything that would calm his dick the fuck down.

Luke was encouraged to see that although Abbey was still angry with him, she wasn't completely unaffected. He'd noticed her hard nipples poking against the lacey bodice of her pretty bridesmaid dress. And he bet if he checked, he would have found her pussy was nice and wet for him too. She'd been so responsive to him back in the day and it appeared she still was.

Luke had been Abbey's first. He was still proud and humbled by that fact. He'd been the lucky one to introduce her to everything. The pleasure of getting her nipples sucked and teased, moving past her embarrassment of having him eat her pussy until she yanked on his hair and came so hard she shook. He'd taught her how to suck his dick so well he nearly went cross eyed when he came in her mouth. And the sex. Still to this day he'd never felt as connected to or as in sync with someone as he did when he'd fucked Abbey.

His sweet little princess had been so trusting and open to experimenting he couldn't have asked for more. Her tight little pussy fit his dick perfectly, so snug, hot, and wet. It was the only place he ever wanted to be. It was home. *She* was home.

Luke cursed himself for getting hard in front of a church full of people. The damn tuxedo jackets provided no cover. They were cut leaving their crotches exposed.

Suddenly, Jake turned to him with tears streaming down his face. Shit, Luke hadn't been paying attention. He'd been lost thinking about Abbey.

"Jake, buddy, you all right?"

Jake wiped his eyes with the back of his hand and shook his head. "No, I'm not. I gotta go."

Luke panicked. Jake was leaving Cassie at the altar? He looked to Pastor Jenkins for help and the pastor shook his head slightly. Pastor Jenkins seemed calm.

Before Luke could say anything more, Jake took off toward Cassie and her father. Everyone in attendance gasped and whispered amongst themselves. The bridal march stopped playing. The photographer was clicking away, taking photographs of the impending disaster and the videographer was capturing every horrific moment as it unfolded.

Luke looked over to Abbey and Leah to find them both in shock with their mouths wide open. He didn't know what to do. Should he chase after Jake? He turned to Heath, his expression guarded. Not much help at all.

Luke looked to his Uncle Darren, desperate for

guidance. Darren, his father and mentor of twenty years now, would know what to do. Darren looked him straight in the eye and shook his head slightly. Luke raised a brow, not sure if doing nothing was the right thing or not. Darren smiled at him and shook his head again. All right, Luke would butt out.

Luke took a deep breath and waited along with everyone else as Jake made his way to Cassie and her father. No one was sure what would happen next.

Pastor Jenkins was right. Cassie was a vision to behold. She and Jake wouldn't allow him to buy her a designer couture bridal gown like he'd wanted to, but the gown she chose was beautiful none the less. The lace looked like it was floating up her chest and down her arms. Her hair was done up and she looked absolutely radiant. How could Jake turn tail now? He'd wanted to see her *before* the ceremony for fuck's sake. And Cassie was expecting. He couldn't believe Jake would be so cruel.

Cassie's father looked more than a little concerned. "Jake, are you all right?"

Cassie cocked her head with a little grin on her face, poised and calm. "You decided on a top hat?" A few people laughed. Cassie was making jokes?

Jake's hand quickly went to his head, touching the brim of the top hat like he'd forgotten he had it on. "Oh, right. I thought it would be fun?" He took it off, turned to Luke, and tossed it over to him. Luke caught it easily and put it on. A few people laughed nervously. Everyone not quite sure what to make of what they were witnessing.

Jake shook his head and looked at Cassie's father. "No, Phil, I'm not all right. Would you mind if I walked Cassie the rest of the way?"

A collective sigh went through the crowd. Jake

wasn't leaving Cassie, he was overwhelmed and emotional by his beautiful bride. For a moment, Luke wondered if he would react the same way when he and Abbey got married because he *knew* they would. If he had anything to say about it, and he sure as hell did, they'd be getting married in the not-too-distant future. He had no intention of Mission Abbey failing.

Cassie's father smiled warmly at Jake and nodded his head. "Sure, Jake, you go ahead. Take good care of my little girl." Cassie's father kissed her lightly on the cheek and placed her hand in Jake's.

Jake nodded. "Thank you, Phil. And I will. I promise you." Jake brushed his lips against Cassie's knuckles and led her to their place up front. Phil followed behind, steering clear of Cassie's wedding dress train.

Luke's stomach, which had been twisted in knots, relaxed. Everyone sighed. Luke looked to Abbey and Leah. They were both smiling again, appearing relieved like he was. Luke shrugged and flashed Abbey a grin. She shrugged back, still smiling. That smile made his heart race and his dick hard. He wanted to keep that smile on her face for the rest of her life.

"Who gives this lovely young woman to this emotional young man?" Pastor Jenkins bellowed out.

Once the laughter died down, Phil spoke up, pride shone in his eyes. "Her mother and I do."

Luke was grateful the ceremony proceeded with no other incidents. Luke kept a careful eye on Jake just in case, and on Abbey too. Since Jake told Cassie he got the top hat because he thought it would be fun, Luke and Heath alternated wearing it throughout the ceremony. He caught Abbey rolling her eyes at him at a couple of times but she'd always had mirth dancing in them. Luke considered it a win.

After the ceremony was over and pictures were

taken, Luke sat alone in the first pew on the groom's side, enjoying a moment of solitude. He had spent a few minutes with Pastor Jenkins's young sons Noah and Joshua, taking pictures, tossing the ball around, and signing autographs. His Uncle Darren had plenty of merchandise and swag in the trunk of his car to give not only Noah and Joshua but the pastor as well. Luke's shoulder was faring well with only a slight ache.

The clean-up crew were busy tidying up while some ceremony guests were mingling and enjoying light refreshments in the church's Fellowship Hall before everyone headed to the reception being held at Cucina Antonetti's in Elmhurst. Antonetti's was known for their amazing Italian food and they served the best family-style food service in the Chicagoland area.

Luke was famished. The last few stressful days had killed his appetite. He would make sure he ate well tonight. He needed to take good care of himself, especially now.

Darren had asked Luke not to lose his shit until after the wedding. Luke could only do so much without breaking down. His uncle's diagnosis was a hard kick to the gut. He still hadn't fully processed it. Luke's own physical issues didn't help his frame of mind either. Add to that Abbey's hostility toward him, and he wasn't sure how more he could take.

Since he was in a church and had a rare moment of solitude, Luke bowed his head and closed his eyes.

Lord, please help my dad get through this awful time. I know the statistics aren't good but you can turn things around for him. Please don't take him from me too. You took my parents way too soon, give me my uncle for as long as you can. Bless Jake and Cassie in their new life together and grant them many years of happiness. Take good care of Cassie during her pregnancy and bless her and Jake with a strong healthy baby. Please see your way to helping Abbey let go of her anger so we can move on from the past. Open her heart and mind so she can see that we belong together. Guide me with your divine wisdom as I do my best to handle the challenges that lie before me. Thank you for the many blessings you've given me over the years. I appreciate every single one. Please continue to bless me, my friends, and family. They mean the world to me. Amen.

Luke quickly swiped away the tear that slid down his cheek. He turned around to see if anyone was watching him and saw Abbey coming toward him from one of the church's side doors.

God does answer all prayers, doesn't he?

As Abbey walked toward him, Luke's heart rate sped up and he felt his dick twitch in excitement. Damn how she affected him. He smiled at her, and to his relief, she smiled back.

Luke moved over in the pew so she could join him. She sat next to him, with her cell phone in hand, careful not to touch him. Luke was having none of that and scooted over so their thighs touched. He felt her stiffen slightly then relax. She wanted Luke to think she was unaffected by him, but her pretty blue eyes were dilating and he saw her pulse fluttering on her neck.

"The dove release you set up for Cassie and Jake, that was really nice. It was the perfect end to the ceremony," she whispered.

Luke had asked Patty Hailey to tell Cassie and Jake that she wasn't able to get a dove release for them if they had asked. It turned out they hadn't so Luke was able to sneak in a surprise for the couple.

"No need to thank me, I was happy to surprise them with it." Luke was encouraged by their cordial conversation. Did this mean Abbey was warming up to him?

Abbey's phone chimed with a text and she frowned at what she read. Luke knew she was essentially always on call for her job. Office Supply Galaxy was too cheap to get her the help she needed. "Is the office paging you? Don't they know you have important family commitments this weekend?"

Luke was pissed. Abbey's manager took advantage of her kind nature. As soon as he got her back for good, he would ask her to quit her job. There would always be a place for Abbey in the Chicago Cobras organization. They could use someone as intelligent and hardworking as her. He'd prefer she not work at all, but he didn't think she would agree to that. His princess needed to be challenged and contribute. It was one of the many things Luke loved about her and always would.

Abbey quickly replied to the text and shook her head, frowning. "They know I have commitments this weekend, but no, they're not paging me."

Luke couldn't stop himself from wondering why the text was bothering her so much. His protective instincts rushed to the surface. *No one* bothered his princess. Not now, not ever.

"So what's got you upset if it's not the office bothering you?" He hoped she'd confide in him, like she used to so many years ago. Once upon a time, they'd shared everything. He desperately needed to get back to that time. He needed Abbey now more than ever.

She waved a hand dismissively. "It's nothing for you to worry about. Just forget about it."

Luke tried to not let the brush off bother him, but it wasn't easy. He leaned into her a little closer, reveling in the warm feel of her body against his. "I do worry about you, princess. Let me help you."

Just like that, the daggers flew from Abbey's eyes

at him. She shoved at him and he moved away, putting space between them in the pew. He mourned the loss of her touch.

"Shouldn't you be worrying about your *wife*? I doubt she'd be thrilled to know you're coming on to me while she's who knows where, pregnant with your child. I stopped being yours to worry about a long time ago." Abbey made to stand and leave, but he took a hold of her arm and pulled her back down onto the pew.

Luke's ears rang and his heart galloped in his chest. If Abbey wanted to do this the hard way, he'd oblige. "And I told *you*, don't believe everything you read or hear. I also told you, you can't get away from me, so stop trying."

Abbey's phone chimed again with another text message which she ignored. "Okay, fine, so you're *not* married. You're still with someone else. And not just *any* someone else, one of the biggest actresses in Hollywood right now. If Brenna's off on location somewhere this weekend and you're looking for some company so you can cheat on her, look somewhere else. I'm most certainly not going to be *that* girl for you. If you thought you could just breeze into town this weekend and I'd be some quick and easy fuck, you couldn't be more wrong. There are plenty of other women attending the reception who'd be more than happy to screw *the* Luke "Strike 'em out" Stryker, so leave me alone."

Luke needed to calm her down quick before someone heard them. What he really wanted to do was take her somewhere and fuck the hell out of her and shut her up so she could listen to him without being furious.

"Look, princess, it's not like that. I don't think of you that way." Luke spoke in calm, even tones.

"Stop calling me *princess*. I'm not your princess. Brenna is now. Can't you just leave me alone? You're ruining my reboot weekend."

This time, Luke let Abbey stand up to leave as Jake approached them. He didn't want to continue upsetting her, but he didn't know what to do to get her to calm down and listen to him.

What the hell is a reboot weekend? I thought Abbey said the office wasn't paging her?

"There you are," Jake said to Abbey. "Cassie's looking for you. Do you mind helping her out for a minute? She's in Fellowship Hall."

Abbey's eyes widened in a panic. "Oh no, is she all right?"

Jake chuckled and nodded. "She needs your help real quick to go to the bathroom."

Abbey smiled at Jake. "We don't want her dress ruined now, do we?" She kissed Jake on the cheek and took off to help her sister. Luke heard her phone chime with another text message. Abbey didn't stop to look at it.

Jake took a seat next to Luke, a sappy grin on his face. Luke couldn't blame him. He'd married the love of his life at long last and they were expecting. Life didn't get much better than that. If Luke could only get Abbey to calm down and listen to him, life could get a hell of a lot better for him too.

Jake leaned forward, placing his forearms on his legs. He turned to Luke, seeming concerned. "Things didn't sound like they were going too well when I walked up. I'm sorry. I should have asked Leah to help Cassie. Maybe you and Abbey just needed another minute."

Luke blew out a breath and leaned back in his seat, gazing up at the beautiful religious paintings that decorated the church ceiling. He hoped his prayers would be answered soon. He looked over to Jake. "A few more minutes wouldn't have helped. She's pretty angry."

Jake leaned back and admired the church ceiling with Luke. "You didn't *really* think you could just show up after not seeing her for ten years and she'd fall into your lap, did you? That's arrogant, even for you, little brother."

Luke sat up in his seat, smiling at Jake's endearment. It was true. Luke had two big brothers, Jake and Heath.

"I didn't expect her to fall at my feet, but I also didn't expect her to be so angry after all this time either." Luke didn't want Abbey thinking he thought so little of her. She wasn't some quick and easy fuck like she'd suggested. She was his woman, always had been and would be again. He needed to convince her of that fact.

Jake sat up. "Don't give up on her. Give her a chance to let her feelings out, then go from there. The day is still young."

Luke knew Jake was right. But it wasn't easy because he knew he hadn't betrayed Abbey. He needed her to let him explain what she *actually* saw when she had walked in on him ten years ago, not what she *thought* see saw.

"Do you know what a reboot weekend is?"

Jake eyebrows furrowed. "Like the server maintenance they do at OSG? According to Abbey, they reboot their servers on a rotating schedule."

Luke shook his head. "The Cobras' data center does that too. I don't think that's it, though. She got a few texts that upset her but she said it wasn't the office. But she said I was ruining her reboot weekend."

"Sorry, Luke. I don't know what that means. Cass hasn't said anything."

A thought occurred to Luke that had his blood boiling. Was Abbey seeing someone? Were those texts from him? Was he trying to upset her today of all days? The thought of Abbey with someone else now that he was back in town to claim her as his had him fisting his hands. He wasn't stupid enough to think Abbey had pined over him for ten years. He knew through Jake that Abbey had dated over the years, but with her work and night school schedules, it had never resulted in anything serious. That gave him a small sense of comfort.

Luke didn't relish the thought of Abbey fucking another man, even if that made him seem like a caveman asshole. Abbey belonged to him. All of her—her soft full tits, luscious lips, and her tight little pussy. They belonged to him and him alone.

Although Luke had been seen with various celebrities, models, and reality show stars over the years, much of what everyone saw and read wasn't true. Most were strategic photo and publicity opportunities.

Not that Luke had been a monk over the last ten years. He'd done a fair amount of fucking, but never with anyone he had ever considered special. Luke's own schedule had been brutal these last ten years too and the truth of the matter was no one, no matter how famous or outwardly beautiful, compared to his princess Abbey.

Luke needed to know what he was up against though. "I know I should have asked before, but is Abbey seeing anyone?"

Jake shook his head. "Not that I know of, and Cassie hasn't said anything about a man in Abbey's life."

Luke's stomach grumbled. He needed to eat something. He needed more in his stomach than pain pills, breath mints, and a few pulls of beer.

Jake stood and Luke followed suit. "Luke, thanks for the dove release. Cassie was thrilled. But you've got to stop with the gifts. It's too much. I mean it."

Luke walked toward the door leading to

Fellowship Hall and snacks. "Jake, get over it. You know I'm a simple guy. I don't own twenty homes and a hundred fancy cars. It makes me happy to spend some money on my friends and family. What else am I going to do with it? And soon I'll have a new little niece or nephew to spoil."

Jake smiled at the mention of his new baby. He let out a breath. "How about you tell me about all these secrets you're obviously keeping and then *maybe* I'll relax on the gift giving?"

Luke laughed at his big brother and shook his head. Jake wouldn't let it go. "Sorry, man, you need to trust me. Come on, I'm starving."

"I really hate you right now. But don't overdo it. We're doing dinner up well at Antonetti's tonight."

Luke had no intention of stuffing himself on snacks. He loved Antonetti's. Cucina Antonetti's had been an Elmhurst staple for years and one of Chicagoland's favorite Italian restaurants. It was one of Jake and Cassie's favorites and when they decided on their wedding date, both Luke and his Uncle Darren contacted the owner Carlo Antonetti to ensure they had an available banquet room. Luke smiled to himself. Not all of his wedding-related gifts had been obvious. Jake and Cassie didn't need to know.

With the ceremony behind them, Luke could now refocus on Abbey. He'd told her earlier she wouldn't be able to get away from him and he meant it.

Chapter Six

Abbey stood outside the entry doors of Cassie and Jake's banquet room at Cucina Antonetti's. She was still irritated after her heated conversation with Luke in church after the ceremony. Why did he continue to push her? She had made herself perfectly clear. She wasn't interested in being Luke's plaything for the weekend. It hurt her to know that he thought so little of her. That he thought she'd help him cheat on his famous girlfriend. She had no intention of becoming tabloid news.

Abbey's phone chimed inside her evening bag with another text message. Her stomach clenched. Besides Luke being an ass, Tom Murphy wouldn't stop texting her, begging her to let him attend the wedding to make Luke jealous. Playing those kinds of games didn't interest her at all.

So far her reboot weekend was off to a terrible start. Not wanting to deal with Tom's barrage of texts which she would not read for at least the rest of the weekend, she stepped into their banquet room.

She smiled as she looked around the room. The room's dark hardwood floors and wood-paneled walls gleamed. The matching wood bar appeared well stocked, with the bartender doing a last-minute inventory. Cassie and Jake opted for an unlimited open bar, which Abbey knew would be would be well frequented throughout the night.

The room was filled with tables of eight that were draped in bright white tablecloths and napkins with printed dinner menus on top of each place setting. The chairs were covered in white satin covers with cornflower-blue bows tied around the middle of the chair backs. The florist and her assistants were finishing up by putting the white and cornflower-blue centerpieces at each table. The long rectangular head table with large captain's chairs for the bride and groom had a gorgeous elongated centerpiece that coordinated with the smaller guest table centerpieces.

Abbey went to her chair at the head table, placed her evening bag on the seat, and sighed. Another one of Luke's bright ideas was to have Leah and Heath sit next to Cassie and the two of them sit next to Jake. Young Amy was sitting with her parents. Abbey took a deep breath and rolled her neck. It would be all right. After dinner was over, she could ditch Luke and kick her reboot weekend into high gear.

Cassie stood in the entryway, smiling as she inspected the room. Abbey went over to her and smiled back. "It looks amazing doesn't it?"

Cassie's eyes glistened and she nodded. "Yes, it's even better than I imagined it."

Abbey heard her phone chime again and growled. She'd just turn the damn thing off after they sat down to dinner.

Cassie gave Abbey a sidelong glance. "Everything all right? Jake told me about your argument with Luke in church after the ceremony."

Abbey should have known Jake would tell Cassie about their argument. They told each other everything. There was a time when Luke and Abbey shared everything too. It felt like a lifetime ago.

"It's not just Luke. Tom Murphy's insisting on being my date to your wedding to make Luke jealous. I've been telling him no all day, but he won't let up. What if he shows up and makes a scene?" That last thing Abbey needed was to bring that kind of drama to her sister's wedding. She also wasn't sure about Tom's true intentions. Now that Abbey was no longer working at OSG, she didn't want Tom to think he could pursue her. She wasn't interested in any way. The thought of being with Tom Murphy made her shudder. Man-whore.

Cassie's brows went up and her eyes danced with excitement. "Tom Murphy's cute. Why not have him be your plus one? We have plenty of room for another person. Reboot weekend, remember?"

Abbey shook her head. Absolutely not. "No way, not Tom. That's just disgusting, no matter how cute he is. He pounces on anything with a vag," she explained.

Cassie laughed, causing Abbey to laugh a little too. "Well, that's what you're looking for this weekend, right? Just some fun, not a marriage proposal. Tom's perfect for that, don't you think?"

Technically, yes, Tom would be perfect for Abbey's reboot weekend. He was all about having fun. But they worked together, used to anyway. She knew too much when it came to Tom. He was a total pig and although he was attractive, she wasn't attracted *to* him at all. Which meant he couldn't be her plus one.

"Oh yeah, he's all about fun. Maybe *too* much fun. But I'm not attracted to him, Cassie. So no, I'm not inviting him."

Hannah Hailey and her assistant dashed into the banquet room and did a scan of the setup. Her assistant straightened the table place cards, brushing lint from the table they were arranged on. Hannah moved the wedding card holder on the gift table and sprinkled white and cornflower-blue rose petals on top of it. She quickly sprinkled rose petals on the on the place card table.

"Would you like petals on the head table too?" Hannah asked Cassie.

Abbey and Cassie both turned to look at the head table. The head table centerpiece was set along the front edge of the table and was about half of the length of the table itself. Other than the place settings, there were no other decorations. Rose petals would make a lovely finishing touch.

Cassie looked at Abbey and she nodded. "Yes, I think petals on our table would look so pretty. Thanks, Hannah."

Hannah sprinkled petals along the head table and took another quick look around the room. She nodded to herself, seeming pleased with the arrangements for the night. She came to Cassie and Abbey and smiled brightly. "I think everything is set and ready to go."

"Thank you for everything, Hannah, and your mother too, of course." Cassie and Hannah hugged briefly. "And you and your assistant are staying for dinner, right? I'm sure you noticed your table place card. It's a shame your mother isn't available."

"Yes, I'm staying. Thank you for the invitation. I love the food at Antonetti's! My assistant can't. He and his boyfriend have another commitment. As for my mother, she's already back at the office working on another event. She normally doesn't attend events we plan." Hannah frowned for a quick moment then replaced her frown with a happy smile.

Maybe mother and daughter don't get along so well, Abbey wondered. How sad since Hannah had worked her ass off today. She agreed with Cassie. Hannah should stay and celebrate all her hard work.

Cassie nodded. "I'm glad at least *you're* staying then. I have you seated with Pastor Jenkins, his wife and a few others. I think you'll enjoy yourself tonight."

"I know I will. I'm going to check in with Carlo Antonetti about the food real quick, then I'll be ready to relax." Hannah dashed off. If anyone needed to relax, it was Hannah. Abbey didn't know how she did it. She and her mother had been going full steam all day.

Cassie leaned in to Abbey. "Apparently from what Jake said, there are sparks flying between our Hannah and Rocco. I already had them sitting at the same table but this just got much more fun."

Abbey shook her head at her sister. She wasn't surprised though. Cassie was happy and in love and she wanted everyone else to be too. Thoughts of love brought her own thoughts back to Luke. How she wished her heart would get on board and move on. The hole Luke put there when he'd betrayed her was still there. She hoped her reboot weekend would be a turning point to get on with her life where Luke was concerned.

"So back to you and Luke. What were you arguing about?" Cassie asked.

Abbey sighed, wishing Cassie would let it go and Luke would get lost. When Luke hadn't been able to make the rehearsal, she had selfishly hoped he wouldn't be attending the wedding either. No such luck.

"Really, Cass? Do we have to do this right now?"

Cassie nodded at her. "I'm the bride, remember? I get whatever I want today."

"Thanks a lot. Using the bride card on me, huh?" Abbey smiled at her sister. She couldn't be mad at Cassie, not today at least. "He's been coming on strong. I don't even know what the hell for. He's with Brenna Sinclair, probably married to her if what I've heard is true."

Cassie shook her head. "No, he's not married, Abbey. We're certain of it."

She wanted to believe Cassie. But what difference did it make? If Luke wasn't married, he was still dating Brenna, which meant he was looking to cheat on her and Abbey would not go along with that plan. But why did the prospect of Luke not being married give her a spark of hope? *Because you're an idiot, that's why.*

"Okay, if you believe that, fine. But he's still seeing her though. So he's still the lying cheating jerk he was when we were together back then. Which means, I'm *not* interested. We've been over for ten years. He sure thinks a lot of himself if he thought he could breeze into town and expect me to just—"

Cassie put a hand up to stop her from continuing. "Look, whatever this thing is between Luke and Brenna Sinclair it's … not like we're all being led to believe on TV and the tabloids. I don't think it's anywhere *near* serious or if they're even really together at all."

Abbey didn't know what to make of that. It made no sense. "What do you mean? They've been together for three years. There are pictures of them kissing and cozy all over the place."

"Oh, I know that. But I don't think those pictures are real either. Or what they're supposed to represent."

Abbey's brain couldn't process what Cassie was trying to tell her. "How can you be sure? Those pictures looked pretty convincing to *me*."

Cassie sighed. "I'm sure for a few reasons. First, Luke doesn't look at Brenna the way he *used* to look at you. Second, the pictures that have been taken of them seem staged. They both have brutal schedules. It's like they came together from wherever they were to get some shots acting affectionate, then they went their separate ways until they got together to have more pictures taken. Most importantly, we've never met her."

That surprised the hell of out Abbey. "Really? What about the string of blondes he's been seen with over the years before he got together with Brenna?" Luke had been seen with several well-known blonde celebrities over the years until he started seeing Brenna Sinclair three years ago.

Cassie shook her head. "We've never met any woman Luke has supposedly been with, including Brenna. Isn't that *odd*, considering he's been with Brenna for three years?"

Abbey felt like she was in the Twilight Zone. She didn't know what to make of any of this. "I don't know what to say, Cassie. And why should I care one way or the other? We haven't been together in years. Luke can do whatever he wants—except me."

"I think some of Luke's relationships and especially this thing with Brenna have been more about publicity than anything else. It's good press for the Cobras and it's brought a lot of attention and donations to the Cobras Children's Foundation. You know how important the foundation is not only to Luke and Darren but to the organization as a whole."

Cassie had a point there. The children's foundation meant everything to Luke. Abbey herself had donated generously over the years. The foundation did wonderful work with disadvantaged children. They arranged for housing, meals, after-school programs, college scholarships, and more. Many of the players spent time with the kids too. The foundation made a difference.

If what Cassie was saying were true, and Luke wasn't *actually* involved with Brenna Sinclair, that didn't mean *Abbey* needed to hook up with him this weekend. There was too much bad history, too much baggage. If she let loose and had some fun, it would have to be with someone other than Luke. Abbey chastised herself for feeling disappointed at the prospect of not sleeping with Luke. *Fucking him good* as Luke used to say. She needed a drink to calm her mind and take the edge off, then she could continue with her reboot weekend.

Jake strode into the room with a goofy grin on his

face. She and Cassie couldn't help but laugh. "It was my turn with the top hat." He kissed Cassie on the cheek and placed a gentle hand on her stomach. "Hello there, my beautiful wife."

Cassie placed her hand over Jake's on her stomach. "Hello to you, my silly husband."

Abbey's eyes welled up. A tinge of jealously took hold. Cassie and Jake were so happy and in love. She didn't want to begrudge them their happiness, but she wanted the same happiness for herself.

Jake turned to the bartender. "Hey, my man, hors d'oeuvres are ready for cocktail hour. Are you ready to roll?"

The older gentleman behind the bar, with gray hair and a friendly smile, gave Jake the thumbs up. "Yes, sir! Ready whenever you are."

"All right then. We've got a few guests sitting on the leather couches against the wall right outside the doors here and a few others milling around. Luke and Heath are chatting people up. Leah's glued to Heath's side." Luke waggled his eyebrows.

Abbey had to hand it to Leah. When she wanted something, she went after it. "You think they'll get together this weekend?"

"I hope they give it a try, for both their sakes," Cassie said.

Jake took Cassie by the hand and led her to the banquet room entry doors so they could greet their guests as cocktail hour began. Abbey went to the head table and took a couple singles out of her evening bag. She cringed when she heard her cell phone chime as she walked away from the head table. She ordered a Long Island Iced Tea and dropped the bills into the bartender's tip glass. With her drink in her hand, she joined Cassie and Jake.

For the next several minutes Abbey helped Cassie

and Jake greet their guests. She knew many of the guests already and was introduced to those she didn't, including several of Jake's single college buddies and co-workers. Feeling a little buzzed from her strong drink, she considered a few potential candidates for her reboot weekend. She tried not to, but she'd looked for Luke a few times. When she'd found him, he winked and smiled at her. That made her heart flutter and her pussy slick. Damn him and her body!

Luke's security detail had done a good job keeping the press away. A few of the restaurant patrons and staff had asked for selfies with him and autographs. Luke turned no one away. He had been gracious and kind. That turned Abbey on even more.

She smiled as Mrs. Antonetti and Carlo Antonetti, her oldest son and current owner/manager of the three-restaurant chain, approached. Mrs. Antonetti, a lovely Italian-born woman in her mid-sixties, was a dead ringer for the famous Italian actress Gina Lollobrigida. Carlo was a handsome man, about six feet tall with a nice build, thick, wavy, dark-brown hair, and chocolate-brown eyes. Abbey noticed Carlo held a small white envelope in his hand.

Mrs. Antonetti double-cheek kissed Jake and Cassie. "Congratulations! Thank you for share your special day with us," she began. Abbey found her accent and broken English adorable and smiled. Mrs. Antonetti held out a hand and Carlo placed the envelope in it. She handed it to Jake. "This is little something for you. Come back after honeymoon for date night. Bring pictures, okay? Don't say no." Could the woman be any sweeter?

"We won't say no," Cassie assured her. "We'll come back with plenty of pictures to show you. Thank you."

Carlo smiled at Abbey and she smiled back. She

thought see saw interest in his eyes. Maybe her night was looking up. *Go reboot weekend!*

Mrs. Antonetti smiled and looked between Cassie and Abbey. "Your sister?" she asked Cassie.

Cassie smiled and nodded. "Yes, and she's single too!"

"Cassie!" Abbey was mortified. She didn't need Cassie's help. She felt herself blush.

Mrs. Antonetti elbowed Carlo in the ribs lightly. "See? She pretty, no?"

"Ma!" Carlo blushed and shook his head. He looked up at Abbey and mouthed *sorry*.

Abbey noticed Luke marching over toward her with fire in his eyes. His long strides quickly ate up the space between them.

Oh shit. He's pissed.

****

That was it. Luke was done. It was one thing to watch Abbey be hit on by some of Jake's college buddies and a few of his co-workers, but it was another to watch as Mrs. Antonetti try to play matchmaker for her son Carlo with *his* Abbey. Not a fucking chance.

He turned away from the conversation he was having with Jake's cousins, stomped over to Abbey, and put his arm possessively around her waist. Luke felt her stiffen. Yes, it was a Neanderthal move, but he didn't care.

Recognition dawned on Mrs. Antonetti's and Carlo's faces. Carlo extended his hand. "You're—"

Luke was in full asshole mode now. "The *best* man." *Yeah, that's right dickhead, she's mine. Don't even think about it.*

"Luke!" Abbey yelled at him and tried to pull away. Luke was having none of *that* either and pulled her closer. She was so soft and warm against him. And cozied up next to him was *exactly* where she belonged. It was time she ditched the attitude and got on board with Luke's plans for their future.

Jake looked at Luke, disappointed shown in his eyes. Crap, Luke was making a scene. "Mrs. Antonetti, Carlo, this is Luke Stryker, from the Chicago Cobras and my best man."

Mrs. Antonetti smiled at him and nodded. "I thought so. Welcome to Cucina Antonetti's!"

"Luke," Abbey warned.

Luke looked at her pleading eyes and took a deep breath. He turned back to Mrs. Antonetti with a smile and shook her hand. "It's a pleasure to meet you. I'm looking forward to dinner tonight."

Mrs. Antonetti beamed with pride. "Dinner will be *delizioso*. You no worry about that."

Abbey nudged him and Luke turned to Carlo and extended his hand. Carlo hesitated for a second but then shook Luke's hand. "It's nice to meet you, Carlo."

"Same here. The Antonetti family are huge fans."

With Abbey, Cassie, and Jake watching him closely, Luke wanted to be mindful of his temper. He'd never been rude to a fan, and didn't want to embarrass Jake or Cassie, but where Abbey was concerned, all bets were off.

Luke felt her relax beside him. He'd missed being close to her like this and felt his temper ease. "Thank you. That means everything to me and the team." He meant it. Where would the team be without their fans?

Luke knew Abbey was looking at him. He turned to her and saw those beautiful blue eyes of hers were slightly dilated. Relief washed through him knowing he hadn't upset her too much.

"Why don't you sign some autographs and take a few pictures for the Antonettis?" Abbey suggested.

Luke didn't want to leave her side, but Jake chimed in. "That's a great idea, Abbey. We still have twenty minutes before introductions and dinner service starts. What do you say?"

Luke regarded everyone's expectant expressions and relented. He didn't want to be a complete ass. He nodded his head. "Of course, I'd be happy to."

Mrs. Antonetti clapped her hands, clearly pleased. "*Bene, grazie*. Carlo, you go with Luke, I check the food. *Andiamo*." Mrs. Antonetti started toward what Luke assumed was the kitchen. Carlo shrugged and followed. Luke glanced at Abbey, Jake, and Cassie. The three of them seemed grateful.

Crisis of his own making averted, Luke followed Carlo down a short hallway into the restaurant's hot busy kitchen. Fortunately, Luke thought no one had noticed him during their walk to the kitchen.

The kitchen itself was a different matter. For a moment, he watched in awe as the chefs, assistants, and wait staff performed a sort of choreographed dance of among each other between prep work, cooking, baking, plating, boxing leftovers … until they noticed him.

Some of the wait staff had their phones out, snapping pictures. Luke was used to that, but he didn't want to draw the press's attention to his whereabouts. The amazing scents of authentic Italian cooking made his mouth water and his stomach growl so loud Carlo heard.

"Get back to work and don't tell anyone, *capire*?"

Carlo's employees shot a few more pictures, nodded, and got back to work, talking excitedly to each other but sneaking glances Luke's way. "*Antipasti per Tyler e Jayne*, my office, *subito*."

Carlo led Luke down another short hallway to his office. Done in the same dark wood tones as the restaurant and banquet rooms, Carlo's office was decorated with a large mahogany desk and executive leather high-back chair. Two luxurious leather captain's style chairs were set in front of the desk and a leather couch was placed against the back wall of the office. The walls were decorated with various pictures of the Antonetti family and their well-known Italian wine vineyards. And a picture of Carlo with the band Kiss in full makeup? There were several pictures of Carlo and who had to be his son, a younger, spitting image of his father. Luke felt the annoying pang of jealousy. If things had worked out differently, he'd most likely have little mini me's of his own by now.

Carlo gestured for Luke to sit as he took a seat behind his desk. Luke sat down and waited, feeling awkward from his earlier Neanderthal display. "First, let me apologize for Ma. She's been trying to marry me off since before my son CJ was born. I meant no disrespect to you or your woman. She's beautiful, of course, but I had no intention of acting on Ma's enthusiasm about her being single," Carlo began. Before Luke could respond there was a knock on the door.

"*Entra.*"

The office door opened and Luke was surprised to see the head chef. Luke sat at attention when he saw the chef was carrying a large plate filled with Jake and Cassie's hors d'oeuvres—mozzarella-stuffed bacon-wrapped shrimp, Italian sausage-stuffed mushrooms, and mini Italian meatballs. Luke's stomach grumbled again and the chef and Carlo laughed.

The chef handed him the plate, a white cloth napkin, and a fork. "Mr. Stryker, I hope you enjoy this."

Luke happily took the plate of delectable hors d'oeuvres from the chef. "Thank you, Chef. Although I'm surprised you're bringing this in." He speared a mini meatball with his fork and popped the entire thing in his mouth. So fucking good. He moaned as he devoured the delicious Romano cheese and herb-seasoned beef meatball. He could easily eat a dozen.

Carlo shook his head. "Don't be fooled, Luke, he was sent by the staff."

Luke ate a stuffed shrimp in one bite, savoring the salty bacon and warm mozzarella cheese. He could guess why the staff sent the chef in with his plate, and he would not be a jerk, especially after sampling the chef's amazing food. "No worries, Chef, I'm happy to take a few pictures and sign autographs. Can you give Carlo and me a few minutes?"

The chef looked over to Carlo. When he nodded in agreement, the chef said, "Thank you Mr. Stryker. And don't worry, the staff won't take much of your time."

"Find CJ for me and tell him to bring the camera, *per favore*," Carlo said as the chef left his office.

"Will do." The office door clicked shut.

Luke thoroughly enjoyed an Italian sausage-stuffed mushroom and looked up at Carlo apologetically. "Thank you for this, I haven't eaten much today. It's been nonstop busy."

Carlo nodded his head in understanding. "You're very welcome. Why should you miss out on cocktail hour? Again, I'm sorry about the misunderstanding with Ma and your woman."

Luke grunted and munched on another shrimp. Everything *does* go better with bacon, he thought. "Abbey *was* my woman ten years ago."

"Ah, the one that got away, eh?" Carlo frowned and shook his head sadly.

Carlo must have let someone get away too, from the sad but knowing expression on his face. "Yes, but I'm getting her back—this weekend. She's not making it easy though, but I'm determined to make her come around. You've lost someone too, I take it?"

Carlo sighed and nodded. "Yes, years ago, when CJ was just three weeks old. He's eighteen now."

Well shit, Carlo wasn't over *his* girl either. Luke estimated Carlo to be in his late thirties, early forties at the most. There was still plenty of time if he wanted to pursue her.

"You should reconnect with her. See if the attraction and chemistry are still there." Now Luke felt like a total dick for being rude earlier. Carlo wasn't interested in Abbey. He was still pining over his *own* long-lost love.

Carlo shrugged, sadly. "I don't know. She had big dreams she wanted to work toward when I last saw her. I didn't want to stand in her way so I didn't even tell her I loved her. I was twenty-three years old with a newborn. She was eighteen and off to beauty school and then she wanted to open a salon and spa with her sister and friends. I didn't want to tie her down. It was for the best, I think."

Luke felt like a complete jackass. "That was then, and this is now. It couldn't hurt just to find her. If anything, just to catch up. Get a haircut? You could try finding her on Facebook."

There was a sudden knock at the door and it flew open. Carlo's son CJ bounded into the room with a camera in his hands. He went right to his father without looking in Luke's direction. The resemblance between father and son was striking. Luke felt another pang of jealousy deep in his gut. "Hey, Dad. They said you wanted the camera?" Carlo nudged his head in Luke's direction.

CJ's eyes grew wide and his mouth fell open. "Holy shit! Luke Stryker!" CJ shoved the camera into

Carlo's chest and rounded the desk with his hand extended.

Luke placed his plate of mostly eaten hors d'oeuvres on Carlo's desk and stood. He shook CJ's hand. The young man had a strong grip. "It's good to meet you, CJ."

CJ's smile was infectious. "Oh my God, did you and Brenna Sinclair get married? Are we doing your reception?" CJ was nearly bouncing out of his shoes with excitement.

Carlo put the camera on his desk and came around the desk to CJ and Luke. "No, son. Luke's not with Brenna Sinclair anymore." Carlo looked to Luke. "I take it that's not common knowledge though, is it?"

Luke was beginning to like Carlo Antonetti more and more. He was a decent man. "That's right. But please don't say anything, okay?"

CJ nodded. "I won't say anything, I promise. But what's with the tuxedo?"

"I'm the best man for the Tyler and Jayne wedding here tonight."

"Oh, great. I hope you enjoy your time with us," CJ replied professionally. All right, Luke liked the young Antonetti too. "So the camera is for a few pictures for the restaurant?"

Luke and Carlo both nodded.

"Before we take pictures, can I run a business proposition by you, Luke?" CJ asked, a hopeful expression on his face.

Carlo's brows furrowed. "What kind of business proposition, son?"

CJ grinned at Carlo and Luke, keeping them both in suspense. "I was thinking of a fundraising event at our three restaurants for the Cobras' Children's Foundation.

Luke *definitely* wanted to hear what CJ had in

mind. He was a whore for the foundation. Whatever he could do to raise awareness for the wonderful work they did, he was all for it.

He made his way back to the banquet entry doors with a few minutes to spare before introductions were due to begin. He'd taken pictures with Carlo, CJ, and some with Carlo's staff, and signed menus, napkins, and blank restaurant survey cards. What he was most pleased about was CJ's idea for a fundraiser. He had a signed copy of their discussion in his pocket. They would arrange a time to get together soon with each of their attorneys to hammer out the details. Carlo was a lucky man. He had a great son. Luke hoped that one day soon, he'd have some of his own. Daughters, too. He needed to get Abbey on board. Fast.

Jake approached him with the top hat in his hand. He handed it to Luke. "Your turn."

Luke put the top hat on and smiled. He was in a great mood. Ready to get the evening started and successfully complete Mission Abbey.

"I was just coming to find you. We're ready to get started. You must be starved, man. You only had some fruit in Fellowship Hall."

"Carlo had them give me a few of your hors d'oeuvres when I was in his office. Fucking awesome. But I'm ready for chicken carbonara and chicken marsala too." Luke rubbed his stomach and laughed. "How's Abbey? Is she pissed?"

Jake shrugged. "She doesn't seem to be. But she's had a couple of strong Long Island Ice Teas on an empty stomach, so make sure she eats well tonight, okay?"

Luke nodded. He intended on staying very close to his princess tonight. "I'll take care of her, don't worry."

Luke and Jake joined the others already in place for the introductions. Abbey seemed calm and had a serene smile on her face. His heart swelled with a love that had endured for the last ten years.

Time to get this party started.

Chapter Seven

Abbey stood in place at the banquet room entrance doors, waiting for the evening's festivities to begin. Young Amy would be first to enter, followed by Leah and Heath, her and Luke, and finally the happy couple. She had a little buzz going but was looking forward to dinner. She hadn't sampled the delicious-looking hors d'oeuvres being served during cocktail hour. With nothing in her stomach but the pastries she ate earlier in the day, she was starving.

Cassie stood behind her, looking as beautiful as she had for the ceremony. The makeup bags they were each given were a godsend. She'd thank Angel again at her next hair appointment. "Oh look, Jake found Luke." Cassie pointed down the hallway.

A few feet away Jake and Luke stood talking. Apparently, it was now Luke's turn to wear the top hat. Abbey was annoyed at herself for thinking the top hat looked good on him. He turned to her and winked. Her traitorous body warmed, and she felt her center get wet.

Stupid body. There are plenty of other available men here tonight.

Abbey was still angry at the spectacle Luke had made of himself in front of Mrs. Antonetti and Carlo. Pulling that *best* man crap. He needed to give that shit a rest already.

You liked the attention though, didn't you? Luke acting all possessive and caveman-like.

She looked away, not liking the direction her thoughts were taking. Whatever game Luke was playing, even if Cassie was right and Luke and Brenna weren't together, Abbey wasn't playing along. That didn't change the fact that Luke had betrayed her. She couldn't trust him.

Love is complicated.

What? Where did *that* come from? Abbey didn't love Luke anymore. That was the alcohol talking, right? Before she could explore her thoughts a little deeper, Jake and Luke stood before them.

Luke grinned at her like he didn't have a care in the world. "You miss me, princess?"

Yes. "Of course not. Don't flatter yourself. Did you at least apologize to Carlo Antonetti for your childish behavior?"

Luke shrugged and waved at Amy. Amy giggled and enthusiastically waved back. "We had a good conversation. Met the head chef, took pictures with some of the staff, you know, the usual stuff. Best of all, Carlo's son CJ had a great idea for a fundraiser we're going to do for the children's foundation. The Antonetti family, they're good people. And they know how to cook!"

Despite all her misgivings and anger toward Luke, Abbey's heart ached for him a little. Having lost his own parents at ten years old, Luke put his heart and soul into the foundation. Sometimes, she wondered if the work the foundation did for disadvantaged children meant more to him than his baseball career.

Luke reached out, took a lock of her hair, and spun it around his finger. Abbey's heart skipped a beat and her skin warmed. How could he still have such an effect on her after all this time? And especially considering how he'd tossed their love aside ten years ago?

Luke waggled his eyebrows at her. "I think maybe you missed me a little. I don't mind that you don't want to admit it. I'm man enough to admit I missed *you*. Have for a long, long time, princess." He leaned in closer.

Luke was going to kiss her, right there in the banquet area hallway of Cucina Antonetti's. Abbey should have pushed him away, but she couldn't find the will. Just one kiss wouldn't hurt anything, right? She could be angry afterwards. *It's reboot weekend, right?*

Luke was closing the distance between them and was going to kiss her when Hannah emerged from the banquet room. "All right guys, the DJ is ready to announce everyone and dinner is ready to be served."

Abbey pulled away from Luke, startled back to reality. She hated to admit she was a tiny bit disappointed at Hannah's timing. It was just as well. She didn't know which way was up where Luke was concerned.

"And you promised my wife you would relax and enjoy yourself, right?" Jake asked. It was too sweet to hear Jake refer to her Cassie as his wife now.

Hannah smiled and nodded. "Yes I did, and I will as soon as everyone's introduced. I do find my assigned table *interesting*." Hannah blushed prettily. "The DJ will announce we're getting started and then he'll announce each of you. Have fun!" She dashed back into the banquet room.

Luke grunted. "That was real bad timing."

"Welcome everyone," the DJ bellowed out. "Let's get the evening started by introducing the bridal party." The guests and the bridal party applauded.

"Please put your hands together for the pretty little flower girl Amy Tyler."

The rest of the bridal party moved up in line and the guests applauded for Amy. Leah hooked her elbow with Heath's and smiled up at him with adoration in her eyes. Abbey was surprised but pleased to see Heath smile back warmly at her. *Maybe Leah and Heath will actually get together. Good for them.*

"Up next we have groomsman Heath Jackson and lovely bridesmaid Leah Tyler."

The guests erupted in applause. Abbey clapped happily for the two of them. She and Luke stepped up to where Leah and Heath had just stood.

Luke whistled and clapped. "Go Marines!"

"Go for it, Heath!" Jake shouted from behind Abbey. She turned around and found him and Cassie laughing. Jake shrugged and Cassie winked at her.

Abbey went to hook elbows with Luke, but he took a hold of her hand instead and squeezed tight. Fond memories flooded her. Years ago, they'd always held hands. Luke's large powerful hand made her feel small and delicate. She tried to let go, the emotions too powerful. *Holding his hand now shouldn't feel so perfect, so right.* He wouldn't let go of her hand though.

"I told you, you're not getting away." Luke kissed her lightly on the lips. "Our turn, princess."

Luke's lips were warm and firm against hers. Perfect. She missed kissing him. She missed so many things. Her body lit up like the fourth of July.

"Now we have best man Luke 'Strike 'em Out' Stryker and the beautiful maid of honor Abbey Jayne."

Abbey was nearly frozen in place, stunned by Luke's surprise kiss. He pulled her along into the banquet room while guests applauded and cheered.

"Smile pretty, princess." Luke smiled down at her. She thought she saw love shining in his sparkling blue eyes. *No, he's just flirting. That kiss meant nothing. But you wanted it to. Yes. No.*

Abbey righted herself and walked with Luke to their spot at the head table. She tried her best to smile as if she was perfectly fine. Shouts of "Strike 'em Out" and "Go Cobras" were heard from several guests. Leah looked at her with a raised brow and a smirk on her face.

"And now, everyone please stand and welcome, for the first time as man and wife, Mr. and Mrs. Jake and Cassie Tyler!"

The guests and head table roared as Jake and Cassie stepped into the banquet room. Jake raised his and Cassie's joined hands high in the air in victory. He gestured to Cassie and she did a little twirl, and they continued to the captain's chairs at the head table.

Tinkling from guests hitting their glasses with utensils could be heard above the applause. Jake took a hold of Cassie, dipped her, and kissed her passionately.

"Get a room!" someone yelled.

"I already got them one!" Luke yelled back.

Once everyone took their seats, Pastor Jenkins made his way to the DJ's table. "Everyone, Pastor Jenkins would like to lead of our evening off with a prayer."

Everyone bowed their heads and the entire head table held hands. Abbey felt the stirrings of arousal again as Luke held her hand firmly. She pressed her knees together, trying to relieve the pressure.

"Thank you, Pastor, for that wonderful blessing. Once everyone has their champagne, the best man and maid of honor will come on up for the toasts and then dinner service will begin."

A moment later, a server was pouring champagne into Jake's and Cassie's toasting glasses. Abbey had never seen such an unusual bottle before. The dark glass champagne bottle was encased in an elegant, shiny silver sleeve which had some sort of engraving on the front of it.

Jake looked over to Luke with a concerned expression on his face. Was he upset that Luke got them champagne? "Luke, what the fuck?" he whispered. "We were supposed to have a *wine* toast."

"What's the big deal, Jake? It's a nice gesture," Abbey said, defending Luke for some stupid reason.

"The big *deal* is this is Moët & Chandon Dom Perignon White Gold," Jake answered.

Abbey shrugged, still not understanding why Jake was so upset.

Jake let out a breath, like he was trying to calm down. "The bottle casing is plated in *real* white gold *and* it's almost twenty-five hundred dollars a bottle."

Well, Abbey hadn't expected *that*. Even so, Luke's generosity shouldn't be this upsetting to Jake. Something else had to be wrong.

Jake looked at the servers pouring champagne for the other guests and glared at Luke. "What are the guests getting, Luke?"

Luke sighed and shrugged. "Just Moët & Chandon Bicentenary Cuvée Dry Imperial 1943. It's no big deal."

Jake growled. Actually growled at Luke. "No big deal, at around fourteen hundred dollars a bottle, with the number of guest we have, that's probably around thirty five grand. Unbelievable. You said you would stop going overboard with the gifts."

Luke glared back at Jake. Were they going to have a throw down before the toasts? Over champagne? Crazy expensive champagne, but champagne none the less.

"And *you* said you were going to relax about my wedding gifts," Luke countered.

Jake shook his head. "Wrong. I said *maybe*. If I recall it had something to do with *secrets*. Remember?"

Secrets? Disappointment filled Abbey. Secrets. She *knew it*. Any hopes she may have entertained, however briefly about Luke, were all but dead now. She should have known better. Now she did and she would behave accordingly.

Abbey regarded Cassie as she examined their champagne bottle. When Cassie teared up, Abbey didn't know what to do. Cassie looked at Luke with gratitude.

Jake gazed at Cassie, concern etched on his face. "Babe, what is it? Are you all right? Is it the baby?" he whispered.

Cassie shook her head and pointed to something on the front of the bottle. "It's engraved with our names and today's date."

Jake studied what Cassie was pointing to and the fight in him disappeared. He looked at Luke and nodded. "All right, Luke. You win. Thank you."

Luke smiled warmly at Jake. "I'm not trying to win. Just trying to do something special for my big brother and his new bride on their wedding day. Stop making it so difficult."

"I'll stop. You have my word," Jake conceded.

"Now that everyone's glasses are filled, the best man and maid of honor can come on up for the toasts. Then dinner service will start," the DJ announced.

Luke stood up, grabbed his champagne-filled glass, and held out a hand to Abbey. She looked at it, hesitating. *Secrets.*

"Princess," Luke warned.

Abbey sighed, picked up her own glass, stood up, and took Luke's hand. The guests and head table applauded as Luke led her to the DJ's table. They both placed their glasses on the DJ's table. The DJ, a dark-haired man in his early thirties, wearing a white dress shirt, black slacks, and welcoming smile, shook Luke's hand and give him a microphone.

"Strike 'em out Luke!"

"Go Cobras! All the way!"

"World Series for sure this year!"

Luke smiled graciously, nodding his head. Abbey felt for him, regardless of Jake's cryptic mention of secrets. She couldn't imagine what it must be like for him now. All the press, attention, the constant demands that went along with being a successful professional athlete. Regardless of what happened between them before or now, she hoped he was happy.

She couldn't deny it still stung that Luke felt he couldn't be happy with *her*, but Abbey didn't wish him ill will. She just wanted to know what the hell he was trying to do regarding *her* this weekend—what game he was playing. What the secrets were that Jake alluded to. Luke held her hand tightly and cleared his throat.

"Thank you. Your support means the world to me and the team. The Cobras are off to a great start so far this season, but today isn't about me or the team. It's about Jake and Cassie."

Abbey looked at Jake and Cassie across the room. Both of them beaming with love and happiness. *Don't be jealous. You love them both. Don't let Luke distract you from your reboot weekend.* Luke squeezed her hand and continued.

"Normally, the best man speech would start with some embarrassing childhood stories, but unfortunately I can't tell you any."

Abbey laughed as guests booed.

"Come on, Luke! Don't hold out on us."

"Yeah, come on!"

Luke retrieved a slip of paper from his pants pocket and held it up for everyone to see. "Sorry everyone, but my top secret mission request clearly states I can't."

"Mine too!" Heath held up a note and waved it for everyone to see.

"Jake, you're a spoilsport!"

Luke put his mission request back in his pocket. "Moving on … Jake and I met when I was two years old and Jake was four. My folks had moved us into the house that was in between Jake's and Heath's here in Elmhurst. Right from the start, Jake treated me like his little brother instead of his little kid neighbor. Heath did too."

Abbey smiled when Heath raised his glass. "That's right, little brother," Heath said.

"Most of the time, when you're friends with someone and you're that young, as you get older and your lives change, you begin to grow apart, see each other less and less until finally that friend becomes just someone you knew a long time ago. That didn't happen between Jake and me though. No, when Jake decides something or someone is important to him, he doesn't give up on it or them."

"Over the years our lives *did* change—*a lot*. Mine especially." Some guests laughed. Abbey didn't though. She knew not all the changes in Luke's life had been positive ones, especially the death of his parents when he was ten years old.

"Some of life's changes don't always have us being our best. That certainly has been the case for me. But that didn't matter to Jake. He never gave up on me. When I've been at my best, he's been there. That's easy though, right? But more importantly, when I've been at my absolute worst, Jake was still there. That's what I want you to understand, Cassie. No matter how your lives will change after today. And they *will*. Whether you're at your very best or your very worst, Jake will be there. That won't ever change. I love you both and wish you nothing but the very best."

Abbey looked at Cassie and Jake, both appearing moved by Luke's speech. Jake wiped a tear from Cassie's face and smiled at Luke, nodding his head slightly. Abbey laughed and felt a little misty herself.

Luke squeezed her hand, her body feeling the warmth of his. Or maybe it was the alcohol, she wasn't sure. He held the microphone out to her. "Your turn, princess." The guests "awwed" and Abbey felt her cheeks burn. She wondered what they all thought of Luke's PDA. Everyone was looking at her expectantly, so she grabbed the microphone from Luke and took a deep breath. She'd worry about them later.

"You would think that since Cassie and I are only a year apart that we've probably always been close. I can tell you that is not the case. When we were younger, she and I didn't get along very well at all."

"I can attest to that," Abbey's mother concurred.

"I know you can, Mom. How many fights have you had to break up over the years?"

"Too many," her mother called out.

"To me, the problem was that Cassie was just so *bossy*."

Cassie nodded at her and smiled.

After the guests stopped laughing, Abbey continued. "That made for a rather strained relationship, to say the least. We essentially tolerated each other for a long time. That was until I got a little older and realized that Cassie wasn't necessarily trying to be bossy, she was trying to guide me and support me.

"You see, I've always been a bit of a nerd. My head was always in books when I was younger, then when I got older, plastered to a computer screen. I'm not going to apologize, either. Being a nerd is *in* right now. Thank you Bill Gates, Mark Zuckerberg. My nerdiness has turned into a pretty great career for me."

"Can you take a look at my laptop?" a guest asked.

Abbey laughed along with many of the guests.

"Cassie's bossiness came from her concern that I was inside my head too much. That I wasn't allowing myself enough time to just relax and give my brain a rest. To enjoy life, have fun, unwind. I hate to admit it, but she was right. Once I understood that she was looking out for me, not trying to be the *boss of me*, we went from tolerating each to being close. For that, I'll always be grateful."

"I'm again taking her great advice or counsel, as lawyer Jake would say, and allowing myself a personal reboot weekend, giving my brain a rest and enjoying the weekend for whatever it brings. I'm sorry, but that means I can't provide any computer support."

"I'll call you next week then!"

The guests all laughed, including Abbey. "Jake, I want you to understand that if Cassie seem bossy to *you*, she's just looking out for you. I'd also like to offer Cassie's advice back to you both. Like Luke said, after today, your lives are going to change. I want you both to remember to get out of your heads occasionally and enjoy the journey of your lives together, now as man and wife."

Abbey handed the microphone back to Luke and picked up her champagne glass. As the guests applauded, Luke let go of her hand. She chided herself for missing his touch. He picked up his own glass and raised it.

"To Jake and Cassie, may you have many happy years together!" Luke clinked his glass with Abbey and they both drank to Cassie and Jake. The champagne was crisp and delicious, tickling her nose. Guests tapped their glasses again as she and Luke returned to their seats and she smiled when Jake kissed his new bride again.

"Dinner service will begin shortly. Enjoy the wonderful food here at Cucina Antonetti's." The DJ started what Abbey assumed was a mixed CD of appropriate dinner music. The volume was just right so it didn't prevent guests from hearing each other speak.

Just as Abbey was making herself comfortable in her seat, she heard her cell phone ring from underneath their table. Her stomach clenched. *Now what?* She reached down and retrieved her evening bag and pulled out her ringing phone. Tim Webber? Her former manager? Why was *he* calling?

Anger flowed hot in Abbey's veins. How *dare* her call her, especially now. *Did he forget he told me my skill set wasn't needed anymore?* Abbey let the call go to voicemail.

Abbey felt Luke looking at her. She turned and saw the worried expression on his face. "Princess, is everything all right? Who was that?"

Abbey just shook her head. She was too angry to respond. She heard the chime of a new voicemail. She knew she shouldn't bother. She didn't work at OSG any longer, but she played the voicemail anyway. She couldn't help it.

"Abbey this is Tim Webber. There's a problem with your system. It's down. No one can log in. It keeps giving an authentication error. Call me after you get this message." That was it. He didn't even bother apologizing for disturbing her on her sister's wedding day or even acknowledging that he was asking her for a huge favor since she no longer worked for him. What an asshole. In a way, she was glad she no longer worked for OSG because she couldn't stand Tim Webber. There was no way she was calling him back. *Fuck* you, *pal, and* your *system, not mine.*

Abbey deleted the voicemail and the fourteen unread text messages from Tom Murphy. She felt relieved and happily turned off her phone. She needed to get back to her reboot weekend. "I need another drink."

Yes, that would make her feel better.

Luke took her phone and put it back in her purse. "When was the last time you ate?"

Abbey had to think. "I guess it was earlier at the Fairchild Hotel before the ceremony. We had some pastries and Mimosas." Her stomach growled. It had been hours since she'd eaten.

"How about this? You still have some champagne in your glass. Why not finish that and have some dinner before getting another drink? I know they're making them pretty strong tonight. What do you think?" Luke looked deep into her eyes, like he could see into her soul.

Her soul that had belonged to him since the day they met so many years ago.

"Then you can get back to your reboot weekend. I'm having one myself in a way. Maybe we could reboot together?" When Luke smiled at her the way he did, she couldn't resist. *Secrets. Jake said Luke has secrets.*

"Secrets," Abbey whispered.

Luke frowned, taking a moment before responding. "I know Jake said that. But it's not what you think. You know I barely have any privacy anymore. For me, some things have to be announced. The damn press, you know? That's why I hired an extensive security detail for today."

In her head, Abbey understood. The last thing any of them wanted was for Jake and Cassie's wedding day to become a spectacle because of Luke's celebrity. So far that hadn't happened, other than Luke's little display in front of Mrs. Antonetti and Carlo.

She supposed it didn't matter. By the end of the weekend, Luke would be off to the next city for another game or whatever else he had scheduled. Abbey would go back to her life too.

Maybe they could reboot their weekend together.

It would be so easy to fall back into old habits with Luke. Just for a couple of days. A couple of fun, sex-filled days with Luke might be just what she needed to get out of her head and relax.

"Yes, I know, Luke. Maybe we can reboot our weekends together. It might not be such a bad idea." Abbey held her breath, wondering what he would say.

His mouth fell open. "Really? I think that's a great idea. But before we reboot, I want to have a chance to explain that night, Abbey."

Abbey got angry all over again. They didn't need to talk about that fateful night ten years ago. It didn't matter. They were over and a reboot weekend wouldn't change that fact.

Before she could tell him she didn't want to rehash the past, servers brought out the first course. He was right, though. She was hungry and the food at Antonetti's was wonderful. She joined in with everyone else tapping their glasses and laughed when Jake placed a napkin over his and Cassie's faces while he kissed her.

****

Luke couldn't believe Abbey had finally agreed to let him explain what happened the night she walked in on him. He was confident once he explained what happened she would find it in her heart to give them another chance. He was ready to pick right up where they'd left off. Fuck a reboot weekend. Luke was looking for a lot more than a weekend. And he had every intention of getting it. He would *not* stay on the ropes any longer.

Luke filled Abbey's and his plate with chicken carbonara and Antonetti's chopped salad. The room quieted down as everyone started eating. He couldn't help but wonder about her secrets. He'd overheard a little of the voicemail message she'd listened to and then immediately deleted. It sounded like a work issue. And it was not like her to ignore a work issue even though she had taken a few days off because of the wedding. In a way, he was glad she ignored the call. From what Cassie had told him, OSG needed to hire at least one additional person to help Abbey with the amount of work they dumped on her. They were just too cheap to do it.

As the first course bowls and plates were being cleared, Luke leaned over to her. "While we're waiting for the main course and side dishes, let me explain what happened that night real quick. I want to clear—"

Abbey shook her head at him. "No, that's not necessary. It was ten years ago. We've both moved on, right? Let's enjoy our dinner and have some fun tonight, okay?"

No. That was *not* okay with Luke. The prospect of getting between Abbey's legs again had his cock getting hard, but he was determined to clear the air *first* before fucking her later. And he *would* fuck her later, over and over until he had his fill. He had ten long years to make up for.

Luke looked out at the guests as he enjoyed his chicken marsala, made with Antonetti Vineyard's own blend of sweet Marsala wine. He'd been looking forward to dinner all day. The chicken was moist and a perfect companion to the sweet flavor of the Marsala wine, and the sliced mushrooms were an excellent finish to the dish. He glanced at his Uncle Darren's table and his uncle seemingly sensing him looking, turned to him and nodded. Luke smiled and nodded back, trying to keep his feelings about Darren's recent diagnosis pushed aside. *There's nothing that can be done about it right now anyway.*

"All right folks, as you can see, the sweet table is just about ready for everyone. Enjoy," the DJ announced.

Luke felt Abbey perk up next to him as the servers finished setting up Antonetti's Signature Sweet Table. He couldn't blame her. Antonetti's served up some delectable desserts. Not as delectable as his sweet princess's pussy though, he thought to himself. He'd be eating *that* later. Luke would make sure of it.

"I'm *so* ready for dessert," Cassie announced beside Luke.

"Me too, babe," Jake agreed.

Luke turned to the happy couple, love and joy radiating from both of them. "Jake, you making sure your baby mamma's well fed?" Luke whispered.

"Damn straight." Jake laughed and kissed his bride on the cheek.

Abbey made to get up and get dessert, but Luke guided her back down to her chair. "How about I get us something and we can share?"

Luke held his breath, not sure what she would say.

"Thanks, that sounds … nice."

Jake had shared the evening's menu with him, so Luke knew which items were on the sweet table. "There's cheesecake, taffy apple pie, brownies, those mini dreams with chocolate dipping sauce, lemon pound cake, tiramisu, and assorted cookies."

Abbey smiled her angelic smile and Luke's heart swelled. God, he loved her. "Yes."

"Me too—all that sounds perfect," Cassie agreed beside him.

Jake stood with Luke. "I'll go with Luke and get some of everything for us too," Jake said to Cassie.

"Get extra." Cassie grinned and discreetly patted her tummy.

Luke leaned over and called over to Heath. "We're getting desserts to share with the ladies. You want to come along and get some for you and Leah?"

It hadn't escaped Luke's attention that Heath and Leah had cozied up during dinner. He hoped Heath took Jake's suggestion about pursuing a relationship with Leah to heart. Luke's oldest brother deserved some happiness in life too. What was the point of making out of Afghanistan alive to then end up alone?

Leah looked at Heath expectantly, waiting for him to answer. Heath offered a small smile and nodded. "Yeah, sounds like a good idea." Leah's smile warmed Luke's heart. Maybe there was a chance for her and Heath after all.

As the three of them approached the dessert table, Rocco rose from his seat next to Hannah and joined them in line. Luke was relieved someone had the forethought to stack larger dinner-sized plates in addition to smaller dessert plates.

Luke's phone chimed in his pants with a text message. Not even trying to be subtle, Heath, Jake, and Rocco looked over Luke's shoulder at his phone.

Brenna: **How is Mission Abbey coming along**
Luke: **Been difficult so far, but working on it**
Brenna: **Don't strike out**
Luke: **Trying my best not to**
Brenna: **Good, don't give up, keep me posted** ☺
Luke: **Will do**

Luke felt the three of them staring at him. He wished he could come clean about everything, but he couldn't. Not right now.

Jake shook his head and spoke to the group. "Don't bother asking him, guys, he's not going to tell us anything."

Not wanting to start an argument, he turned to Rocco. "So, how are things going with Hannah?"

Rocco looked down at his shoes and shrugged. Was he blushing? Luke hadn't expected that from the big Italian Marine.

Rocco looked up and glared at Jake. "Interesting seating arrangement."

Jake held his hands up in surrender. "Don't look at *me*. Cassie did the seating arrangements before you and Hannah even met. It worked out though. Admit it."

Rocco just shrugged, looking unsure.

Rocco and Heath needed a pep talk. "Just get some desserts and share with her. You too, Heath," Luke suggested.

"Luke's right," Jake said.

Neither Rocco nor Heath appeared convinced. Luke sighed and tried again. "How about you guys consider this a part of your *own* reboot weekend, like Abbey said in her speech? She's agreed to let me reboot with her this weekend."

Three sets of surprised eyes looked back at him. "But you're looking for more than a weekend though," Heath said.

Luke nodded. He sure as hell was. He was looking for *every* weekend from now on. "I know that, but Abbey's been running hot and cold on me all day. I got her to agree to the weekend at least. She doesn't understand that I intend on getting *all* of them. Yet."

The four of them moved up in the line. "But *first* I want to explain to Abbey what she actually walked in on ten years ago. She says she doesn't care. Says she doesn't want to hear it. But I don't want to start anything until we clear the air, you know?"

"Like Brenna said, don't strike out," Jake teased.

"Seriously, though, don't give up," Heath said.

Luke nodded. He wasn't going to give up. He never would. He and Abbey belonged together, and that was that. Once he had his chance to clear up the misunderstandings of that night, Abbey would finally let go of all the hurt and anger she'd been holding onto and they could move forward. Happily and together. Like they always would be.

They moved up in the line once more. Luke grabbed a large plate from the stack. "Jake, maybe you better get two plates. Cassie didn't seem very *sharey*." He chuckled and filled his plate with everything the sweet table offered. Maybe some tasty sweets would sweeten Abbey's attitude toward him.

Luke sat down with his plate overflowing and nearly drooling, not only for dessert but for Abbey. She was about to find out exactly what Luke meant about sharing.

She worried her lush lower lip. Luke's mind immediately went back to the many times he'd had her luscious lips wrapped around his hard dick. He'd taught his princess exactly how he like it sucked and she'd become exceptional at blowing him. He felt his cock harden in his tuxedo pants. He could hardly wait until he had her in his bed later on. He intended to spend the entire weekend in bed with her. Maybe they could beg off of meeting everyone for brunch tomorrow morning.

"There's only one fork," Abbey observed.

Luke nodded. "I know. That's because I'm going to feed you."

Her eyes widened. "What?"

Chapter Eight

Luke was going to feed her? He couldn't be serious. Everyone would see them. She must have misunderstood him. No, that couldn't be right.

He had a wicked gleam in his eyes and a grin on his face. She felt herself blush. "Did you say you're going to feed me dessert?"

"Yes, that's exactly what I said."

She didn't think that was a good idea. It was much too obvious. Too intimate in a way. In a room full of people, many of whom were family members?

"Luke, that's really not necessary. Plus everyone will see us. I can feed myself." Surely he could be reasoned with. They'd agreed on rebooting their weekend together, but him feeding her in front of an audience seemed like too much.

Luke shook his head and looked out at the guests. "Princess, no one's paying attention to us. They're busy getting their own desserts and stuffing their faces. Look for yourself."

Abbey glanced around the banquet room. There were guests chatting in line at the sweet table, some were leaving the room to use the restroom or have a cigarette outside, and many were at their tables enjoying the sweet treats they'd filled their plates with. No one was paying much attention to the head table at the moment. Still, she wasn't sure.

He held out a forkful of chocolate brownie with walnuts to her lips and raised a brow in challenge. Abbey's heart galloped in her chest. She took a deep breath and opened her mouth. *So this is a part of my reboot weekend? All right then, here we go.*

It was one of the best brownies Abbey'd ever eaten. She moaned when the rich flavor of chocolate fudge hit her tongue. It was the perfect combination of cake and fudge with crunchy walnuts mixed in.

She watched, transfixed, as Luke took a bite himself and swallowed, his Adam's apple bobbing up and down in his throat. She couldn't help but stare as his tongue licked chocolate frosting off his kissable lips.

Abbey remembered Luke's talented tongue. He'd spent hours using it all over her. Kissing her senseless with just the right amount of firmness. Licking her nipples relentlessly until they ached so good. And when he used his tongue between her legs, it hadn't taken many swipes against her throbbing clit to set her off like a rocket ship.

For the next few minutes, he continued to feed them from their dessert plate. Although Abbey enjoyed the delicious treats she was being fed, she enjoyed watching Luke's mouth as he ate even more. She imagined his mouth, lips, and tongue on her, and by the time they'd had their fill of dessert, she was hot and aching. Her panties were damp and she desperately needed relief. The kind only Luke could provide.

She was practically vibrating in her chair, her breaths reduced to quick pants. Luke licked his lips and she couldn't wait another minute to get a taste of him. She leaned in and he met her halfway.

Abbey startled and quickly pulled away at the amplified sound of the DJ's voice. "All right, everyone, we're going to get the evening's festivities underway. The photographers have set up in the corner next to the gift table for anyone who would like to have pictures taken. Jake and Cassie, come on up for your first dance as man and wife."

Abbey shivered and tried to calm down. She

looked over to Luke and saw him frowning. "Bad timing, DJ dude," he mumbled.

She giggled at him as she joined the guests and applauded while Cassie and Jake went to the dance floor for their first dance. Luke reached over and held her hand, and they both watched, hand in hand, as the newlyweds danced to "The Way You Look Tonight" by Tony Bennett. From the way Jake was looking at Cassie—with love, lust, and contentment—it was the perfect song. Abbey teared up. Once upon a time, Luke had looked at *her* the same way.

She felt his warm fingers brush away a stray tear on her cheek. His simple touch made her insides sizzle. *This is so unfair*. He turned her head, so she faced him. "No tears, princess."

Luke leaned in and her eyes drifted shut. She should have pulled away but didn't have the will left in her to do that. The soft, warm brush of Luke's lips on hers left her reeling. The world around them fell away. She'd missed Luke so much. Missed *everything* Luke. Abbey's head was swimming. She wanted him, needed him so badly.

Luke licked the seam of her lips, seeking entry, and Abbey opened her mouth, happy to let him inside. The first taste of him was a sweet mix of the delicious desserts they'd just shared—chocolate, tart apples, cheesecake, and more. His big warm hands cradled her face as their tongues tangled and danced. More decadent than any dessert.

Abbey lost herself in him. Her heart raced and her skin felt hot and tight. Her breasts were swollen and heavy and her panties were soaked. Luke moaned sexily and she was ready to toss him under the table and—

"If the bridal party and parents of the bride and groom would like to come to the dance floor now, please."

Abbey quickly pulled away from Luke as if she were burned. She took a deep breath, then another, trying to center herself.

The heat in Luke's gorgeous blue gaze nearly scorched her. She felt a sense of female pride knowing she had affected him like he had her.

"That fucker has shitty timing," Luke mumbled. He frowned, stood up, and offered her his hand.

Abbey looked up at Luke and giggled. She couldn't help it. He looked like an aggravated little boy who'd just been told he couldn't have cookies before dinner. "Strike 'em Out" Stryker had gotten too used to getting his way over the years.

She stood and took Luke's hand. So big and strong wrapped around hers. Leah was already leading Heath to the dance floor. He wasn't putting up much of a fight. *Good for them.* Abbey was rooting for them well beyond the weekend.

"So you think DJ cock blocker over there is funny, huh?"

Abbey shrugged, giggling as Luke led them to the dance floor. They were the last to arrive. She reached for Luke's hands but he placed her hands around his neck and placed his around her waist.

For a moment, Abbey stiffened, unsure if she was comfortable with their intimate display in front of everyone. Luke pulled her in close against his muscled body as "Unforgettable" by Nat King Cole began to play.

Luke was exactly that to her. Unforgettable, even though she'd tried hard *to* forget him over the years. Abbey was aware she and Luke were getting knowing looks and smiles from the dance floor and from wedding guests.

The feel of Luke in her arms after so many years

apart, so strong and warm and perfect, had her not concerning herself with what anyone else thought. She'd announced her reboot weekend, so everyone most likely assumed Luke was a part of it.

Abbey placed her cheek against Luke's chest and inhaled. Luke's own musk mixed with the exotic scents of sandalwood, rosewood, and oud wood from Tom Ford's Oud Wood which he wore had her happily drifting off to a sensual place as they slowly swayed to the music. Like an addict, she'd pined over Luke when she'd seem him in many Tom Ford Oud Wood commercials over the years. Tom Ford was one of Luke's many and lucrative endorsement deals.

She couldn't miss the feel of Luke's erection pressing against her belly. Was he *bigger* than she remembered? Her body simmered with anticipation, knowing later she'd have Luke's long, thick dick inside her once again. No one had elicited the kind of mind-blowing pleasure that Luke had. Not that she had had many lovers since she and Luke had broken up. But every sexual encounter after Luke had left her unsatisfied and wanting.

"You've been unforgettable to me, princess," Luke whispered.

Abbey looked up at Luke, surprised. He gazed at her with such tenderness she wanted to believe him, but how could she? He'd cheated on her just as his baseball career had taken off. Abbey stayed silent, not trusting herself to speak. Luke didn't really mean it, she reasoned. It was a wedding. Everyone was emotional. That was what happened at weddings. Everyone became sentimental. Single guests wanted to hook up. He was just caught up in the moment.

The song ended and she extricated herself from Luke, feeling a little off kilter, but missing his touch immediately. *Damn him.* After the applause died down, the DJ announced the dance floor was open to everyone.

Abbey needed a drink. That would take the edge off. Calm her down so she could enjoy the reception and go with the flow of whatever the evening held in store. A quick dance number began playing and Abbey made to head to the bar, but Luke took a hold of her arm.

"Look, Abbey, can we go somewhere quiet to talk for a few minutes? Just to clear the air about that night? Please?"

Not this again. Luke was like a dog with a bone. Why couldn't he let it go? What difference did it make now, anyway? After all this time? There were supposed to have a good time this weekend, not dredge up the past. After the weekend was over, who knew how long it would be before she even saw Luke again.

"Luke, it's not necessary, so drop it. We're supposed to be having a fun reboot this weekend right? So let's do that."

Luke pulled a face and just as he seemed ready to argue the point, little Amy came up to them and tugged on Luke's jacket sleeve. "Wanna dance with me, Luke?" Amy looked up at Luke expectantly.

His face softened. "Of course. It would be my pleasure." Amy dragged a reluctant Luke deep onto the dance floor and Abbey made her escape to get some dollar bills from her evening bag.

Thank you, Amy.

At the bar, the bartender gave Abbey the champagne that had been served to the guests. Why not? Today was a celebration, right? Jake and Cassie's wedding day. Her reboot weekend.

Abbey took a small sip, the bubbles hitting her tongue and tickling her nose. It was dryer than the head table champagne. Very good, but she preferred the Moët

& Chandon Dom Perignon White Gold they'd drank at the head table.

Abbey giggled and took a long sip. *Now I'm a champagne snob.* She watched Amy keep Luke on the dance floor longer than he'd probably expected. Amy was dancing, or rather bouncing around like little girls did, with Luke showing off his best moves. He could move all right. Abbey could attest to that.

Lost in memories of past sexual exploits with Luke, she hadn't noticed she was no longer alone until a man spoke to her.

"Jake really did things up right today, didn't he?" The man on her right, whom Abbey didn't recognize, was about six feet tall, and had dark-blond hair styled with a little too much product and calculating, deep-brown eyes. His nose was slightly crooked, possibly from being broken. He was a decent-looking man in his tailored gray suit and a deep-red tie, holding a tumbler with a finger of scotch. *He's no Luke though.*

He extended his hand and she shook it. Firm enough grip, but his hands weren't as large or powerful as Luke's. Touching him left Abbey feeling cold. "I'm Mel Johnson. I'm a corporate attorney with the Cobras. I work with Jake."

Attorney. Abbey should have known by his demeanor. "I'm Abbey Jayne. Jake's new sister-in-law. Nice to meet you. Yes, Jake wanted today to be special for Cassie. I think he's done a great job so far." Abbey wanted to be cordial to Jake's co-worker, but she wasn't the least bit interested in Mel Johnson, corporate attorney for the Cobras. Mel was at a wedding, for Pete's sake. He could *turn the attorney off* for a few hours, couldn't he? Abbey appreciated when Jake wasn't "lawyering", he was a laid-back, easy going guy. Not like his pal Mel.

Mel took a business card out of his jacket pocket

and handed it to Abbey. Wanting to be polite, she accepted it and then noticed Luke gracefully pass Amy over to Heath and Leah to continue dancing with.

"It's obvious that Luke Stryker is a part of your reboot weekend, but after the weekend is over and he's left, give me a call. Let me take you to dinner sometime."

Abbey tucked Mel's business card into her evening bag as Luke stalked toward them. His determined, purposeful strides made quick work of eating up the distance between them. *He looks more than a little angry.* She held her breath.

"Johnson. I'm not interrupting anything, am I?" Luke's tone dripped with sarcasm and disdain.

Mel's eye grew wide and he shook his head. "No, not at all, boss. I was just introducing myself to the maid of honor, and enjoying a celebratory drink together, right, Abbey?" Mel looked nervously to her for corroboration.

A little part of Abbey got turned on by Luke's alpha male behavior, but she didn't care for Luke's intimidation tactics toward his employee. There was no need for it. Mel was harmless.

She rolled her eyes. "Don't be an ass, Luke." Abbey saw Mel wince. Poor guy. He'd probably never consider of insulting the great Luke Stryker.

Luke raised a brow, glaring hard at her. He turned to Mel, who downed his scotch in one gulp. "Oh, I'm sorry. I didn't realize I was an *ass*. Was I an *ass*, Mel?"

"Shit," Mel muttered under his breath. He glanced down at his shoes like they were the most interesting things in the world. He looked up at Luke and shook his head. "No, of course not. Not at all."

Abbey's temper bristled as Luke continued to behave like an ass toward Mel. He needed to stop. Now. "Luke, that's enough."

Luke nodded tersely. "You're right, princess. I've

had *enough*." Luke turned to Mel and gestured to his empty tumbler. "Looks like you need a refill, Mel."

Likely relieved to be given an out, Mel held his tumbler up in salute and bolted to the bar without saying a word.

Abbey was ready to throttle Luke. He was out of control. "I really don't appreciate—"

Luke grabbed the champagne glass out of Abbey's hand, drained the contents, and slammed it onto the nearest table. "You want to know what *I* don't appreciate? I don't appreciate you throwing yourself at some stiff when you're supposed to be with *me*."

Abbey gasped. How *dare* Luke say that? Was he serious right now? "Look, I wasn't *throwing* myself at anyone. I was having a drink. Mel came up to *me*. I know you know that because I saw you watching me from the dance floor, so *back off*."

Luke balled his hands into fists. "Not happening, princess. In fact, I'd say now is a good time for us to have a private chat about that night. You've put me off long enough."

Not this again. Why won't he let this go?

Abbey's temper rose to a full boil. She would make different plans for her reboot weekend. Luke had left her no choice. "I *told* you. There's nothing to say about that night. And I've changed my mind about this weekend. Reboot with someone else."

Luke stepped up close. Abbey had to crane her neck to look him in the eye. His beautiful blue eyes bore down on her, fierce with rage. Abbey wasn't afraid. She knew Luke wouldn't hurt her, not physically. Her heart was a different story.

"Not happening. We're going to talk privately and continue on with our weekend *together*." Luke took her by the hand and led her to the banquet room doors.

Abbey tried to pull away but Luke wouldn't let her go. "I told you, I have nothing to say about that night. And our weekend is over. Maybe I'll really go throw myself at Mel." She didn't know why she said that. She didn't mean it. She wasn't interested in Mel at all. She'd been looking forward to spending time with Luke—in bed, even if for just the weekend. Come Monday, she'd deal with the harsh realities of her life—unemployed and alone.

"Really? You have nothing to say? Nothing at all? You walked out that night without a word. After ten years, you expect me to believe there's not one thing you want to say to me?" Luke dragged her through the banquet room doors despite her best efforts to resist and the questioning looks from wedding guests.

Once they were in the hallway, Abbey noticed the several of Luke's security goons stand at attention. All of them wearing dark suits and ear pieces. *Real subtle, Luke.* Luke's security detail had kept the paparazzi away, at least. She was grateful for Jake's and Cassie's sake.

"Yes, that's what I'm saying. I have nothing to say to you about that night." Abbey was lying, of course. There had been so much she had *wanted* to say. Back *then*. Now, though, she didn't see what difference it would make. *What's done is done.*

Rocco burst out of the banquet room with a concerned look in his dark eyes. The other members of the security team looked to him for guidance.

"That's such *bullshit* and you know it. I think you have plenty to say but you're afraid to say it."

Abbey scoffed. She wasn't afraid. She was hurting. Still hurting almost as if she had walked in on him with that groupie slut yesterday. The old wounds she had hoped were healed after ten years had burst wide open when she'd seen Luke in the church vestibule.

She'd been trying to ignore it, shrug it off, but the hole he'd left in her heart ten years ago was now open and bleeding. After all this time, she still loved him and hated him at the same time. There it was. Abbey didn't know what to do about it. What *could* she do? Luke was the one who had dealt their relationship the death blow. Not her.

He dragged her down the hallway past the restrooms. Abbey tried to pull away but was no match for Luke's strength. "Stop it! I'm not going anywhere with you!" She didn't care she was shouting, calling unwanted attention to them.

Luke turned to her, his anger seeping out of every pore. "Yes, you fucking are. And you're going to tell me what you've wanted to say to me for the last ten years."

To her surprise, Luke tossed her over his left shoulder in a fireman's hold, held on to her legs, and continued down the hallway. Abbey's hair fell down around her, obstructing her vision. She hit him in the ass repeatedly with her evening bag and kicked her feet. "You asshole! Put me down right now! I'm not saying anything to you!"

Luke ignored her, and she bounced on his shoulder as he stomped his way to their destination. Abbey felt her shoes fall off but kept on kicking. "My shoes! They're expensive! I had them dyed special to match my dress!"

"Rocco, get her fucking shoes!"

From Abbey's limited vision she could tell Luke was walking through a doorway. She heard the door click closed. He gently set her down on her stocking-covered feet and she felt dizzy as the blood rushed out of her head. She panted, and she swayed, pushing Luke away when he tried to steady her.

Abbey pulled her hair away from her face and

tossed her evening bag on the large dining table that looked like it sat about twenty people. It was covered in a bright white tablecloth with bright white, elegantly folded cloth napkins placed around the table at each chair.

Abbey sat down in the nearest chair and took a few deep breaths, slowly feeling the dizziness subside. Luke sat down next to her but said nothing. His expression was unreadable.

"Now, tell me what you've wanted to say to me about that night." Luke's demeanor seemed calm and relaxed but Abbey could sense the tension he was holding in. He was wound tight.

Abbey didn't care though. She'd had enough of this game he was playing. "I told you, I have nothing to say." She started getting out of her chair but he pushed her back down by her shoulders.

"And I told *you*, that's bullshit. Tell me." His tone was low, growly.

She shook her head, anger simmering just below the surface. "I don't care what you think, Luke. Not anymore." *Liar. You care a lot. That's the problem, isn't it?*

"Also bullshit, now tell me." His voice was a little louder now. She wondered if it could be heard outside the room they were in.

"Luke, stop already. I want to get back to the reception. So should you." Her voice rose and her stomach clenched.

"Not until you tell me!" He slammed a fist on the table with a thud.

Abbey's stomach churned as she thought about that night. The sight of Luke and that skanky groupie naked was permanently burned into her brain. The disappointment, betrayal, and anger seared her soul and her heart.

"No," she shouted back. Fuck Luke and what *he* wanted. What about what *she* wanted? She had wanted to believe Luke loved her and wanted to marry her one day and have a family and all the other things they talked and dreamed about. But life didn't always give you what you wanted.

"Tell me right the fuck the now! Say it!" Luke was shouting like Abbey had never heard him before. She didn't care. He could throw a temper tantrum all he liked.

"I said no!"

"Do it! Say it!" He slammed his fist on the table again.

Abbey's pulse raced and her temperature rose. Her insides shook with a rage she'd held inside for much too long. Ten fucking years.

"Fine! You want me to tell you! I will! Her breaths came out in quick pants. "You fucking broke my heart, okay? As soon as you won your first World Series Championship and your career as a pro pitcher took off, you just tossed me aside like was nothing! Nothing! I loved you so much! So fucking much and you didn't even care! I gave you everything, my virginity, my heart and soul, and you just tossed me aside the first chance you got. And for what? Some groupie whore! There. Is that what you wanted to hear so badly? Are you happy now!"

Abbey shook, and a flood of tears she'd held in for years streamed down her face. She covered her face with her hands and allowed herself to sob for the first time since she'd walked in on him. All the pain and anger wrenched through her. She heard him get out of his chair, relieved he would finally leave her alone.

Except Luke kneeled down in front of her and

turned her chair to face him directly. He put his hands on hers and pulled them away from her face. She kept her eyes closed, and the tears continued to fall.

He held her hands tightly. Abbey was annoyed she felt comforted. "No, Abbey, I'm not happy at all. Please open your eyes and look at me."

Abbey shook her head. She just wanted to get out of there and be left alone. What a mess. She was Cassie's maid of honor and was in some small banquet room sobbing her heart out instead of at the reception where she was supposed to be.

"Please, Abbey," he said gently.

She slowly opened her eyes, surprised and heartbroken to find tears streaming down Luke's cheeks. She was at a loss for words and physically drained.

"Now please just let me talk and tell you what happened."

Abbey wanted to get up, but Luke held on to her hands.

"Please, let me have my say, and when I'm finished, if you still want to go, I won't stop you. You have my word."

Abbey scoffed. "I'm not sure that means much, Luke." She hated herself for sounding like a bitch, but when it came to Luke, he had some real credibility issues.

He took a deep breath and exhaled slowly. "I know it seems that way, but I'm hoping you'll change your mind in a minute."

"All right, then." Abbey didn't have it in her to fight anymore. She grabbed one of the cloth napkins nearest to her and wiped her face. Some of her makeup stained the napkin. She'd let Luke have his say and leave. They would be done once and for all. Although she should be happy to finally get closure, the thought hurt deep down to her soul.

Luke nodded sadly. "You didn't see what you *thought* you saw that night."

Abbey shook her head. She knew what she saw. Luke and that groupie slut naked after they'd had sex.

"Listen to me, Abbey. *Hear* me. I *didn't* and would never cheat on you. I swear to you on my parents' souls."

She sighed, not sure what to believe. "But I saw you two, naked."

Luke squeezed her hands firmly. "Think back. Try to remember clearly. That bitch was naked, not me. Oh, she got my shirt off, sure, but my jeans were on and zipped. She was a strong drunk. I was a little drunk, but I was fighting her off when you walked in. I kept trying to tell her I was waiting for *you*, that I was going to celebrate my first World Series win with *you*."

Abbey startled in her chair when a knock sounded at the door. "Luke," Rocco called out.

Luke turned to the door. "Everything's all right, Roc."

"Okay, just checking. Take all the time you need," Rocco said.

A sliver of hope bloomed in Abbey's heart. If what Luke was saying were true, how the hell did the groupie get in his room to begin with? Something didn't add up.

"How did she get in your room then?" Abbey wasn't sure she wanted to know.

Luke sighed and shook his head. "How do you think? My scummy *ex*-agent Earl Jepson."

Abbey stomach clenched again. She'd hated Earl Jepson. He'd been a slimy sleazeball as far as she was concerned. He hadn't been shy about letting her know he didn't like her. He thought she was holding Luke back and was in the way.

"Asshole," she whispered.

"Fucking right, he was. I've never seen Darren so mad when he found out what happened. Fired his ass right away and we've been happy with Glenn Milner's representation ever since. I wish you had let me explain this to you a long time ago." Luke kissed her knuckles softly. "I loved so you much, Abbey, still do. The way you shut me out all these years broke my heart."

She began crying again. Mourning all the years she and Luke had lost because she'd been too hurt and stubborn to let him explain what happened. But what about Brenna? She needed to know the truth about their relationship.

"I'm so sorry, Luke. I still love you too, I never stopped. But what about Brenna? Cassie suggested you two weren't really together, whatever that means. What's going on with her?" Abbey held her breath, waiting for his answer.

Luke sat back down in his chair. He ran a hand through his hair and pinched the bridge of his nose. "Cassie's right. Brenna and I weren't really together. I've been doing her a favor, a *huge* favor by pretending to be her boyfriend for the last three years."

She didn't understand. That made no sense. Why would Brenna Sinclair, international film star need a *fake* boyfriend? Luke must have sensed her confusion and continued.

"It's no secret her conservative Baptist minister father doesn't think much of Hollywood, or her acting career. He'd think even *less* of Brenna if he knew she preferred women to men. Using me as cover wasn't so bad. We'd meet up every few months and get some shots taken of us in public, being all PDA and shit until we met up again. I was able to accompany her to a couple of movie premieres. Fans ate it up. She even got me those two small parts in her movies. It was fun, not that different from doing commercials, and I've done a *ton* of those over the years. Bottom line is I consider her a friend. I think you'd like her."

That wasn't what Abbey had expected at all. Luke was right, though. Brenna's father would have a field day if he found out she was a lesbian. He'd been public about his disappointment in his oldest daughter's chosen profession. Abbey didn't even understand his issue with her. Brenna Sinclair was an amazing actress, well-respected, and professional, and she had remained above the fray of drama and scandal typical of Hollywood.

"Three years is a long time to pretend though," Abbey heard herself say. She hadn't meant to say it out loud.

Luke nodded. "I know. We never meant for it to go on that long. But with both of our schedules being so crazy, before we knew it, three years had passed. But our *relationship* is over. I'm leaving it up to her as to how she wants to make it public."

Abbey felt a renewed sense of hope where she and Luke were concerned. Could they forge a future together after all this time? She looked at him, longing, love, and lust in his sparkling blue eyes. Her heart swelled with the love she'd always felt for him and her body flooded with desire as her core slickened. Her heart and body were on board with the possibility of reuniting. *Game on!*

Needing to get close to him, she bolted out of her chair and kneeled between his legs. She put her arms around his neck and crushed her lips against his. She felt him smile against her lips as he pulled her closer, wrapping his arms around her tightly.

Luke ran his tongue along the seam of Abbey's lips and she joyfully opened for him. Their tongues hungrily explored and tangled with each other, both of them ravenous for the other. Abbey deepened the kiss and tugged on Luke's thick hair. She felt satisfaction as he moaned into her mouth. Abbey put all the emotions she was feeling into their kiss—love, hope, joy, and desire until they pulled apart, both panting.

"Christ, I love you, princess," Luke gasped.

Abbey smiled up at him, a sea of emotions overflowing inside her. "I love you too, so much, Luke. I always have." She needed him so badly. Her long dress, lingerie, and hose would make getting undressed quickly impossible. She smiled when she looked at Luke's lap and saw his big dick straining against his tuxedo pants zipper. *Is he bigger than I remember?* That thought made her even wetter, soaking her panties even more.

She looked over at the door. "Do you know if there will be an event in this room tonight?"

He shook his head. "No, there isn't. As a precaution, I paid the Antonetti's to keep the other banquet rooms free tonight."

Abbey couldn't believe the lengths Luke had gone through to keep the press away for Jake and Cassie. It made her love him even more. She would show him just how much.

She unbuttoned his pants and he put his hands on hers to stop her from going any further. "What are you doing?"

Abbey looked up at him, smiling slyly. "What do you think? I'm going to suck that big dick of yours, just the way you like it." She started to unzip his pants but he held her hands still.

"But I want to fuck you. So bad. Let's just go back to my hotel room." Luke started zipping up his pants but Abbey stopped *him* this time.

She chuckled. She would have loved to leave and go back to his room. But they couldn't, not yet. "We can't leave right now. There's still the cutting of the cake and bouquet and garter toss to get through, at least. We're the maid of honor and best man. We should stick around until the end of the night, don't you think?"

He leaned back in his chair and sighed. "I guess so. But I think Jake would understand if we bailed out now." Luke stuck out his lower lip, pouting like cute a little boy. *Cute for a thirty-year-old, six-foot-four professional baseball player.*

She laughed at his logic. "Maybe, but I doubt my family would. Let me take care of you now and then later you can fuck me real good." Abbey had never been much for dirty talk, unless it was with Luke. She found that with Luke, she felt free enough to be something other than the computer nerd she normally was. She could be fun, flirty, or filthy and he never judged her. Never made her feel self-conscious or ashamed. In fact, the dirtier the better as far as he was concerned.

With an exaggerated sigh and nod of his head, he acquiesced. "Fine, but after the reception your tight little pussy is *mine* and maybe we skip brunch tomorrow so I can fuck you all day. How about that?"

Abbey unzipped his pants, pulling his boxer briefs, t-shirt, and shirt out of the way. "How about we worry about brunch tomorrow?"

Her mouth watered once his long hard cock was fully uncovered. *He is definitely bigger than I remember.* Luke's engorged purple head glistened with pre-cum at the tip. The long blue vein stretching along his length pulsed.

Abbey leaned forward and licked the tip of his cock, his salty essence exploding on her tongue. She breathed him in, loving the scent of his cologne mixed with his natural musk. So sexy, masculine … so Luke. She'd missed this. Luke had been her first. He'd taught her everything about sex. Taught her exactly how to please him.

Luke hissed when she sucked on the head and gripped her hair. The little sting of pain turned her on even more. "Take all of me, Abbey," he whispered.

Emboldened, she sucked Luke's hot, hard cock as far down her throat as she could. She breathed through her nose to avoid gagging. *So big*. He groaned loudly and she sucked him in earnest.

Abbey found a comfortable rhythm that he seemed to enjoy and when she looked up at him, he had his eyes squeezed shut. His mouth was open, panting. The muscles in his neck strained and his jugulars pulsed.

Thrilled to her very core, she gently squeezed his heavy sac, feeling the coarse hairs in her palm. Luke pumped his hips, fucking her face with a steady rhythm.

"I'm not going to last, Abbey. Oh God. Swallow every fucking drop."

He pumped his hips faster and held on to her head tighter, the sting of her scalp almost too much. "Oh fuck, Abbey!" Luke shot ribbon after ribbon of hot salty cum down her throat. She struggled to swallow it all down. *Does he come more now too?* She managed not to miss a drop although she wasn't sure how. He slumped back in his chair, gasping for air, and let go of her head.

Abbey licked Luke's deflating dick clean, carefully tucked him into his pants, and zipped him back up. She stayed put, proudly kneeling between his legs, waiting for him to drift back down to earth.

Luke slowly opened his eyes, his pupils still dilated, and flashed Abbey a cocky grin. "Best head ever, princess." Luke sat up straighter and reached out to her.

Abbey rolled her eyes even though she knew she'd taken good care of her man. At that moment, it felt like Luke was once again *her* man. She didn't want to get ahead of herself but hoped he would be from now on. She had to admit though, she was afraid.

Luke moved her so she sat across his lap. He pressed his lips to hers and she opened to him without hesitation. His tongue gently massaged hers, as though he didn't care if he tasted himself on her. *So hot.* She felt Luke start to get hard again beneath her and giggled.

"Like I said. Best. Head. Ever." He nuzzled her neck, his breath warm on her skin. "I'm starting to get hard again, princess. I can't get enough of you. You sure we can't quietly slip out of here?"

Abbey was tempted, *so* tempted. She couldn't do that to her sister, though. Luke would have to act like an adult and behave until it was the appropriate time for them to leave.

She stood up and finger combed her messy hair. She cringed at what she thought she must look like now. First from crying and then from being with Luke. And she needed to put her shoes back on. She hoped Rocco still had them.

Luke stood and grabbed Abbey's evening bag, handing it to her. "I know what you're thinking, but you're wrong. You're beautiful, princess." He kissed her lightly on lips, forehead, and the corner of each eye. He made her feel like a princess, he always had.

"Good thing Angel gave us all a makeup touch up bag," she said as Luke led them out of the room into the hallway. Rocco and the rest of Luke's security detail were waiting a few feet away near the leather couches against the wall across from the restrooms.

She and Luke must have been overheard as a few wedding guests and restaurant patrons were milling around with curious expressions on their faces. Abbey felt herself blush as she and Luke walked over to Rocco. He handed Luke her shoes and winked.

Abbey went to take them from him, but he shook his head, indicating she should sit. She plopped down on one of the couches and he kneeled down in front of her. He made a show of putting her shoes on for her. To add insult to injury, she could hear a few people clicking photos as he hammed it up. *Goofball.*

Abbey got up and walked toward the ladies restroom door with Luke hot on her heels. "Luke, just give me a minute to freshen up, and we'll rejoin everyone, all right?"

"Fine." He leaned in and kissed her on the cheek. "Then when you say the time is right, we go back to my hotel room and I get to fuck you," he whispered.

Abbey's body warmed and hummed with anticipation. She could hardly wait.

Chapter Nine

Luke posed for a few photos with the servers cleaning up Jake and Cassie's banquet room. It was a quarter past midnight and although he'd wanted to leave the reception much earlier, he was glad Abbey insisted they stay.

Maybe he was sentimental or some shit, but Luke had enjoyed watching Cassie miss Jake's mouth with his piece of wedding cake. Jake had been a good sport about it and had carefully fed Cassie her piece, but then *she* ended up playfully biting his thumb. It was sweet and Luke couldn't be happier for his big brother.

The cake was delicious. Luke had gobbled up a huge piece himself. Moist yellow cake filled with real strawberry filling and rich buttercream frosting. Abbey was around here somewhere with a huge chunk of it in a to-go container. He had plans for that cake once they got back to his hotel room.

"How fun! You caught the garter," the sweet brunette server told Luke as she double-checked the selfies they'd just taken.

"Go figure. I guess I can catch too, huh," Luke answered her with a smile. He was wearing the white lacy garter with a blue satin ribbon on his left arm. The silver charm with Jake's and Cassie's names and wedding date sparkled from the overhead lighting.

"Oh right, because you're a pitcher. Thanks for the pictures, Luke. I appreciate it. I better finish up so I can head home. Bye." She put some dirty glasses in a plastic container on top of a wheeled cart and rolled it to the kitchen.

Luke exited the banquet room doors and met up

with Rocco and Jake. Jake looked as happy as he had the minute he'd married Cassie earlier that afternoon. Cassie was pregnant but Jake was nearly glowing himself.

Rocco clapped Jake on the shoulder. "The gifts are loaded up and we'll drop them off at your condo. Your folks have the wedding card box."

"Thanks, man. We'll see you at brunch around noon then?"

Rocco gave Jake a curt nod. "I'll be there."

Luke had been amused, watching Rocco and Hannah circle each other all evening. Both of them reluctant to fully relax and enjoy each other's company, It was obvious there was something going on between the cute event planner and the Italian.

Luke hadn't missed that Rocco seemed disappointed when Hannah hadn't caught the bouquet. Hannah hadn't intended on joining the single ladies in the tradition at first, but Abbey and Leah had dragged her out on to the dance floor. Leah had made an aggressive play and caught it. Although the big Italian Marine had put in a good effort, Luke had easily snagged the garter nearly out of Rocco's hands.

He couldn't resist teasing the man. "So, after Jake and Cass come back from their honeymoon, are you going to bring Hannah to their place for the wedding gift reveal party?"

Rocco didn't respond.

"Did you ask her, at least?" Jake asked.

Rocco ran a hand through his hair and shrugged. "I asked her, what's the big deal?"

Thank God for small miracles. "The big deal is you're both obviously interested but holding back for no good reason." Luke blew out a frustrated breath. Why was Rocco being so difficult about this? Hannah Hailey was a terrific woman. Pretty, smart, hardworking—

DANIA VOSS

Rocco could do a hell of a lot worse.

"Did she agree to come with you?" Jake asked.

Rocco nodded sadly but from Luke's perspective, he should have been happy. "Yes."

Jake's smile beamed. "All right then, that's great news. I like her, Cassie does too. This is a good thing, Roc. Relax and go with it."

Rocco took a deep breath and shrugged again. He seemed unsure. "We'll see. I better get going. See you at brunch." Rocco man-hugged Jake and turned to Luke.

"Your shoulder holding up okay?"

Earlier in the evening Luke, Hannah, and Rocco has used Carlo Antonetti's office to quickly reapply the emu oil cream to Luke's sore shoulder. Carlo had helped Rocco re-secure his shoulder support and Luke had taken another couple of pain pills.

Luke rolled his shoulder, feeling only a dull ache. He would be fine. He wasn't about to let a little shoulder soreness keep him from getting his hands on Abbey and fucking her until she begged him to stop. Not that he would.

"Yeah, man. I'm fine," he told Rocco.

Rocco nodded and left, leaving Luke and Jake in the hallway alone. "Heath gone?"

"Leah dragged him out of here a little while ago." Jake thought a moment. "He wasn't resisting too much."

Luke chuckled. Leah was determined, he'd give her that. He only hoped she didn't live to regret it. "You think those two will be all right?" Luke wasn't sure what Heath's issue was with getting together with Leah, but he didn't want to see either of them get hurt. Leah had been like a kid sister to Luke all these years and Heath his other big brother. Things could get complicated. He didn't want to have to take sides if things went south.

Jake appeared somber. "Win, lose, or draw, I

hope they give a relationship a shot. As long as Heath gives it his best, I'll be all right with whatever happens. I think there's real potential for them."

Luke nodded. He hoped so. *Good luck, you two.* His heart swelled and his dick twitched when Abbey emerged from the ladies' restroom with Cassie. Both of their smiles lit up the hallway.

Jake made a beeline for Cassie and took her hand. "Ready to head out Mrs. Tyler?"

Cassie beamed at Jake. "You bet I am, Mr. Tyler."

Luke took the container of wedding cake from Abbey and the four of them walked to the curb where two limousines were waiting. It was still warm out with a gentle breeze. Antonetti's outdoor lighting wasn't too bright but allowed for them to see fairly well, even late at night.

Luke had insisted on a separate car for each couple and Jake, for once, hadn't put up a fight. Jake wanted some alone time with his new bride on the way to the Fairchild Hotel. Luke couldn't blame him.

After Jake helped Cassie into the waiting limo, he turned and hugged Luke tight. "Thanks for everything today, Luke. We appreciate it."

Luke hugged Jake back, happy he was able help make the day special for him and Cassie. "No need to thank me, big brother. I only wish you would have let me do more."

Abbey held on to Luke's hand as they both watched Jake's and Cassie's car make its way through the parking lot. Abbey's hand, small and warm in his, made Luke feel protective and grounded. He'd missed touching her so much. She had a way of making him feel at peace.

Once they couldn't see Jake's and Cassie's car

taillights any longer, their driver helped Abbey into their limo. Luke slid inside beside her, sinking into the plush leather seat.

The dim lighting inside the limo cast a halo around his princess, making her seem almost ethereal. To Luke, she was and always would be.

"Let me know when we're close to the Fairchild," he called out to the driver.

"Yes sir, Mr. Stryker," the driver replied and then rolled up the privacy partition.

Abbey worried her plump lower lip. Luke felt the blood rush to his cock as he recalled the amazing blowjob she'd given him in the small banquet room earlier that evening.

"Are you upset we stayed until the end of the night?"

Luke reached out to her, pulling her onto his lap. She snuggled into him, warm and soft. *I've missed this. Being close like this.*

"Well…" he began. "At first I just wanted to leave so I could fuck you. But I have to admit, staying was nice. I'm glad you talked me into it."

She kissed him lightly on the lips, her warmth spreading through him. "Good, I'm glad. I think their reception was amazing. I think everyone had a great time."

Luke kissed her neck against her fluttering pulse, causing her to moan softly. "I think you're right, princess. But *now*, I get you all to myself."

He felt her shiver and he couldn't help but feel ten feet tall. She appeared to want him as much he wanted her. He shifted her on the seat until she was below him and he was stretched out on top of her. He pressed his hard cock against her belly and she squirmed beneath him.

Abbey ran her fingers through his hair. Luke couldn't get enough of her touch. He claimed her lips and demanded entry. He was finished waiting, he'd waited all day for her. She was *his*. Always had been, always would be.

Luke growled in satisfaction when she eagerly opened for him, plunging his tongue into her waiting mouth. Their tongues wrestled vigorously as they rode to the Fairchild Hotel, the motion of the moving car adding to their excitement.

Luke pressed his hard dick against Abbey again, and she pulled at his hair, the sting of his scalp driving him crazy. They ended their kiss, both of them gasping for breath. "See what you do to me? I'm hard as a fucking rock."

"I'm so glad. I love your hard dick, Luke," she murmured.

Abbey would have to wait for his dick. Luke had something else in mind for this princess. His mouth watered for a taste of her. He quickly positioned her so she was sitting upright. He kneeled down in front her on the carpeted limousine floor and took her shoes off.

She placed her hands on his shoulders. "What are you doing?" she whispered.

Luke smiled up at her and waggled his brows. "Going to get a taste of what I've been craving all day."

Even in the dim light of the limo, he could see the excitement in her eyes. His girl loved getting her pussy licked. When they were younger, and he'd first asked her if he could eat her out, she'd been too shy. Eventually, he'd convinced her to trust him and let him try it. Since the first time she came from his tongue, she'd never refused him again.

Luke ran his hands up her legs, disappointed to find she had full hose on, not thigh highs. She had a full-length slip on too. *Too many clothes.*

Abbey helped him by lifting her ass up and bunching the skirt of her dress up to her waist. Luke yanked the hose off, not caring if he tore them. She wore sexy lace panties the same color as her dress. He admired them for a second, noticing the damp stain in the middle. Good, she was wet and ready for him. He tore her panties off and brought them to his nose. He inhaled her musky essence and groaned. So sweet, so Abbey.

"Hey! I got those special. They match my dress," Abbey complained, though there wasn't much bite in her tone.

He snickered and put the panties in his pocket. "I'll get you another pair. Now spread those legs, baby, let me look at my pussy."

Abbey smirked. "*Your* pussy?"

Luke raised a brow and took a hold of her legs. "Damn *straight* it's mine."

She placed her hands on his and spread her thighs wide for him. *Good girl.* The sight of her glistening wet pussy had him throbbing in his pants. His cock was so hard it hurt. He had wondered if Abbey shaved or waxed but was relieved to see her blonde pussy hair was neatly trimmed. He preferred a more natural look. Fuck, he just preferred Abbey. Period. Pussy hair or bare, it didn't matter.

He pulled her hips forward so she sat right at edge of the car seat. She leaned back and closed her eyes. He got the hint and leaned in, inhaling the sweet musky fragrance that was Abbey. That belonged to *him.* "Spread your pussy lips apart for me, baby."

Abbey didn't hesitate and pulled her labia apart for him. *That's my girl.* With him, he knew she felt less inhibited. She could turn that amazing brain of hers off for a little while and turn herself completely over to *him.*

It was a heady feeling. Made him feel fucking amazing.

The sight of her glistening wet cunt make his mouth water. He could see her swollen clit peeking out from under its hood. She was perfect. She was *his*.

Luke swiped his tongue along the entire length of her slick pussy, from hole to clit. Abbey's tangy natural flavor was like ambrosia on his tongue. One little taste would never be enough. Abbey's sweet little whimper had him smiling. It wouldn't take long to get his princess off.

Like a starving man, he devoured Abbey's pussy, licking and laving at her. Tonguing her hole and nipping at her hard little clit until she was writhing against his face. She'd let go of her pussy lips and grabbed his head, tugging at his hair, pulling him closer, gyrating her hips against his probing tongue.

"Luke, please," Abbey moaned.

His princess didn't have to beg, not *this* time. He doubled down and inserted a finger inside her hot pussy. She clenched tightly around it. Luke's cock throbbed, knowing it would be balls deep inside her hot, tight channel soon. If he wasn't careful, he'd come in his pants like a teenager.

He flicked her clit over and over, her juices now coating his face, and he added a second finger. He worked over her clit and finger fucked her until she crashed over, screaming his name, sending a new wave of juices flowing from her pussy.

Abbey went limp in her seat, gasping for air. She let go of her death grip on him and gently stroked his hair. Luke removed his fingers and sucked them clean, savoring her taste. He tenderly licked her pussy clean as she squirmed, still sensitive after her orgasm. He placed a few soft kisses along her thighs and wiped his mouth with her hose, then put them in his pocket with her torn panties. He'd have to replace the hose too. He'd get her thigh highs instead. They'd be much easier to work with.

"Mr. Stryker, we're two minutes from the Fairchild Hotel," the driver announced through the speaker system.

Abbey startled, sitting up straight, trying to right herself. Luke gently moved her back against the car seat. He leaned in close, touching his lips to hers. "Taste yourself, princess."

She tentatively ran her warm tongue along the seam of Luke's lips. He plunged his tongue deep inside her mouth and she greedily lapped at him.

Reluctantly, Luke pulled away. He didn't want to linger too long and risk embarrassing her if she didn't feel put together by the time they arrived at the hotel. He never wanted to make her feel uncomfortable, especially in public. "You're the best thing I've ever tasted, baby."

Abbey shook her head and giggled. "I seriously doubt that." She pulled her slip and dress back down into place.

Luke grabbed her shoes, holding them in his hand. Abbey reached for them, but he wouldn't let them go. "Don't doubt it, princess. Best. Thing. I've. Ever. Tasted."

She rolled her eyes at him, took her shoes, and slipped them on. "Okay, if you say so."

He gathered her evening bag and their cake container just as the limo stopped and the engine shut off. "I *do* say so. I almost came in my fucking pants."

Two of Luke's security detail met him and Abbey inside the Fairchild Hotel lobby doors. The luxurious hotel, located in Oak Brook, Illinois, minutes from Chicago O'Hare Airport was normally bustling, but at nearly one in the morning, it appeared quiet. The last thing he needed was to get deterred by Cobras fans when he wanted to get Abbey to his room as fast as possible so he could finally fuck her. He held on to her dainty hand, not wanting to lose their connection, even for a minute.

Luke noticed one solitary hotel front desk agent busy on their cell phone. "It's quiet, Mr. Stryker. No issues," one of the security men said. "Two men are waiting on your floor at the elevator doors to escort you to your room."

Luke had reserved and paid for a block of rooms on the top floor for family and friends, including the honeymoon suite for Jake and Cassie. He'd ensured his and Abbey's rooms were several rooms away from the block of reserved rooms and next to each other.

"Great, thanks. Let's go, then." Luke kissed Abbey gently, her essence still lingering on her warm, luscious lips. They were escorted through the vacant hotel lobby to the golden elevator banks. *So far so good. No one's noticed us.*

They waited for the next available elevator and as the doors opened, a middle-aged couple dressed to the nines appeared out of nowhere. The man with a receding dark-brown hairline and a slight paunch in a designer black suit recognized Luke immediately. *Shit.* The man's companion, a statuesque woman with red hair that obviously came out of a bottle, too much dark eye makeup, and a skin-tight, dark-blue cocktail dress showing off way too much cleavage, eyed Luke like he was a piece of meat. *Double shit. So much for going unnoticed.* Luke squeezed Abbey's hand for assurance.

Luke's security men stood at alert, watching the couple closely. Luke sighed. He just wanted to get to his room for shit's sake. He needed Abbey something fierce. It had been ten long years. He should have been buried deep inside her by now.

Receding Hairline Man extended his hand and

shook Luke's hand firmly. He had a decent handshake, at least. "Luke Stryker! It's great to meet you. I'm a Premier season ticket holder." The redhead winked and slowly licked her lips.

Luke cringed inwardly. He wished Abbey didn't have to witness this. He took a quick glance over at Abbey and she looked … amused. *Great.*

Premier season tickets were expensive, so Luke couldn't just brush the man off. "That's good to hear, sir. I hope you're enjoying yourself at the games."

The man laughed and reached inside his jacket pocket. Luke was pushed aside as his security detail descended on the man. The redhead squeaked and Luke placed himself in front of Abbey, his heart racing. He'd die first before letting anything happen to his princess.

The man held his hands up in surrender, a panicked look in his eyes. "Wait. Stop! I was just getting my business card, I swear. You can take it out of my pocket yourself. I'm not armed."

"He's never fired a gun in his life," the redhead said.

Luke watched, cautiously optimistic as both security men patted the man down and removed a business card from his inside jacket pocket.

The man took the card and held it up. "See? My name is Alfred Gleason. I'm the best real estate broker in the area. I wanted to offer my services, that's all. I handle properties here in the area, Oak Brook, Hinsdale, Elmhurst—anywhere the Chicago Metro area."

Luke sighed, relieved there wasn't an imminent threat. He took Gleason's card and put it in his pants pocket. The one with Abbey's hose and torn panties. He needed to get her to his room *now*.

"Thank you, Mr. Gleason. I'll certainly keep you in mind when I'm in the market for property in the area."

Luke shook Gleason's hand. "I have to be careful. I'm sure you understand."

Before Gleason could comment, the redhead chimed in. "The least you could do is take a picture with us, don't you think?"

"Please excuse my wife, it's late. We're tired as I'm sure you are. Gloria, honey, don't be upset."

Luke wasn't tired, he was wired, horny as shit, and ready to sink into Abbey. But he would do his duty and pose for some shots with the Gleasons.

Luke posed patiently with a smile on his face as one of his security men snapped several shots with Gleason's iPhone. Abbey snickered when Mrs. Gleason squeezed his ass behind her husband's back. *Christ.*

They all rode up in the elevator silently, with the Gleasons looking through their photos. The elevator chimed and the doors opened to the third floor, the Gleasons' floor. They said their goodbyes and Luke held Abbey tightly as they rode to the tenth floor.

Luke and Abbey were escorted, without further incident, to his room. Once inside, he tossed the cake container on the kitchenette counter and reached for her.

"Princess, I've got to have you, right *now*." Luke plunged his tongue inside Abbey's mouth, desperate for her. She responded in kind, tangling her tongue with his until they were both breathless.

Luke took her by the hand and led her to the bedroom he was using in the two-bedroom suite. He couldn't get her naked fast enough.

He shrugged out of his tuxedo jacket and tossed it aside. Abbey turned her back to him.

"Can you unzip me?" She kicked off her shoes while Luke worked the zipper down her dress. "And don't forget the little hook at the neck."

Luke unhooked the tiny hook for her after two

attempts, his hands shaking with need. He watched as she shook out of her dress and removed her slip, leaving her bare-assed and in her sexy cornflower-blue bra. The sight of her perfect ass had his dick pulsing in his pants. He wanted to take a bite of the succulent globes of flesh. He realized the panties he'd ruined were part of a set. *Lucky me.* Abbey unhooked her bra and slowly turned around, smiling seductively.

Luke's mouth watered at the sight of her. Smooth porcelain skin with rounded hips and full tits with hard, dusky nipples, just waiting to be sucked and teased. Her pussy glistening with her juices. *Mine.*

Abbey came toward him and started in on his shirt buttons. "Someone's got too much on, don't you think?" she purred.

"Hell yeah," Luke agreed. He made quick work out of the buttons she hadn't touched and shrugged out of his shirt. He pulled off his t-shirt and Abbey gasped. Shit. He'd forgotten about the shoulder support. He felt fine. She didn't need to worry.

Her eyes glistened with tears. "Oh my, God. What happened? Is that why you missed rehearsal? Because you were hurt?" Abbey gently touched his support-covered shoulder, a tear rolling down her cheek.

He took a hold of her hands and squeezed gently, trying to calm her down. "I'm all right, really, baby. Nothing's broken or dislocated. I'm badly bruised, that's all. A little sore, but that's it. I promise, I'm fine." He pulled the support apart and took it off. He felt better with it off. "Go on, princess, get on the bed. Please. I need you."

Abbey hesitated briefly before nodding and climbing onto the king-size bed, positioning herself in the middle, lying against multiple fluffed pillows and the soft white sheets. She watched with a concerned expression on her angelic face as Luke made quick work out of undressing.

He gripped his throbbing hard cock and stroked himself from root to tip a few times, using his pre-cum as a lubricant. He noticed Abbey watching him stroke himself with avid interest. Good. His princess wanted him. "See what you do to me? I've been hard for you almost the entire damn day."

He crawled onto the bed and she spread her legs for him. Her pussy glistened with her juices, her clit swollen and pink. "Someone's eager, aren't they?"

He slowly kissed his way up her body, starting with her ankles, calves, and up her quivering thighs to her drenched pussy. One quick lick ending at her pulsing clit had Abbey squirming beneath him and moaning. "Mine," he whispered and kissed the light dusting of trimmed blonde hair on her mound. He could feast on her all day and night and never get enough.

Working his way further upward, Luke licked and kissed her abdomen. He paused a second, imaging what it would be like when she was swollen with their first child. He couldn't help but feel a tiny bit jealous of Jake at that moment. His big brother was one lucky fucker with a baby on the way. Luke would do his best to catch up fast. If things hadn't gone to shit between him and Abbey ten years ago, he suspected they'd have a couple of kids by now.

Luke licked her belly button, causing her to giggle. He placed tiny kisses further along her flat stomach until he reached her full, swollen breasts. He took a hard, dusky nipple in his mouth and laved it mercilessly with his tongue, making the tip even harder. Abbey grabbed a hold of his head, pulling him closer. He worked it over good and then turned his attention to her other breast, licking, nibbling, and biting her nipple until she was gyrating beneath him, her skin hot and flushed.

"I'm going to fuck these perfect tits real soon. Would you like that, princess?"

Abbey nodded her head enthusiastically but Luke was having none of that. "Tell me."

"I'd love for you to fuck my tits, Luke," she breathed.

He smiled and placed a quick kiss on her soft luscious lips. "But not right now. Right now, I'm going fuck your tight little cunt. That's what you *really* want, isn't it? My big dick inside you, right?" Luke positioned himself at Abbey's entrance, rubbing the head of his cock along her slick folds, waiting for her answer.

"Yes, Luke. I want your big dick, please." She moaned and rubbed herself along the tip of his hard cock. She was soaking wet, ready for him.

"Good girl, princess." Luke pushed his way inside her hot, wet channel. Although Abbey was drenched for him, she was still incredibly tight, nearly strangling his dick. It took him a few strokes before he was fully seated inside of her.

She wrapped her arms and legs around him and he nearly lost it. She was everything he had ever wanted. Hot and sweaty, skin to skin had never felt this good with anyone else. He knew it never would be. Nothing compared to the feel of his princess—soft, warm, willing, trusting. She was perfection. She was home. She was *his*.

"Oh God, Luke. My big strong Viking feels so good." Abbey groaned.

Luke pulled out and pushed back inside her tight pussy and groaned himself. *Too good.*

He'd forgotten she'd referred to him as her Viking when they were younger. And right now, fucking her after so many years, he *felt* like a Viking. Strong and powerful, even with a sore shoulder.

Luke thrust inside Abbey harder, her tight hot pussy gripping him like a vise. He wasn't going to last long. Not this first time. He'd make it up to her next time. And there *would* be a next time, and another and another.

Luke pistoned into Abbey harder and harder, causing the headboard to bang against the wall. He didn't care if anyone heard. In fact, he'd feel proud if everyone knew he was pounding into his woman.

He quickened the pace of his thrusts, Abbey moaning each time he pushed his cock back inside her, his balls slapping against her ass. He adjusted his hips, allowing his dick to bump up against her G-spot over and over until she was scratching at his back. He welcomed the pain, her desire for him bringing him closer and closer to the edge.

"That's right. I'm your big bad Viking and you're my hot little Shieldmaiden, baby."

"Luke, I'm close. Make me come," she panted.

Luke felt his own orgasm building. His balls drew tight and the base of his spine tingled. He stroked Abbey's little clit as he continued to drive into her. She screamed his name as she tumbled over, causing him to go over too, shooting his load deep inside her waiting pussy. He'd never come so hard in his life. He felt it from the top of his head down to his toes. *Because it's Abbey.*

Once he'd unloaded every drop of cum inside Abbey and he felt himself soften, he pulled out and lay down on his back beside her. The only sound in the room was their heavy breathing. She quickly snuggled up to him and he wrapped his arms around her, their skin still damp with sweat.

When their breathing returned to normal, Abbey sighed and lightly stroked his chest. He'd missed her touch so much over the years. Always so gentle, loving and tender. That was his Abbey.

"I've missed you so much, Luke. I love you. I tried so hard to get over you, but I couldn't."

Luke held Abbey tighter and kissed the top of her head. He didn't want her having any regrets. The past was the past. Now they could move forward. *Together. Like it should be.*

"I've missed the hell out of you too, baby. You are the love of my fucking life, Abbey. Never doubt that. There were so many times over the years that I needed to talk to you. About so many things. Life on the road, each time we won the World Series, graduate school."

Not having Abbey as a sounding board hadn't been easy for him. He trusted her completely. Took her advice to heart. She'd never had an agenda when it came to him either, like most everyone else in his life did. Abbey's agenda had only ever been to love him.

"I know I wasn't there physically, but in spirit I was. As far as graduate school goes, it was tough, I know. And even though I was so hurt and angry, I watched every game. I cheered you on every time. I was thrilled every time you guys made it to the playoffs and won the World Series. The Cobras are what they are today, in large part because of *you.*"

Luke grunted. *Not anymore.* He pulled out of their embrace and laid Abbey down on her back, positioning himself halfway on top of her with his head resting on her warm chest. She wrapped her arms around him and gently stroked his hair.

He smiled as the bed smelled of them and sex. If only he could bottle it and carry it with him everywhere he went. "Yeah well, I'm done now. The team will have to continue on without me as their star pitcher."

Luke felt Abbey stiffen beneath him. "But I

thought you said your shoulder was just bruised? After a little recovery time won't they put you back on the roster? You helped them win four World Series championships over the last ten years. Darren's going to let them screw with you like that?"

God, he loved this woman. Fierce until the end. Ready to stand up and defend her man no matter what. How had he gotten so fucking lucky? He didn't know or give a shit how, but now that he had Abbey back, he'd do everything in his power to make her happy. To make *them* happy.

He kissed her left breast and smiled when her nipple pebbled, humbled by her responsiveness. "My shoulder is just bruised, I wasn't lying about that. But if you've been following my career, you must have noticed my pitching speed has slowed down. Not a lot, but it has. I'm thirty now and after ten years it's not surprising or unexpected."

He'd had a stellar career, no two ways about it. But physically, there were limits as to how long he could continue and remain effective. He'd always known that. He and Darren had planned for that eventuality.

Abbey growled in Luke's defense. She knew he was right. "I know. You're still one of best pitchers in the Major Leagues though, even with a slightly slower pitching speed."

The events of the last few days had finally caught up to Luke. His eyes stung. Darren had stopped Luke from crying at the hospital when he'd told him about his diagnosis. But here, alone with Abbey and with only the soft light from one of the bedroom nightstands on, he felt free to release the pain and sorrow he'd been holding in.

"Even without my injury, though, you know Darren and I planned for this. If I hadn't gotten hurt on Wednesday, I might have given myself another year, possibly two." Luke finally allowed his tears to fall.

Abbey held him tightly, giving him the space he needed to just be. She sniffled and gently stroked his hair, comforting him the best way she could.

"But Abbey, Darren's sick. The prognosis isn't good, so we decided I'd transition to ownership of … everything now, rather than later. I haven't talked to him in detail because of the wedding, but I'm guessing there'll be a press conference early next week."

Luke's tears ran unchecked as he wept, holding his true love in his arms. He mourned the end of an amazing career, one he was so very proud of. He mourned what he believed would be the eventual loss of his uncle, his second father, his mentor, his advisor, the last of his immediate family. Although Darren could easily afford the best of care, money couldn't fix everything. Rich or poor, cancer was a motherfucker. It didn't play favorites.

Luke positioned himself fully on top of Abbey, resting on his elbows so he didn't crush her. "It's going to be all right, baby. As long as I have you beside me, I know everything will be all right."

She brushed away the tears from Luke's face and smiled affectionately at him. "I'll be right here with you, Luke. I promise. I love you. I'll help you and Darren however I can."

Hard again since Abbey was naked beneath him, Luke easily slid his cock inside her. She was still slick from both of them coming earlier. Her pussy gripped his dick tight as he slowly thrusted in and out of her, taking his time, savoring the feel of her.

They tenderly made love as they kissed and whispered words of love and affirmation to each other. They were bound together heart and soul. When Luke shot his cum deep inside her, he prayed they'd created a life. The perfect combination of the two of them—smart, caring, ambitious, athletic. He hoped their first child would be a boy, chauvinistic as that sounded. He couldn't help it. Men wanted mini versions of themselves. That was just how it was. Luke wanted daughters too, though. Pretty little versions of his princess. He couldn't help but smile at the thought. His future family would be amazing.

"Luke, that's the second time you didn't use a condom. Do you normally not wear one?"

Shit. Luke had hoped she was so caught up in reconnecting after so many years that she wouldn't notice they'd not used protection. He'd always used a condom, never went bareback. Too risky for many reasons. But Abbey was his forever. Luke had every intention of getting her pregnant as soon as possible.

"I've always suited up, baby. Every time. I'm clean though. You don't have to worry about that." Luke pulled out, immediately missing Abbey's warmth around his dick. He placed her head on his chest and wrapped his arms around her. "You're not on the pill?"

She sighed and snuggled against him. "Well, no. The last couple of years have been brutal with night school and work. I didn't do much dating, let alone have sex."

Hope bloomed in his heart at the possibility that she could get pregnant this weekend. He knew he was being underhanded about it. He wasn't letting Abbey get away again. Pregnant or not.

"So there's a chance you could get pregnant?" Luke waited patiently while Abbey seemed to do the calculations in her head. *Let it be the right time of the month.*

Abbey stiffened against him, but Luke stroked her arm gently, hoping to calm her down. "Yes, maybe.

Luke we have to be careful next time."

Thank fuck. "Princess, would it be so awful if you happen to get pregnant from fucking me today? I'm not going anywhere, either way. You can trust me." He knew he was moving fast, but he felt like he wasn't moving fast enough. He had ten years to make up for. From his perspective, he and Abbey were behind schedule.

She blew out a breath and relaxed against him, her warm skin comforting and soothing. He wanted Abbey to believe they were together again. For *good* this time.

"I suppose not, although knocking me up like this might not go over well with my folks. Even as much as my father likes you. I'm his youngest daughter, his little girl. I think he has a shotgun." Abbey giggled and kissed his chest. "I've always wondered what our children would be like. I was hoping for little mini Lukes to join the Cobras' roster."

He vowed to do his best to make Abbey a mini Luke as soon as he could. "Challenge accepted, princess. And don't worry, I'll handle your father." He was pretty sure her father wouldn't be too upset. Luke had an important surprise locked up in his hotel suite safe.

Chapter Ten

Abbey slowly woke to the decadent feeling of Luke's warm body spooning hers. His leg hair tickled the back of her legs and his arm was protectively around her waist. She smiled, feeling his morning erection pressed against her ass. His long even breathing suggested he was still sleeping. She could definitely get used to waking up like this every morning. And if he had meant what he'd said earlier this morning, she would be.

She still couldn't believe she was here after so many years. Abbey had wasted ten long years being angry, hurt, and stubborn when she could have spent it being with Luke. If only she would have let him explain. Then who knew where they'd be by now. Married most likely. Probably a kid or two. Little mini versions of Luke.

Her hand instinctively went to her abdomen. Based on her cycle, there was a chance she could be pregnant. The thought should have made her nervous, considering she and Luke had only just reunited, but because she loved him so much, she was hopeful. Hopeful of the amazing future they could build together. Finally, after being apart for so long.

Abbey thought back to everything they'd talked about. She was humbled because he trusted her enough to tell her about his amazing career coming to an end and his Uncle Darren's condition. She wasn't ready to use the C-word just yet. Abbey had always known Darren to be a strong, vibrant man. Driven. Ambitious. Well respected in the sports community as well as the business community. *He'll beat this. He has to, for Luke's sake and his own.* It hurt her heart to think Luke could lose another parent.

She looked over at the digital clock on the nightstand. The red display showed it was nearly ten thirty. She and Luke had managed a few hours of sleep, at least. Instead of feeling tired, Abbey felt refreshed with a renewed sense of optimism.

Needing to use the bathroom, she gently eased herself out of bed. Luke moaned in his sleep and turned onto his back. She frowned at the bruises on his shoulder, the deep red and dark purple spots a harsh contrast against the bright white bedsheets.

In slumber, with his hair tussled and his face peaceful, he looked young and carefree. Unfortunately, at the moment, he was anything but. Abbey meant what she'd told him when he confided in her earlier. She'd do anything she could to help him and Darren through the transitions that were being thrust upon them now. She would let Luke sleep a little longer before they needed to get ready for brunch.

She quietly padded to the luxurious en suite bathroom, clicking the door closed. She'd never seen anything so lavish. It was nearly the size of her apartment, with heated, white Italian marble floors, an oversized white jetted tub, a ceiling dripping with glistening chandeliers, and a plush, eight-foot long, white backless couch conveniently placed in front of an enormous glass-enclosed shower with too many shower and steam heads to count.

She took care of business and washed her hands. Abbey looked at herself in the vanity mirror. Her eyes were bright and her skin glowed. Several hickeys and love bites on her breasts and stomach stood out against her light complexion. Luke had marked her as his and she couldn't help but feel thrilled.

She was sticky. Sticky because Luke had decided

he *needed* to eat wedding cake off her body before they'd fallen asleep. She stretched, feeling pleasantly sore in all the right places, especially between her legs.

Luke's cock was bigger than the last time they were together. Almost painfully big, but she didn't mind, welcoming the pain. Just as she finished brushing her teeth with the hotel-provided toothbrush, Luke stumbled in, rubbing the sleep out of his eyes.

Abbey stood there looking her fill at the god of a man in front of her. *He's beautiful.* Golden-blond hair mussed up from sleep, long, powerful legs, six-pack abs, lean, muscular arms, and nearly fully erect. Aside from the angry-looking bruises on his shoulder, Luke was perfect. *And mine.* She felt her nipples pucker and her pussy slicken just watching him stand there, not fully awake yet.

"You left me," Luke muttered as he walked toward her. Stalked toward her.

"I didn't leave you. I had to use the bathroom."

He stopped in front of her, leaned over, and gently kissed all the marks he'd left on her body. His warm lips on her skin had her body humming. How could she want him again? *He's turned me into a nympho.*

Luke grunted and used the toilet, unbothered by her presence. Rather than feel uncomfortable, she felt content by the intimacy they shared. It felt right to her. As it should be between them now.

After he finished, he washed his hands and brushed his teeth using items from his black leather toiletry bag. He stroked his hard dick a couple of times and took Abbey by the hand, trying to lead her out of the bathroom.

"Back to bed, princess. I need you."

She gently pulled out of his grasp. "Luke, we

have to get ready for brunch, remember? We're all meeting at the restaurant at noon."

Luke sighed and shook his head. "Forget brunch. I'd rather spend the day in bed fucking you, trying to make a little mini Luke," he whined.

Abbey quivered at the thought. Not only of spending the day in bed with Luke, but of the possibility of making a baby. *Luke's* baby. She knew he would make a wonderful father if his work with the kids from the children's foundation was any indication.

As if on cue, both their stomachs growled. They had worked up an appetite. "See? We're both hungry after all that strenuous physical activity, right? I hear the brunch buffet has prime rib, honey-glazed ham, and turkey carving stations. Doesn't that sound delicious?"

Luke's stomach growled again, even louder than before. He shrugged. "Yeah, I guess so, but we can always order up room service, you know," he countered.

Abbey chuckled. *Poor Luke.* He couldn't get what he wanted exactly when he wanted it. If they were going to start a family, which she still couldn't wrap her head around just yet, he'd have to get used to delayed gratification.

"I know, but we promised Jake we'd be there. It's just for a little while. We can build up our strength with some great food and then we can come right back up here, like you want to. What do you say?" She smiled at him, amused as he seemed to contemplate whether they would keep their promise to Jake.

Luke blew out a frustrated breath. "Fine, but we take a shower together before heading to brunch." He turned knobs and pressed buttons, and the shower magically came to life. Luke let the shower run for a few moments and guided Abbey into the warm spray.

She sighed as the warm, pressured water eased

her sore muscles. Heaven. Pure heaven. She felt Luke at her back, wet and warm, and he wrapped his arms around her. She could feel his hard dick pressed against the crack of her ass. She wiggled and Luke groaned.

Shivers went down her spine when he placed light little kisses along her neck and shoulders. "Here, let me work some of the kinks out, baby," Luke murmured softly and rubbed her neck, shoulders, and back, easing her tension away.

He worked his way down her back and kneaded the globes of her ass with his warm slippery fingers. *So good.* She felt him kneel down behind her and he slowly rubbed her thighs and calves. The feel of Luke's strong hands and fingers on her body had her nipples tightening and her pussy moistening.

Abbey felt so relaxed and turned on she leaned against the shower wall for support. She startled when she felt Luke's tongue between her legs, licking her slick folds. She arched her back, sticking her ass deeper into Luke's face.

She groaned and moved her hips back and forth, riding his tongue. Luke nibbled and laved at her clit with his talented tongue until she couldn't hold on any longer. Abbey squeezed her eyes shut and rode the wave of pure bliss that roared through her. How was he able to make her come so quickly? No one else had been able make her respond the way he did.

Before Abbey could catch her breath, Luke thrust his hard cock deep inside her, bumping up against her G-spot. She shuddered and pushed back against him, feeling another orgasm building.

"Princess, you feel so fucking good," he groaned as he pounded into her from behind, his balls slapping against her ass each time he slammed back into her. "You like my big dick fucking you from behind, don't you baby?" He pulled out and thrust back in, hitting her G-spot again.

Yes. She loved it. Any way she could have Luke, she'd happily take him. God, she was going to come again.

"Yes, Luke. You feel so, so good." She groaned, pushing back against his cock. She was close. As if Luke sensed her, he reached between her legs and stroked her still-sensitive clit until a wave of ecstasy thrummed through her again. "Luke!"

"That's it, baby, come all over my dick. I'm right behind you, princess." Luke grunted and pulsed inside her, filling her with so much cum she felt some trickle out of her. "Take all my cum, baby. Take every last drop. I'm going to keep fucking you until we make a baby. Count on it."

Luke held her tightly as they both came down from their orgasmic high and their breathing slowed to normal. The warm shower spray continued beating down against their sensitive skin. She felt Luke soften and pull out of her. She immediately missed him inside of her.

Luke turned Abbey around and devoured her mouth while steam billowed around them. Their tongues danced and tangled until they were breathless again. Luke broke the kiss and touched his forehead against hers.

"I love you so much, Abbey. So fucking much. I can't wait to see you swollen with our baby." He held her close as the warm shower water continued to sluice over them. She leaned into him, reveling in the warm, strong feeling of his powerful body wrapped around hers.

Abbey had dreamed of moments just like this over the last ten years. The two of them, together, content, and wrapped around each other. She'd been so lonely over the last ten years. Abbey hadn't realized just how lonely until this weekend.

They gently swayed in the shower, happy right where they were. The prospect of having a baby scared Abbey a little, but she was looking forward to it, too. What a crazy thing to possibly end up pregnant at the same time as her sister.

"I love you too, Luke. I'm excited but scared, too," she admitted.

What if this was all just a dream? What if trusting Luke so easily after so much time was a huge mistake? Then where would she be? Alone again, heartbroken *and* pregnant? How would that even work? Would they share custody like divorced couples did? Would Luke be angry and sue for full custody? Abbey felt tears sting her eyes.

"Hey princess, where did you go just then?" Luke lifted her chip up so he could look at her.

Abbey saw the concern in his eyes. She didn't know how to verbalize her concerns. "I'm scared."

Luke smiled down at her and shook his head. "No need to be, princess. I'm not going anywhere. I'm going to take such good care of you and our baby, you'll see. Trust me, Abbey. We belong together. I'm in this for the long haul."

Abbey wanted to believe. Very much. Her stomach growled, then his did.

"Okay, let's finish up and get you fed. You might be eating for two now," Luke suggested.

Laughing, they made quick work of getting cleaned up. The Fairchild Hotel's spa supplied the most lush bath products Abbey had ever used before. The lavender-scented body wash left her skin silky smooth and soft. The matching shampoo and conditioner did wonders for her golden locks. *No more store brand for me.* Abbey would pick some up before she checked out of the hotel.

She had no idea if she was pregnant or not. It was probably too early for a pregnancy test, regardless. *Don't stress out over it. It'll happen when it happens.* "Maybe. Either way, I'm starved."

Luke turned knobs and pressed buttons, shutting the shower off. Abbey's hot flesh chilled, and she shivered. He led her out onto the heated floor and wrapped a fluffy white towel around her. *Much better.* She towel dried her hair the best she could. It would have to do until she got to her room where her toiletries and blow dryer were.

Luke dried off and wrapped a towel around his waist. She admired the blond Viking in front of her for a moment before heading to the bedroom to get her things. He followed behind her.

"What are you doing?" Luke asked as she picked up her clothes strewn all over the bedroom floor. Her room was right next door. Maybe she could sneak next door in her towel and avoid the hassle of getting dressed and then having to change again.

"I have to go to my room, Luke. My clothes are there. I have to dry my hair. You know, I have to get ready. You go ahead and get dressed, then come get me when you're ready." Abbey glanced at the nightstand clock. Damn. A quarter to twelve. They would be late for brunch.

Abbey dug her suite key card out of her evening bag and went to the door with Luke right behind her. "I'll walk you next door, princess."

Two of his security detail stood in the hallway. Abbey peeked and didn't see anyone, only the housekeeping cart. Not that she was ashamed, but walking around in nothing but a towel wasn't the norm for her.

"I'll be right back," Luke told the men. One of

them held his suite door open while Luke escorted her to her suite and opened the door for her.

So this is what it will be like to be taken care of—by Luke. I think I can get used to this.

Luke ushered Abbey inside her suite. Just as lush and well-appointed as his suite, hers had one bedroom. He held on to her suite key card and kissed her softly on the lips. His lips were warm and inviting.

"Go and get ready. You're probably freaking because we're going to be a little late, aren't you?"

How did he still know her so well? "Not completely freaking out, but do I hate to be late. That hasn't changed."

Punctuality was one of Abbey's biggest pet peeves. She'd always prided herself for being on time, usually early for appointments. Chronically late people annoyed the hell out of her. She knew Luke wasn't normally late either. They'd been pleasantly distracted this morning.

He kissed her on the forehead and headed toward the door. "I won't take long. I'll let myself back in when I'm ready." He left with the suite door clicking closed behind him.

It's so much easier for a man. All they did was towel dry their hair and throw on a pair pants and a shirt.

She tossed her wedding clothing in the closet and ran to her bathroom to get ready. The spa's haircare products left her golden-blonde tresses luxuriously soft and shiny. She'd buy some before she left the Fairchild.

Abbey hurried through but didn't skip her skin care routine. She'd considered applying a little makeup since she had all the products that Angel had given her yesterday. When she examined her face in the mirror, she had to admit she looked refreshed and glowing with nothing on her face at all. *This is what happiness looks like.* Smiling at her reflection, she applied a little lip gloss and made quick work of slipping into a white satin and lace bra and panty set. Abbey chose not to look at the clock, but instead concentrated on getting ready.

She'd just slipped into a short-sleeved, floral-print sundress that showcased her boobs without showing off too much cleavage when Luke walked into the bedroom. Abbey cinched the waist ties behind her, accentuating her narrow waist and rounded hips. She loved this dress. Sexy without being slutty. Perfect for Sunday brunch.

Luke looked her over slowly, his gaze searing her as it made the journey from her face down to her bare feet. She felt her nipples react and her core slicken. Abbey shook her head. There was no time for *that*.

He stalked over to her and kissed her so ferociously they were both panting when he finally pulled away. "Damn, princess. You're the most beautiful thing I've ever seen."

Abbey shook her head but still flushed at his compliment. Luke had traveled in the same circles as the most gorgeous women in the world. There was no way she could ever compete with that. Not that she wasn't pretty, but she wasn't the *most* beautiful. She knew that.

Luke frowned at her, shaking his head. "Don't do that, princess. Don't compare yourself to who I've been exposed to. To *me*, you are the most beautiful, the most precious person in the entire world. You always have been. Believe it, all right?"

When Luke looked at her with such tenderness, love, and desire, how could she not believe him? She wanted to because he was that to her. Beautiful and precious. He always had been.

Abbey nodded. "Okay, I will. Let me put my sandals on and I'll be ready to go." She looked at Luke and laughed to herself. *Just like I said, pants and a shirt, although very expensive pants and shirt.* He had on a black pair of Gucci Genius jeans and light-blue Gucci dress shirt nearly the same shade as his eyes.

This was Luke's life now. He could afford anything he wanted. She wondered now that she was with Luke, how her life would change in addition to having their baby. She'd bet he wouldn't want her to work, arguing she wouldn't *need* to. Abbey didn't have a job at the moment, but wasn't sure if she saw herself as a full-time stay-at-home-mom kind of woman.

She pushed those thoughts aside. It was still her reboot weekend. There was plenty of time to decide about work and family starting tomorrow.

"So I was talking to my boys while I was getting ready. We decided we're having two boys then a girl," Luke announced as they and the two security detail reached the elevator banks. She was thankful no other guests were around.

Boys? What? "What boys? Jake and Heath?" Abbey had no clue what Luke was talking about? Two boys *then* a girl?

Luke grabbed his crotch. "My boys, my swimmers, my baby makers," he replied.

Abbey rolled her eyes. "You spoke to your *sperm*? And what? Put in an order for two boys and a girl? In that specific order?"

If the security detail thought Luke was crazy, they made no indication of it. They stood quietly with her and Luke waiting for the next available elevator to arrive.

He flashed her a smug smile and shrugged. "Yes. We need two boys first *then* a girl. The order is important."

An elevator dinged and the doors opened. *Thank God, it's empty.*

"First, I don't think you can order the birth order of children like that. Not yet anyway." Maybe you could, with technology what it was these days. She'd have to look into that. "Second why is the order so important?" He seemed so determined.

Luke put his arm securely around Abbey's waist, pulling her close. "I've got four World Series championship rings and three Cy Young awards. I can do whatever I want, princess," Luke said confidently. "But we need two boys *before* the girl because our daughter will be so gorgeous I'll need our sons' help to protect her and keep all the other boys away from her. *That's* why."

Aww. Abbey's heart squeezed. He couldn't say things like that. *So sweet.* Abbey looked over at the two security detail and saw they were grinning and nodding slightly.

"See? The guys agree, don't you?" Luke kissed her forehead and smiled brightly.

"Yes, sir," both the men replied.

They reached the lobby floor and the elevator doors sprang open. Luke didn't acknowledge the few guests waiting to enter that had recognized him. "So, it's settled then. That's the plan." Luke led her by the hand to the restaurant, determination in his stride.

Abbey just smiled. How could she argue with that logic? This was her Luke. She'd play along with his plan, knowing full well Luke would adore their children regardless of their birth order or gender.

It looked like she and Luke were the last to arrive at the bustling restaurant, not quite ten minutes late, with Leah and Heath just sitting down. Leah looked positively radiant, with Heath a little more subdued but not able to take his eyes off her. Good for them. Abbey hoped the two of them gave being together an honest try. They deserved to be happy.

Luke and Abbey took their seats with Leah, Heath, and Rocco to Abbey's left and Darren and Maureen to Luke's right. Across the table from them, the newlyweds sat center stage with Abbey's parents to her right and Jake's parents to Abbey's left, along with Abbey's grandmother Ruth and Jake's grandmother Beverly.

"Now that we're all here," Jake began and took Cassie's hand in his, "go ahead and fill your glasses. We have pitchers of Mimosas, water, cranberry juice, and plain orange juice in the pitcher with the white straw tied around the handle."

As everyone busied themselves filling their glasses, mostly from the Mimosa pitchers, Luke turned to Abbey and whispered, "Cranberry?"

Abbey knew she needed to refrain from drinking alcohol on the chance she could be pregnant already, but she knew Jake and Cassie were watching her and Luke with interest, their brows raised. She trusted they wouldn't say anything out loud when Abbey nodded and Luke filled her glass with the burgundy-colored juice.

Once everyone had filled glasses, Jake continued. "Cassie and I would like to thank everyone at the table for helping to make yesterday the best day of our lives. No one could ask for a better group of people to call family than the ones sitting around this table. There was a lot of toasting to Cassie and me yesterday, but this afternoon I want to toast all of you." Jake and Cassie raised their glasses and everyone around the table followed suit. "We love you all and consider you an amazing blessing in our lives. To our family."

"To our family," everyone around the table echoed and took a sip of their chosen beverage.

"Make sure you eat and drink up. I was told Luke has already taken care of our bill." Jake flashed Luke a phony glare and helped Cassie out of her chair. Abbey heard the click of camera phones around them, but no one at their table, including Luke acknowledged them.

This is what it's going to be like, especially after I become pregnant? "It's okay, Abbey," Luke whispered as everyone made their way around the generous brunch spread. "Come on, let's eat so we can head back to my room." He took her hand and led her to the carving stations and got them both plates.

Abbey's mother seemed to notice their interlocked fingers and gestured to her father. Abbey's father looked over, surprised at first, and then smiled at her and Luke, nodding with approval. Her mother flashed them a huge grin and went to the omelette station. Abbey was relieved but not surprised. Her parents had always been fond of Luke. *Everything's going to be okay.*

Luke signed a few autographs and took photos with some diners while Abbey filled her plate with turkey, scrambled eggs, sausage links, country fried potatoes, and sautéed vegetables prepared for her at the omelette station. Abbey hoped she had a good mix of nutrients, just in case. She needed to research the proper pregnancy eating plan as soon as possible.

Abbey had just begun digging into her food when Luke returned the table with his plate piled high with prime rib, ham, country fried potatoes, and a variety of other food stacked on top of each other she couldn't decipher what was what.

Luke leaned over and kissed Abbey's cheek, his warm lips searing her skin. Her body reacted immediately. *Hold it together, Abbey.*

Jake laughed at Luke. "Damn, Luke, you sure you got enough? You didn't have it pile it on so high. You can go back up for more, you know?"

Luke shrugged Jake off. "What can I say? I'm

starved. Had a busy morning, need to replenish my energy."

Leah snickered beside Abbey and she felt herself blush. She needed to get the subject back to the newlyweds.

"So, are you both excited about your honeymoon in Aruba? What's it like there in June?"

With the conversation steered to topics other than her and Luke, everyone relaxed into their meals and enjoyed post-wedding chitchat. Although Abbey could still hear cell phone photos being taken, she was thankful no one bothered them.

Abbey was nibbling on dessert when Darren spoke up.

"We're holding a Cobras press conference Monday afternoon at one o'clock."

Luke stiffened beside her. She took a hold of his hand and gently squeezed it for assurance. He squeezed back. Everyone around the table stopped what they were doing, all eyes on Luke and Darren.

"That's quick," Luke muttered, seemingly not thrilled with Darren's announcement.

"Is everything all right?" Abbey's father asked.

Everyone at the table had troubled expressions on their faces. Abbey's stomach fell to her feet, her heart aching for Luke. Even though she and Luke had discussed the upcoming transitions, it was probably still difficult for him. Talking privately was one thing. A press conference was something different. It made everything real.

Darren nodded, but he had a frown on his face. "Yes, we have a few important announcements to make. They can't wait."

Jake looked pissed. "And you can't *at least* tell the family? *Now?*" Everyone at the table murmured in

191

agreement.

"Jake, look…" Luke began, but Darren put a hand on his shoulder.

"Jake, have you noticed everyone around us is taking pictures? Many are recording on their phones."

Jake's eyes widened as if he hadn't considered the possibility. He looked at the surrounding diners, anger flaring from his eyes. "Don't you people have better things to do? Can't you see we're having a private family meal? Back off."

Some diners walked away embarrassed, while others who were sitting nearby just placed their phones down, trying not to be so obvious. They didn't fool anyone.

"Jake, it's going to be all right. You have my word. There's no reason to get upset. You just married your beautiful bride. You're leaving on your honeymoon tomorrow. Focus on that. It's what's most important."

Jake blew out a frustrated breath and Cassie reached out and laced her fingers through his. "I'm really tired of this shit, you know? All damned weekend with secrets."

"Everything's going to be all right," Cassie said. Jake nodded sadly and pulled her close for comfort.

"Your bride is right, Jake. I didn't mean to dampen everyone's happy mood, but I wanted the family to know before the press conference was announced. It will be later this afternoon," Darren added softly.

Luke suddenly stood up, surprising everyone at the table. He looked down at Abbey tenderly. "I'm going for more dessert. Would you like more cheesecake, princess?"

Abbey nodded and Luke kissed her lightly on the lips before heading to the dessert tables. She sighed when she heard the click of cell phones behind her. *After a little more dessert, I'm ready to get away from all these prying eyes.* Abbey wasn't sure if she'd ever get used to the attention. She wondered how Luke did it. He never seemed too bothered by it.

****

Outside the restaurant entrance, Luke stood with everyone from their table, chatting after they'd all stuffed themselves. He'd been ravenous, but he was still distraught his Uncle Darren had scheduled their press conference for the following afternoon. *Too soon.* He was pissed that some brunch diners had paid too much attention to their group.

He held Abbey's hand tightly, comforted by her support. He was eager to get back to his room, not only so he could fuck her until they were both worn out, but for some much needed privacy. He was tired of having his every move watched. He needed a break. He needed to get the focus back on him and Abbey and their plans for the future.

Jake checked his watch. "Well, Darren booked us a couple's massage, so we really should get going to the spa."

"Oh, that sounds so nice," Abbey commented and looked at Luke with a gleam in her eyes.

He'd get them a couple's massage since his princess liked the idea. Maybe they could get a private massage in his room so they wouldn't attract unnecessary attention at the spa.

"Abbey! There you are. What the hell?" Luke and his family turned to find some angry, dark-haired, bad boy wannabe dressed in black jeans, a black Harley Davidson t-shirt, and tatted-up arms storming over to them.

Abbey flinched and that pissed Luke off. Was she *afraid* of this asshole? He didn't give a shit who this dude was. *No one* fucked with his woman.

"What are you doing here, Tom? I told you to I didn't need you as my date this weekend," Abbey told the asshole. She had considered this douche as her date for the wedding? No *fucking* way.

Tom gestured at his and Abbey's linked hands with disgust. "Oh yeah, I got that after I saw at all the pictures of you posted on Facebook."

Shit. Luke had hoped very little of their time together ended up on social media. So much for everyone's word they wouldn't post anything. Regardless, what business was it of Tom's if Abbey had refuted his attempts to muscle in as her date? Fuck him and his attitude.

Luke held on to her as she slumped her shoulders. "I had no idea we're on Facebook. I turned off my phone."

His family checked their cell phones, including Grandma Ruth and Grandma Beverly. Even in their late-seventies those two were fairly computer literate. They were all probably looking for news or posts about him and Abbey. This was not good.

He hadn't heard from Brenna since last night. How was this revelation going to affect their Mission Abbey plans? Brenna hadn't told Luke how she was planning on making the news of their split public.

Tom threw his hands up in frustration. "No shit. Since when do you turn your cell phone off? Your ticketing system was down. Tim and I kept trying to reach you, but you never picked up or responded to our calls and texts. What the fuck, Abbey?"

An angry Grandma Ruth went right up to Tom and poked him in the chest. "Don't you talk to my granddaughter like that, you jerk!"

An angrier Grandma Beverly was right on Ruth's

heels and in Tom's face. "Ruth's right. You leave our Abbey alone. She's a smart, good girl and she doesn't have to listen to your crap."

Tom stepped back and put his hands up in surrender. Abbey let go of Luke's hand and group hugged the upset grandmothers. "I've got this," Luke heard her tell them.

Abbey turned to Tom with anger in her pretty eyes. *Good, she's going to let this dick have it and I'll be her backup.* Unfortunately, their confrontation drew a bit of attention and three of his security detail including Rocco, were at the ready, waiting for Luke's direction. He wanted Abbey to have her say before he let them get rid of this asshole.

"First of all, it's not *my* ticketing system anymore. Tim Webber made it abundantly clear that my responsibilities and skill set were no longer required when he fired me Wednesday afternoon. But I'm sure you already know that, don't you?" Abbey crossed her arms under her chest, exposing more of her tempting tits in her pretty sundress. Luke didn't miss Tom the Douche ogling her.

"You got fired?" the entire family, including Luke, asked. Everyone looked stunned. Abbey worked her ass off at that shit hole Office Supply Galaxy. They were too cheap to hire additional people to help her, leaving Abbey with the workload of at least two people. From what Luke understood, Abbey was the only person supporting OSG's ticketing system. The system was considered mission critical and they fired her? It made no sense.

Tom redirected his gaze to Abbey's face, looking remorseful. "Abbey and about fifty others were laid off, not fired. And I didn't know. Not until the system went down Saturday night and Tim called me when he couldn't reach you. You should have called one of us back. Tim's really pissed off."

Abbey shook her head. "I don't give a shit what Tim or *you* are. I no longer work at OSG, so the ticketing system is no longer *my* problem. Let Tim be pissed off. So am I. I worked my ass off for ten years and what did I get for it?"

"Abbey, think about it a second before you ignore Tim. He's making noise about going to HR…"

Luke's Uncle Darren stepped up beside Abbey and put an arm around her shoulders. "That's *enough*. Abbey, honey, did OSG require you to sign termination documents?"

Abbey nodded. "Yes, I had to so I'd get my six months' severance and three months of paid health insurance."

"So Tom, you tell Tim, Jim, John, Clark or whoever else thinks they can intimidate Abbey, that if they even *consider* withholding Abbey's severance or any other benefits she's entitled to, by the time my legal team is through with Office Supply Galaxy, she'll *own* the damn company. Now get the hell out of here and don't *ever* bother her again. Understand?"

Luke motioned to Rocco and his security detail. Rocco grabbed Tom by the arm, flanked by the others on the security team, and led Tom around the corner to the hotel exit.

Luke and everyone else sighed in relief. Abbey kissed Darren on the cheek and immediately returned to Luke's side, lacing her fingers through his. Her beautiful smile lit up her face. Luke was more than capable of defending his woman, but he knew his uncle was protective of their family. He hadn't had the heart to ask his uncle to step aside.

Abbey's father Phil held out his hand and Darren

shook it. "Thank you, Darren."

Darren clapped Phil on the shoulder. "My pleasure, Phil. No one screws with this family if *I* have anything to say about it."

Some onlookers applauded and snapped photos of Darren and Phil. "Don't you all have someplace else to be?" Luke barked.

His gut clenched. Who knew how much longer they'd all have Darren in their lives? Before Luke could contemplate his uncle's future, two of his security detail ran toward them from around the corner.

"Everyone needs to get back to their rooms, immediately."

"What's going on?" Abbey asked him, concern in her lovely gaze.

Luke wasn't sure. Did Tom do something? Then he saw the press descending, video cameras in hand, cameras flashing, and Brenna Sinclair heading toward them, larger than life, like the movie star she was. She wore a form-fitting, white, knee-length knit dress and high-heeled white pumps, a stark contrast to her silky dark-brown tresses. Brenna Sinclair was the epitome of Hollywood royalty—and she looked pissed. Damn. *What the fuck, Brenna?*

Abbey let go of his hand and stepped away. Why was Brenna doing things this way?

"There you are, Luke! I should have known. I've been waiting for you in our hotel room *all weekend* but you kept putting me off. Because of *her*, I bet?" Brenna flicked her dark-brown locks over her shoulder with dramatic flair. The paparazzi ate it up, the camera flashes nearly blinding.

Abbey looked him with watery eyes, betrayal etched in her delicate features. "Luke?"

"Now I know why you *insisted* I not attend your

197

friend's wedding as your guest. You *said* it was because you didn't want to draw attention away from the bride and the groom. But now I know that was a lie. You wanted to spend time with *her*. Don't even bother trying to deny it. Your escapades are all over social media. What a fool I was. I thought you were going to propose this weekend."

"Luke, what's the blonde's name?"

"How long have you been cheating on Brenna, Luke?"

"Did you think you could have them both? Got a redhead somewhere too?"

Luke was going to kill Brenna for doing this. He thought she would mention they'd stopped seeing other this weekend with *TMZ* or *Access Hollywood*. Not create this unnecessary drama that he would have to untangle with Abbey. Actors.

"I can't believe you did this to me again. I could be…" Abbey whispered as she tried to push her way through the crowd of press and onlookers.

Luke reached for her arm, but she pulled away as if she was repulsed at the thought of touching him. "Princess, it's not what it seems." *Christ, did I just say that? Because it's not what it seems.*

Brenna gasped melodramatically. "You call *her* princess too?"

Fuck. This was getting worse by the second. Luke was relieved hotel security and the local police arrived. *It's about time.* Before they could wrangle the press away, Abbey made a break for it and some paparazzi started after her.

"Rocco," Luke shouted over the roar of commotion.

Rocco ushered Abbey away with the rest of his security detail as some the hotel's security guards fended off the press.

His heart sank as his family stood around him with confused expressions on their faces. It was time for him to make everything right. Once and for all. He hoped it wasn't too late.

Chapter Eleven

"Hey blondie, what's your name?"

"Who colors your hair?"

"Are you sleeping with Brenna Sinclair, too? Are you into threesomes?"

"Who's better in bed, Luke or Brenna?"

As quickly as he could, Rocco led Abbey away from the horde of press that had upended her life, but not before the vile reporters fired off disgusting questions at her left and right. Did they really think she'd answer any of their repulsive questions? What was wrong with them?

Abbey squeezed her eyes shut and let Rocco guide her down a hallway to what she hoped were the elevators. At least Luke's security detail and the local police had finally caught up to them and had dragged the press away before they hurled any more obnoxious questions at her.

Her stomach roiled and her body shook. She'd been utterly humiliated—again. Her heart ripped right out of her chest—again. But unlike the first time Luke had betrayed her, or she believed he had, this time though, he'd truly betrayed her in front of the press. If not for Rocco nearly carrying her, she would have collapsed into a heap on the hotel floor. Wouldn't that have made for some entertaining pictures. Damn paparazzi.

She heard an elevator ding and the doors open. Rocco gently guided her inside. Abbey opened her eyes and pushed away from him as soon as the elevator doors closed.

"Did you know Luke was still with Brenna?" Abbey whispered to Rocco, her mind numb, her heart shredded, hot tears spilling down her cheeks. Then she thought better of it and put her hand up to stop Rocco from replying. "It doesn't matter, does it? You're *his* friend, *his* employee. It's your job to protect *him,* right?"

Rocco sighed and blew out a breath as the elevator ascended to the tenth floor. "I *am* his friend and employee. You're right. It's my job to protect him from crazy fans, from people who might want to hurt him, not from being an asshole and treating people like shit. That's on him."

Rocco's response stunned her. He wasn't defending Luke's awful behavior like she thought he would have. That was a surprise. Just like the surprise that Luke hit her over the head with on the first floor.

Abbey had to know though. How deep did Luke's lies and deception go? "So, you didn't know about Brenna? Has she been staying here at the Fairchild all weekend?"

Rocco shook his head. "I'm not sure. We haven't seen her on the property until she showed up a little while ago. Luke had me, Jake, and Heath convinced he intended on using this weekend to win you back for good." He shrugged and frowned at her.

Abbey snorted. He'd fooled them all. Bravo. Brenna and her acting coaches had trained him well. "Luke's turned into quite an actor, huh? It looks like we can't trust a word he says."

"I don't know what to say, Abbey, other than I'm sorry."

She nodded sadly, not crying at least. The elevator stopped on the tenth floor and the doors opened. Rocco stepped in front of the doors, blocking her. Three hotel guards were on the other side of the elevator doors.

"It's all clear, Mr. Moretti. The rest of Mr. Stryker's security detail is in the hallway and we have hotel guards stationed at both stairwells," one of the hotel guards said.

Rocco nodded and took her hand. Abbey saw six of Luke's security detail stationed along the otherwise empty hallway near their family's block of rooms. She dug her suite key card out of her purse and inserted it. When the door clicked, and the light flashed green, Rocco pushed the door open for her.

Abbey walked inside, turned, and gave Rocco a quick peck on the cheek. "Thank you."

Rocco kissed her gently on the forehead. She was touched. Rocco was a good man. She hoped he and Hannah Hailey got together. They looked like they'd make a good couple. But what did Abbey know? She had stupidly thought she and Luke did too. Clearly she'd been wrong about that.

"Do you want me to come inside and stay with you for a little while? I don't mind," Rocco compassionately offered.

What a nice guy. Unlike Luke. Lying. Cheating. Asshole Luke. "No, I'll be fine. Maybe I'll just pack my things and someone can give me a ride home?" There was no reason for her to stay at the Fairchild. Not now. It would be better for her to be at her place.

Rocco smiled sympathetically at her and nodded. "Of course. Take all the time you need. We'll get you home safely and discreetly. Don't worry about that."

Abbey nodded sorrowfully and closed the door. After it clicked into place, she slid down the door, drained of all emotion. Slumped on the floor with her back against the door, she silently let her tears flow. She vowed they would be the last she would shed over Luke. She was done. It was over. Abbey swiped at her face as tears continued to fall. *Come on, Abbey. He's not worth it.*

She should have known better. She shouldn't have let Luke convince her into more than just a fun weekend. How could she have been so stupid to believe all Luke's bullshit? His so-called plans for the future? His two boys *then* a girl crap? She had to give him credit. He sure had her fooled. She fell for his shit hook, line and sinker.

Abbey would have spent the weekend with Luke without all the false promises. It would have been a part of the original plan for her reboot weekend. There was no reason for Luke to take things to another level with false promises of a future together. They could have had some fun and gone their separate ways on Monday, like she had intended.

But that didn't explain Brenna Sinclair. Luke had obviously lied about not being with her. But why? Just to get Abbey into bed this weekend? That was low, even for him. Or maybe not. Luke had changed since that night ten years ago. And not in a good way.

Obviously Brenna believed they were still together. She had made that painfully clear on the first floor. In a way, Abbey felt sorry for her. To be an A-list actress like Brenna Sinclair and to find out your man was unfaithful on social media like that. Brenna had a right to be upset. She couldn't blame her for going off the way she had.

Abbey lightly banged her head against the suite door and blew out a breath. Shit. Unbeknownst to her, Abbey was now the other woman. Damn Luke. This was all his fault. She hoped the press skewered him over this. He deserved it. Asshole.

Was Luke lying about his shoulder and career coming to an end too? What about his Uncle Darren, did he really have cancer, or what that all part of Luke's act to garner sympathy so she'd sleep with him? Abbey shook her head. It didn't matter. She had to worry about herself now.

Reluctantly, she stood up and took a couple deep breaths. She needed to get her things together, go home, and regroup. The faster she got out of the Fairchild, the better.

Abbey retrieved her carry-on bag from the bedroom closet and proceeded to the en suite bathroom to quickly toss her toiletries inside her bag. She wasn't concerned with being organized. She needed to get a move on.

Someone pounded on the door just as she had finished packing up all her things. "What now?" she muttered to herself. Did the paparazzi get past the hotel security guards and Luke's security detail? She waited silently in the suite's living room.

"Abbey! I know you're in there," Luke shouted.

Her stomach twisted. What the hell was wrong with him? Did he think she would ever want to speak to him again? After what just happened? *He's lost his mind.*

He pounded on the door again. "Abbey let me in. Let me explain what's going on. Come on, princess."

She fisted her hands, her anger building. "Don't call me princess. Save that for Brenna, asshole."

"Calm down and open the door," he pleaded.

"Fuck you, Luke. Don't tell me what to do. I have nothing to say to you. Not anymore," she shot back.

Why couldn't he leave her alone? Why did he insist on trying to feed her more lies? Did he think she'd believe him *now*, after being caught in a lie? He had to be crazy. There was no other explanation.

"That's enough, Abbey. I'm not playing around. Open the damned door. Now," Luke insisted.

She growled. The nerve! Ordering her around like she was his flunky. "And I told *you*, I have nothing to say, asshole. You've had your fun. Go back to Brenna and leave me alone."

"I'm not going anywhere until you open this door. Either *you* open the door, or I'll get someone from the hotel staff to open it. Your choice," Luke threatened.

Choices. Yeah, right. Her choices had been taken away from her when Luke had decided to lie to her all weekend.

Abbey was too emotionally drained to continue arguing. Maybe if she allowed Luke to "explain" then she could leave and get on with her life. Letting Luke in her suite might be the fastest way to get back home.

She opened the door and Luke stormed in. She couldn't look him in the eye. Why was he holding a bag from the Fairchild spa? She sighed. What did it matter? It was probably spa products for Brenna. How insulting that he brought them with him. Was he going to "explain" that away too?

He put his hand under her chin and she backed away. "Abbey, come on, please look at me," he begged, his voice barely a whisper.

Fine. Maybe it would speed things along so she could go home. She looked at him. She tried not to feel sorry for him. He looked haggard. His hair was sticking up all over as if he'd been running his fingers through it.

"Fine, go ahead and explain," she relented, defeated.

"Luke? Did she let you in her room?" Who was that? Was someone outside?

"Yes, Brenna. I'm in her room," Luke said as he took his cell phone out of his back pocket.

What kind of game were Luke and Brenna playing? Was that paparazzo right? Were they into threesomes?

Abbey wanted none of this. She opened her suite

door. "I don't know what you two are doing or what you're into, but I'm not interested. Luke, please leave. Find someone else to play your kinky games with. I'm not the one."

"Abbey, please hear us out. Nothing kinky is going on, I swear." This came from Luke's cell phone. Brenna, she assumed. "Please, Abbey."

Abbey slid down the suite door onto her ass, cushioned by the room's plush carpeting. She crossed her legs and crossed her arms under her chest. "Fine. Go ahead. Let's get this over with."

Luke sat down on the floor cross-legged, directly in front of Abbey, and held his cell phone out toward her. "Go ahead, Brenna."

"First, I want to say how sorry I am," Brenna began.

For what? Luke was the one who should be sorry. "What for? Luke is the one who created this mess. He had me convinced you two weren't together. I'm not some skank, like the paparazzi were trying to insinuate." Abbey glared at Luke. He had the decency to look apologetic. It didn't matter.

"I know that. And Luke wasn't lying. We're not together. We never were," Brenna continued.

"See? I told you," Luke whined.

Abbey wasn't sure what to believe. This conversation could be a part of game Luke and Brenna were playing. Abbey didn't dare to hope what Brenna was saying was the truth.

"Be quiet, Luke," Brenna scolded. "I know you've probably read and heard the hurtful things my father has said to and about me. He's made no secret of how little he thinks of me because of my chosen profession."

In that regard, Abbey knew Brenna was telling

the truth. Mr. Sinclair, a southern Baptist Minister, had been brutal in his criticism of his oldest child and of the acting community as a whole. Abbey had found his remarks way out of line. Brenna's reputation was impeccable, considering how scandalously many others in Hollywood behaved.

Brenna was known as a consummate professional, drama averse and a humanitarian. She had helped to bring a lot of attention to the Cobras' Children's Foundation and many other charitable organizations. From all accounts, Brenna Sinclair was the real deal. Her father's behavior toward his oldest child was unfair and unwarranted.

"Because of my father's disdain for me, I talked Luke into being my cover so I didn't have to endure even more public scorn from my father for my choice of romantic partners."

Hope bloomed in Abbey's chest. Was it possible Luke had been telling the truth? Was what happened at the hotel's restaurant entrance all an act? Why hadn't Luke warned her so she could have avoided the pain and anguish of believing he was a lying, cheating asshole?

"So you're really a lesbian? Not that it matters." Abbey had no issue with homosexuals. It wasn't for her to judge or make issue with who people chose to be with, love, or marry.

Brenna laughed through Luke's cell phone speaker. "Not exactly. I've been dating women for the last few years, but I've had serious relationships with men too. If I had to put a label on myself, which I hate to do, I suppose I consider myself a bisexual."

Was Luke frowning? He looked disappointed. "So you weren't attracted to me at all then?" Luke asked with amusement in his voice.

"Sorry, pretty boy, but no," Brenna replied with a

smile in her voice.

"Have you been staying here at the Fairchild this weekend?" Abbey needed to know. She wanted to fully understand what was going on before deciding about her and Luke. She still had doubts.

Abbey heard shuffling and a clicking sound.

"No, I'm not at the Fairchild. Luke, I just texted you a picture," Brenna said.

After a couple of swipes, Luke held his phone up so Abbey could see. The photo showed Brenna holding up the room service menu and room key card from the Drake Hotel there in Oak Brook, near the Fairchild Hotel.

Abbey felt herself relax a little, but she was still hesitant to fully believe.

"I had intended on contacting *Entertainment Tonight* and mention that Luke and I parted ways with some excuse about conflicting work schedules, blah, blah, blah. But when I saw a couple of social media posts with you and Luke, I thought maybe I'd try the whole drama queen bit—and I failed miserably. Sometimes you need a script," Brenna admitted.

Luke swiped his phone and held it out to Abbey again. "Brenna has been texting me all weekend, hoping I could convince you to take me back for good. She's been on our side the entire time, princess."

Abbey quickly scanned the text message thread between Luke and Brenna, confirming what Luke said. Her heart skipped a beat. Based on their texts, Brenna had been encouraging Luke not to give up on getting her back. Brenna had been fully on board with what Luke was calling "Mission Abbey". Abbey's eyes misted. *Luke really loves me. He hasn't been lying.*

"I'm beyond sorry at how badly I handled things. I've spoken with Darren and he agreed to let me say a few words to clear everything up and come clean tomorrow afternoon at the start of the Cobras' press conference," Brenna explained.

Abbey couldn't let Brenna do that. It could further damage her strained relationship with her father. Although Brenna's sexual orientation shouldn't adversely affect her acting career, unfortunately, it could.

"Brenna, it's all right, you don't need to do that on my account. I agree you handled things really badly, but I believe you. Our conversation is good enough for me." Abbey hoped she could spare Brenna some pain and humiliation.

"I appreciate that, Abbey, but it's not good enough for me. I've been a coward. Luke's been a good friend to me and I let him down."

Luke shook his head vigorously. "Brenna, it's all right. You don't have to…"

"Yes, Luke, I do," Brenna interrupted. "I'm not ashamed of who I am. I'm ashamed of how I've behaved when it comes to the two of us."

"But what about your father? What about your acting career? What if your announcement negatively impacts your current work? Future projects? You have a movie opening soon." Abbey needed to make Brenna understand she didn't need to put it all out there. She could save herself. They would all survive what happened earlier. Nothing more needed to be said or done. The press would move on to another scandal and they'd quickly be forgotten. They'd become old news.

Brenna sighed over the phone. "My announcement might actually end up being a good thing. Garner support. Coming out, so to speak, won't necessarily be the kiss of death for my career. If it is, well … I've invested my income wisely over the years. I've been smart, and I'll be fine. Luke inspired me. I didn't draw attention to it, but I earned my degree in marketing a couple of years back. I have options. If my acting career takes a hit, I can devote more time to my humanitarian efforts."

Luke smiled at Abbey, obviously proud of Brenna. Abbey was proud of her too. Brenna Sinclair was one special lady. Abbey now understood why Luke had helped her. He was a good man. *Her* man.

"And as far as my father goes, we don't have much of a relationship at the moment. The mighty minister has a few secrets of his own that I've been holding on to for a long time. He that is without sin among you, let him cast the first stone. If he *dares* to make issue, the gloves come off. It'll all work out. I have faith. You both should too."

Luke looked at Abbey for support and she nodded. "All right, if you're sure, we'll follow your lead. Thank you."

Brenna scoffed on the line. "I should thank *you*, Luke. Our farce went on for much too long. I've been a coward. I'm looking forward to womaning up. It'll be freeing. You'll be at the press conference tomorrow, Abbey?"

Abbey's eyes went wide and she frantically shook her head at Luke.

"Yes, she'll be there," Luke confirmed. He took one of Abbey's hands and kissed her knuckles gently. Luke's warmth spread through her. "Princess, you'll have to get used to dealing with the press from now on, since you're my woman. The press conference will be a good, controlled, first exposure. We can invite the family too, other than Jake and Cassie, if that makes you feel more comfortable."

Luke's woman. The thought made Abbey heart soar and her soul sing. They could do this. They could be together, have a future, a family—have everything. She'd loved this man for so long. Dreamed of their forever since she was a young woman. Abbey was almost afraid to believe this was real. She would take Brenna Sinclair's lead and woman up herself.

She nodded and squeezed Luke's hand tightly. "No, that's fine. As long as you're there, I'll be all right."

Brenna clapped. "Yay! Thank you, Abbey. Okay, I've taken up enough of your reboot weekend time. From what Luke's said, he has another mission he's been working on. The two boys then a girl mission. I'll leave you to it, then. See you tomorrow!" Brenna disconnected the call.

A laugh burst out of Abbey. She couldn't help it. Luke was a nut. What was wrong with him? "You told Brenna about your baby-making plans?"

Luke tossed his phone and the Fairchild Hotel spa bag to the side and grabbed Abbey, placing her on his lap facing him. He pulled her sundress up to her waist and wrapped her legs around his waist.

Abbey giggled as Luke kissed her lips, cheeks, nose, and forehead. "No, I told her about *our* baby-making plans. My baby makers have already spoken to yours, so we're all in sync."

Abbey pushed Luke down on the plush, carpeted floor so she was straddling him. She bent down and kissed him, her long hair creating a halo around his head. She groaned when Luke grabbed her ass cheeks and squeezed. Her skin felt hot and tight, her nipples pebbled to hard points, and her panties grew damp. She needed Luke. Now. *We have our first son to make.*

She pulled Luke's shirt out of his jeans and went to work unbuckling his belt. He stopped her and tried to pull her dress off.

"Princess, I'll work on my pants, you get that

dress off," Luke said as he toed his shoes off and yanked off his jeans.

Abbey loosened the tie on the back of her dress and pulled it over her head, tossing it aside. She struggled at first but was able to unhook her bra and flung it aside too. Luke took a hold of her panties and tore them off.

"Luke! You can't keep ruining my underwear." Secretly though, she was thrilled by his alpha male behavior. What women wouldn't want her man so desperate for her that he tore her clothes off? But still. Abbey was fortunate she had extra panties in her carry-on bag.

Luke slid a finger through her wet folds. Abbey shivered and rubbed herself against him. "I'll get you new underwear, baby. Better yet, fuck that. You don't ever need to wear underwear again as far as I'm concerned."

She wasn't so sure about not wearing underwear from now on. That was a discussion for another time. "Enough about panties, Luke. We have a little Viking to make, right?" She was fully on board with Luke's baby-making plan.

His gorgeous blue eyes widened and darkened. "Hell yeah, we do. Two little Vikings then a Sheildmaiden, princess. Come here, sit on top of my dick. Let's fuck a little Viking into you."

Abbey shook with need and she positioned herself on top of him. She rubbed her slick pussy along his hard cock, eliciting moans from then both. He was hot, hard, and ready for her.

She lined up Luke's hard cock with her entrance and slowly impaled herself, her wet channel making the journey down his length fairly easily. *So hot, so hard.* Her inner muscles gripped him like a vise and he squeezed his eyes shut. Pride swelled at his reaction to her.

Luke gripped Abbey's hips so hard she wondered if she'd end up with bruises. She didn't mind. She craved his marks on her. She wanted to make some of her own on him.

His beautiful blue eyes opened, nearly black from being dilated. Her big, strong Viking wasn't unaffected. "God, Abbey. You feel so good. Come on. Fuck me, baby."

He lifted her hips and then slammed them back down, bottoming out. He filled her to the hilt and her blood was on fire with need. Abbey bounced on his hard dick in a frantic rhythm, desperate for release. This is how it had always been with Luke. She couldn't get enough of him. She probably never would.

They were together, how they should be. How they were meant to be. Abbey was his, and Luke was hers. She'd always known it and couldn't deny it or fight it any longer. She didn't want to.

Abbey's breasts bounced as she continued to ride Luke hard. She felt her orgasm building. It wouldn't take her long to go over. He tweaked her pebbled peaks with his fingers and it sent shock waves from her head to her toes. Never in her life had anything felt so good.

"Oh, Luke. I'm close." She groaned. She picked up the pace, bouncing up and down on top of him, each downward stroke almost painfully bumping her cervix. Luke rubbed her engorged clit, teasing the hard little bud until Abbey detonated and saw fireworks behind her closed eyelids.

Abbey heard him grunt and stiffen underneath her. She felt his hot seed shoot deep inside her as her channel convulsed around him. Pulse after pulse of Luke's cum filled her as she collapsed on top of him, their warm bodies damp with sweat. All she heard in her suite was the sound of their erratic breathing. She smiled at the prospect that this time, they might have created their first little Viking.

Luke held her tightly as their breathing slowed. He shifted her, pulling out of her. She lay beside him with her head on his chest. He held her close, lightly caressing her, the thick carpeting providing a bit of cushioning.

"Shit, princess. You nearly killed me that time." Luke kissed the top of her head and breathed deeply. "I love you so much, Abbey. Sometimes I feel like my heart will explode with it. I don't ever want you to doubt me. Promise me, baby."

Abbey smelled their combined scents of sex as they lay there, content after uniting physically and emotionally. This was where she always wanted to be. Beside Luke. She knew that would never change.

Abbey looked up at him. Reflected back at her in Luke's soulful blue eyes was so much love and tenderness that tears sprang to her eyes. "I've always loved you, Luke. No matter how hurt or angry I was, my heart always belonged to you. I promise I won't doubt you." She kissed his warm soft lips and placed her head back on his chest. The sound of his strong, steady heartbeat in her ear soothed her.

"So I was thinking, since you're now unemployed, and we're back together for good, what do you think about moving in with me?" Luke asked.

Abbey wasn't opposed to moving in with Luke. Especially since they were trying to start a family. But he lived on Chicago's Gold Coast. Abbey had always lived in Elmhurst. She liked the suburbs and wasn't planning on being unemployed for long.

"I've seen pictures of your bachelor pad in

Chicago, Luke. It's not a family-oriented space." She snuggled up against him, now feeling a chill.

He rubbed her arm. "That's true. Keeping it will be convenient since it's close to Stryker Field and the Cobras' corporate offices. Let's look for a nice gated community around here? My place in Nevada is gated and family friendly. We can do whatever you want. Haven't you heard? Your man is loaded."

Abbey didn't care about that. She'd loved Luke before he was rich and famous. He knew she wasn't some gold digger. She was educated and independent. That would never change.

"Yup. My man is a pretty, rich boy. I do like the idea of finding a secure place here in the suburbs though. A gated community is unfortunately a must, I think. Good thing you're loaded, right?" Abbey giggled when Luke tickled her. "I know his wife is a bit much to take, but if we're going to look locally, Mr. Gleason is one of the best around for luxury properties. He's well respected in the area and works hard for his clients."

Luke groaned. "That wife of his, shit. But hey, if he's got a good reputation, I'd be happy to give him a shot to find us something. Or maybe facilitate the construction of a new place."

Abbey shivered. What a nightmare building would be. She'd heard too many horror stories about new home construction even though it had become prevalent in Elmhurst over the last several years. "You sure you want to go through the stress of building *and* starting a family *and* transitioning to the next phase of your career at all the same time?" Abbey hated the idea.

"Hell no. Not when you put it like that. You're right. For now, let's buy something. We can build something later if we want. So smart, my princess. One of the many reasons I love you so much."

Luke sat up and stretched. Abbey would never tire of looking at his sculpted body. *My Viking.* The bruises on his shoulder looked a little better, like they were healing. Abbey joined him and sat up, feeling soreness between her legs. She didn't mind. She wasn't about to give up having sex with Luke because he was big. She'd just have to get used to it. *It's a cross I'll happily bear.*

Luke brushed some of her hair behind her shoulder and gently kissed it. She warmed up all over again. "Luke, I know I'm not employed at the moment, but I plan on looking for something else soon. I know you're going to say I don't need to work, being loaded and all, but that's not me."

Abbey prayed this didn't cause friction between them. She wanted Luke, a family, and more.

He shrugged and kissed her shoulder again. "I know. I want to take care of you, though. However it makes you the happiest. You could make good use of your MBA with *me*. There are all kinds of opportunities within the Cobras' organization and the foundation. Lots of possibilities. It'll depend on what you want and to what degree you want to be involved. Full- time, part-time, special project work. I want you to understand you have a lot options now that you're not tied to Office Supply Galaxy anymore."

Abbey's heart warmed. She liked the idea of working alongside Luke. She'd be in good company with so many of their family members already for working for the Cobras. She was flattered by Luke's proposal. "You really wouldn't mind us working together?"

Luke shook his head and kissed her lips. *So warm and delicious.* "Of course not. We're a team. The organization would be lucky to have you. *I'm* lucky to have you."

The pounding on Abbey's suite door startled them both. "Luke! Abbey! Family meeting in the fucking honeymoon suite. Now!" Jake sounded angry. *Really* angry. Abbey couldn't blame him, though. The fiasco after brunch must have been the straw that broke the camel's back.

"Shouldn't you and Cassie be getting a couple's massage right now?" Luke shouted back.

"Fuck that massage and fuck *you*. I've had it with all this shit this fucking weekend! You and Abbey clean up and get dressed right now and meet everyone in my fucking room."

Luke laughed. Abbey giggled. "Are we in trouble?" Luke teased Jake.

"Hilarious, asshole. I mean it, Luke. You have ten minutes or I'll drag you to my fucking suite myself, dressed or not. I mean it!" Jake stomped away, but they could hear him cursing as he walked down the hallway.

Luke blew out a breath and frowned. "He's pretty pissed. I don't blame him. Come on, princess." Luke stood and helped Abbey up off the floor. They both groaned and stretched some of their stiffness away. "When Jake's finished bitching me out, we'll come back and use the bed."

She couldn't agree more. The bed sounded much more inviting than the floor. "Sounds good to me."

She collected her clothes, minus the torn panties, and her carry-on bag and then dashed into the en suite bathroom. She tossed her things on the white backless couch and cleaned up as quickly as she could. Ten minutes wasn't much time. She wished there was time for a quick shower. Her parents would be in Jake and Cassie's room. She wasn't thrilled to smell like sex in front of them and everyone else.

Luke swaggered in with his clothes like he didn't

have a care in the world and tossed them on the couch beside hers. Men. He placed the spa bag on the floor beside the couch. *What's up with that spa bag?*

When Abbey felt decently refreshed, she washed her face and brushed her teeth. Luke frowned at her in the vanity mirror. "What's wrong, Luke? Is it your shoulder? Are you in pain?" She panicked. All of his baby making efforts could be hurting him. They needed to slow things down. There was plenty of time to get pregnant. Luke's priority should he his shoulder.

He finished washing up and began getting dressed. Abbey followed. "My shoulder's fine. That emu oil cream Hannah gave me is helping. I hated seeing you wipe and wash away all my cum from between your legs." Luke shrugged and put his shoes on.

Abbey tied the waist tie on her sundress and sat on the couch to put her sandals back on.

Luke was obviously anxious to start their family. She couldn't fault him for that. So was she.

"I'm sorry, but I had to clean up. My parents are in Jake and Cassie's room. And cleaning up won't affect anything anyway. Your *baby makers* have done their job."

Luke kneeled down in front of Abbey and held both her hands. He leaned in and lightly brushed his lips against hers. He smiled up at her. "I know, I'm just being stupid. I'm excited to start our family. That's all."

Abbey smiled and squeezed his hands. "I am too."

He let go of her hands and presented the spa bag to her. *Oh, it's for me.* "I got you all the spa products we used here and some others. I like the lavender scent on you. Take a look." He pressed her to look inside the bag.

Abbey appreciated the gesture, since she liked the products too, but they didn't have time for this. She didn't want Jake any more upset than he already was. Luke's insistent gaze had her taking the items out one by one. "Shampoo, conditioner, body wash, body scrub, facial wash, and scrub. Thank you, Luke. I love all of this, but we need to get going."

He shook his head, holding the bag in front of her still. "There's one more thing in the bag, baby."

Abbey didn't think so. She was pretty sure she'd taken everything out. She felt around what seemed like an empty bag to the very bottom. She gasped in surprise. A little velvet box? No, it couldn't be, but that didn't stop the tears from streaming down her cheeks.

Luke chuckled and took the little blue velvet box out of the bag and held it in his hands. "No reason to cry, princess," he whispered.

Luke flipped the box top open and inside was the most beautiful if not most enormous princess-cut diamond engagement ring Abbey had ever seen. The center stone had to be ten carats with ten small diamonds set down along each side of the band. Even the center stone prongs had diamonds set inside them. She assumed, knowing Luke, it was a platinum setting. It must have been the bathroom lighting, but she'd never seen anything sparkle so brightly. *He wants to marry me.*

"In case you were wondering and so you can brag to everyone we know, a seven-carat princess-cut center stone, two carats' worth of round side stones and almost another carat's worth of round stones around the center stone prongs, platinum, and all the stones are colorless and flawless. Flawless, just like you." Luke removed the ring out of the box and took her left hand in his, his warmth enveloping her.

Abbey shook. Her heart pounded in her chest. *Oh my God.* This was it. Luke was proposing.

"This reboot weekend hasn't gone exactly as I

had hoped, but one thing hasn't changed. I love you, Abbey. More than anything in this world. I always have and I know in my heart and soul I always will. You'd make me the happiest man in universe if you'd agree to be my wife." He looked at her. Hope and expectation gleamed in those sparking blue eyes of his.

"You want to marry me?" Abbey didn't know why she asked him that. She *wanted* to marry him. Had dreamed of this day since they day they met so many years ago. She was nervous, maybe a little afraid too.

Luke kissed the palm of her left hand and slid the ring onto her ring finger. Perfect fit. *Of course.* "Shacking up with you and having babies isn't an option for me, princess. You're mine. I want a ring on your finger and the paperwork to prove it. Will you marry me, baby?"

"Your ten minutes are up, asshole!" Jake pounded on the door.

"Fuck off! I'm busy! Baby? Will you?" Luke chuckled, waiting for her reply.

Abbey giggled as Jake continued pounding on her suite door. Poor guy. He'd have to wait a minute. She wrapped her arms around Luke and squeezed tight. "Yes, I'll marry you. I love you so much. Of course I will." Abbey felt Luke sigh in relief. Did he think she'd say no?

"Luke, I mean it! Open this door right now. I'm serious!"

Luke stood and helped Abbey off the couch. He took her by the hand and led her to the suite door. "Hold your fucking horses a minute! Here we come."

Chapter Twelve

Luke followed his new fiancée into Jake and Cassie's suite and clicked the door closed. *That's right, I'm locking that shit down.* He intended on getting married as quickly as possible. No drawn-out engagement like his big brother Jake. Nope.

Seated around the large living room, in various chairs and couches, were the people who meant the most to him. His family. He looked around and between him and Abbey, Rocco, both sets of parents, Darren and Maureen, Leah, Heath, and the newlyweds he counted only thirteen. Grandma Ruth and Grandma Beverly were missing.

Jake paced in the center of the room. "Nice of you to fucking join us. Didn't I tell you ten minutes, Luke?"

Shit. Jake was angry. He needed to calm him down. "Look Jake, know you're pissed…"

Jake stopped pacing and clenched his hands. "Just shut the fuck up, will you? I'm doing the talking right now."

Damn. Luke put his hands up in surrender. Abbey guided him to chairs closest to the suite door and they sat down.

Abbey looked around the room and frowned. "I'm sorry, Jake, but where are the grandmothers?"

Cassie urged Jake to sit down next to her so they faced everyone in the room. "They were so upset by the fucking circus after brunch, we sent them to the spa to calm down."

Everyone startled at the pounding on the suite's door. "Open this damn door! We know you're all in there!" That was Grandma Ruth.

"That's right! Did you think you could just shuffle us off? We've got news for you, you can't!" And there went Grandma Beverly.

Christ, what a clusterfuck. Luke leaped up and opened the door. Both grandmothers stormed in, looking as angry as Jake.

"See, I told you Bev. They're all here," Grandma Ruth accused.

Jake stood up and calmly walked over to the Ruth and Beverly, placing a hand on each of their shoulders. "Ladies, why aren't you at the spa?"

Was Jake serious? Didn't he see the grandmothers were angry at being left out of their family meeting? Even Luke understood. And rightly so. Ruth and Beverly were tough old birds. Their minds were still sharp, and they were in decent health considering their advancing age. *Come on, Jake, don't be a dick. Treat them like adults.*

Both ladies pulled away from Jake. "Screw the spa. Don't treat us like we're frail and feeble minded. We're an important part of this family and we should be right *here* along with everyone else." Ruth nodded once and looked at Beverly who nodded back in agreement.

Jake, the dope he was, wouldn't let it go. "But we didn't want to upset you any more than you already were. The conversation will get heated. I guarantee it."

Grandma Beverly waved a hand dismissively. "So what? You think we haven't heard curse words before or used them ourselves? Shit, fuck, asshole, bitch."

Luke couldn't help but smile. *Let him have it, Grandma Bev.*

"Prick, cock, crap, balls," Grandma Ruth added. "So enough with the shit and let's get this meeting started."

Jake threw his hands up in defeat. "Fine. I'm sorry for excluding you, even though I thought I was being considerate. It won't happen again. Come on, there's room there on the couch beside Rocco."

Both grandmothers sat down, with Rocco on one end of the couch and Grandma Ruth on the other. "We noticed you spending time with the pretty event planner Hannah at the reception." Grandma Beverly waggled her eyebrows at Rocco.

The big Italian Marine blushed and suddenly found the floor terribly interesting. "Jake and Cassie had us seated at the same table," he mumbled.

"Yes, we saw that. You should ask her out on a date," Ruth added.

Beverly shook her head. "No, it's called hooking up now, Ruth. That's what the young people call it."

"Oh. Well then you two should hook up on a date." Ruth smiled brightly at Rocco and nodded at him.

God, he loved these women. What a riot. The room laughed at poor Rocco's expense.

"Gram, hooking up means having sex," Jake explained with a smile on his face.

"Hannah is a lovely girl. She's beautiful and has a nice figure. Don't you *want* to have sex with her, Rocco?" Beverly asked with all seriousness.

Luke thought Rocco would pass out from embarrassment. He needed to help his buddy out. "Bev, Rocco's bringing Hannah to Jake and Cassie's after they get back from their honeymoon. To their wedding gift-opening party, as his *date*."

Grandma Beverly patted Rocco's leg happily. "That's wonderful news! You can have hooking up sex with her after the party then."

"But be safe. Use condoms. You can get them at

Walmart. They're not very expensive," Ruth advised a beet-red Rocco.

Rocco nodded his head, looking mortified. "Yes, ma'am."

After the laughter died down, Jake cleared his throat to get everyone's attention. Luke wanted to start by apologizing to everyone, but his princess shook her head at him.

Jake held Cassie's hand and looked around the room. "Now that that's settled, we can start this family meeting or, to use Darren's term, our family press conference."

Luke needed to speak up. *Sorry, princess.* "Look Jake, I'm…"

Jake glared at Luke and put a hand up to stop him. "Can't you just shut the fuck up for once? I'm doing the talking right now."

Luke closed his mouth. *So much for trying to apologize.*

Jake continued. "The reason Cassie and I called this meeting or press conference is because we're sick of all the secrets that everyone's been keeping from us all weekend. It stops. Now."

Cassie kissed Jake sweetly on the cheek, love radiating between the newlyweds. "We know it's our wedding weekend and you've all been trying to be considerate of that. Jake and I appreciate that, we do."

"But," Jake cut in, "we're not fucking children. If there is something important going on with any of you, you need to come clean right away. It doesn't matter whatever else is going on. We're all adults and we'll fucking deal with it. Understood?" Jake looked around the room. Everyone nodded in agreement.

"So from now on, no more secrets. And to show you Cassie and I are serious, I'm going to start with a secret we've been keeping even though we're not ready to share it for what you'll understand are obvious reasons." Jake kissed Cassie's hand softly and smiled. Cassie beamed.

"Cassie and I are expecting. She's eight weeks along," Jake announced proudly.

The room erupted in cheers and applause. Luke held Abbey's hand tightly. He hoped soon *they'd* be making the same announcement too.

"But what about the honeymoon? Should you still go? Is it safe?" Monica Jayne looked tearful and panicked, obviously concerned for Cassie and the baby.

"It's perfectly safe. Cassie and the baby are both doing fine. We'll be careful. Our plan was to relax and unwind anyway," Jake assured her. "I'm asking all of you not to say anything until Cassie's safely past the first trimester though. Just in case."

"And Luke, don't go prepay a Harvard degree for the baby. I mean it."

That was it. Luke was done. Abbey squeezed his hand, probably hoping it would calm him down, but it wouldn't work this time.

"You know what, Jake? Fuck you. Since we're all supposed to air our grievances and come clean, I have something to say too. I'm so sick and tired of getting shit whenever I want to buy something for you. You didn't give Darren a hard time when he hired Hailey's Events to plan your wedding. So don't give *me* one when I block and pay for some hotel suites, or snag you a few bottles of Utopias or pay for brunch."

"I think I speak for everyone in the room, other than Darren, when I say we don't want to take advantage, Luke," Heath began. "You're family, we don't care you have money. Hell, Jake and I have known you since you were two—long before you became a professional athlete and multi-millionaire or billionaire."

Jake nodded at Heath and turned to Luke. "Heath's right. Regardless of the money, we're family. You're too generous, man. You don't *need* to buy us so much. We'll love you anyway, asshole."

Luke rolled his eyes. They didn't get it. He'd have to make them all understand "See? I don't think I've done *enough*. All my *millions* as Heath put it, what good are they if I can't fucking share them with all of you? What I've spent is a drop in the bucket and I could do so much more and I'd still have enough to last ten lifetimes."

"None of us feel comfortable asking for things, Luke. We're all working. We're all supporting ourselves. No one wants a handout. Don't you get that?" Jake frowned, looking conflicted.

Luke shook his head. "That's just it. None of you *ask*. I *offer*, happily. And I know if the situation were reversed and one of *you* had this kind of money, you'd do the same thing and you all know it."

Darren nodded his support and Luke he was grateful. His uncle was the most generous man he knew. Not only financially either. Luke's stomach twisted as the thought of losing him. The world would be a lesser place without Darren Stryker in it. He wondered if Darren would "come clean" and share his diagnosis with everyone in the room. Luke hoped so. He didn't like keeping secrets as much as Jake was making issue with it at the moment.

"Speaking as someone who has even *more* money than my boy here," Darren began, "what you might perceive as overly generous or charity, we see differently. The money provides options. It's supposed to help make our lives *easier*. And it's given out of love, not charity. Never. So can you all see yourselves relaxing your position on this for us? Please?"

Luke couldn't have said it any better. Everything he'd ever done and would ever do for the people in the room—all of it—came from a place of love. "I'd like to add one thing to what Darren, Dad, said. When we offer or get you something, we don't expect you to kiss our asses. Don't fuss, don't cuss me out, just say thanks. Can everyone agree to that, at least?"

Luke held his breath, waiting for everyone's response. He had a few ideas he wanted to share right now, if everyone could agree to relax on the gift-giving shit. He looked around the room, and everyone reluctantly nodded their agreement. Darren winked Luke's way.

Thanks, Dad.

Luke rubbed his hands together conspiratorially. Jake and Rocco groaned. *Too bad, guys.* "First, Rocco, dude, it's time for a new truck. Your Silverado is what, nearly twenty years old? And you bought it used. Time for an upgrade. You've honorably served this country and you deserve something better to drive." Luke saw Rocco open his mouth to object and Luke raised a brow. "How about Wednesday we go get you a new Silverado 3500HD?"

"Oh Rocco, that's wonderful! Get a black truck, they're very manly looking," Grandma Beverly said, clapping.

"And you need those steps on the side to help shorter people get in, like Bev and me. Oh, and Hannah too," Grandma Ruth added.

The big Italian blushed and nodded at Beverly and Ruth. "They're called running boards. And yes, I'll make sure to get them. But Luke, the 1500 is what I had my eye on."

Luke would make sure Rocco's 1500 had all the

bells and whistles. Hell, by the time he finished with the dealership, they'd probably throw in an Impala at no extra cost. Luke was pleased Rocco agreed to let him help him out with a new ride. "All right, a fully loaded 1500 it is. What do you say?"

Grandma Beverly patted Rocco's leg and nodded in encouragement.

"Thank you. I can't wait," Rocco said with a nod of his head.

Excellent. One down. One to go. Luke looked over at Jake and Cassie. Cassie glanced back at him curiously. Jake just frowned and cursed under his breath. *Tough shit, big brother.*

"As far as prepaying for a Harvard degree, baby Tyler might want to go to Yale or Princeton," Luke said.

"Damn it, Luke," Jake exclaimed and ran a hand through his hair.

Luke pressed on. "But we're arguing about something that's years away. And if I want to pay for the baby's college education, I will. And like you just agreed to with everyone else, you're just going to let me and say thank you. And on graduation day, I'll be sitting right next to you during the ceremony, proud as hell."

Jake blew out a breath and Cassie looked at her new husband with love and encouragement. "Fine. But you're right, it's a long way off. We can discuss it, not argue about it then, agreed?" Jake sighed in relief.

Luke nodded. He had Jake right where he wanted him. "Agreed. Right now, though, the more pressing issue is little baby Tyler. So I want to buy you and Cassie a house."

Cassie squeaked and her eyes widened.

"Fuck, Luke, really? A house? You want to buy us a fucking house? Just like that?" Jake looked distraught but Luke was sure he could convince him without much arguing.

"Just hear me out. Your two-bedroom condo will work for a little while, but you'll need more space soon. So why not let me buy you a place here in Elmhurst where you're already living, before the baby comes? It'll be a lot less stressful for all of you. Think of it as a belated wedding gift or a pre-baby shower gift?" Luke turned to Darren for support. His dad smiled back at him encouragingly. Abbey held his hand tight and her eyes glistened with tears.

"You could use Mr. Gleason to find you someplace nice in town. We met him last night after the reception," Abbey suggested. "Luke, do you still have his business card?"

"If Alfred Gleason is working for you, you'll be in good hands," Jake's father said.

Luke retrieved Alfred Gleason's business card from his wallet and held it up. "What do you say, Jake? You've said you'd just say thank you, remember?"

Cassie gently kissed Jake and gave him a reassuring smile. "It'll be all right, you know? And Luke's right, we'll need the extra space soon. We all agreed to be gracious with Luke and Darren's generosity, babe."

Luke sensed the moment Jake relented. He knew his big brother, though. Luke understood Jake's reluctance. "Buying you this house does not mean I don't think you can take care of your family. I'm trying to help make things a little easier for you, that's all. Like you'd do for me, right?"

That did it. Luke knew Jake was on board.

Jake nodded and Cassie beamed. "Yes, and thank you. But a *regular* house, nothing crazy. Three or four bedrooms, two and half bathrooms, a nice backyard for kids to play in. That kind of a house. Agreed?"

Yes! "Agreed." Luke made a quick call to Alfred Gleason while the family discussed what Cassie and Jake should look for in their new home. Gleason agreed to find a *regular* house for Jake and Cassie in Elmhurst and something that Jake would probably consider *crazy* in a nearby gated community for him and Abbey. Luke was offering all cash purchases and picking up the seller's moving expenses to speed up the process.

With all of that settled, it appeared Jake was back on the war path. *Here we go.*

"Now, back to the secrets. Don't think a new truck and a house will distract me from the real reason we're here." Jake turned his attention to Abbey. "Office Supply Galaxy laid you off? You were the only person who supported your system. What the hell is that?"

Abbey stiffened beside Luke. He held her hand and waited for her to organize her thoughts.

"Apparently, there was a reduction in force of about fifty people. I suspect that my former manager Tim Webber, who is relatively new at OSG, wanted to get rid of me so he could bring over someone he worked with at his previous company. He had already brought two of his people over. He needed my headcount to be available to bring over his third. Being the asshole he is, when the system went down during the wedding, he called me, expecting me to fix the issue, even though I didn't work there anymore. As you now know from Tom Murphy, the Support Desk Manager, I ignored their calls for help. I was told my skill set wasn't needed any more—so fuck them."

Luke and the rest of the room clapped. Abbey deserved better than what OSG did to her. For ten long years she'd worked her ass off.

"You should work for us, Abbey. Don't you agree, Luke?" Darren asked.

"We've already discussed it. We'll see where Abbey feels most comfortable in the organization or the foundation. There are plenty of opportunities for her." Luke kissed her softly. He felt her smile against his lips. His cock twitched. *Down boy, not now.*

"All right then. I agree, fuck OSG if they're stupid enough to let this Tim Webber asshole get rid of you. And this Brenna bullshit, Luke?"

"Yes, what about that? I got the impression you and Abbey were back together? You know, I've always liked you Luke, but I won't stand for your hurting my girl. So I'm with Jake on this one." Abbey's father glared at Luke. He'd never done that before. Luke didn't like it one bit.

"Dad, don't be mad at Luke," Abbey pleaded.

Luke kissed the hand he'd been holding and she smiled weakly at him. "Phil, Monica, everyone—I'm sorry about the entire Brenna Sinclair fiasco. I promise you all there is nothing going on between Brenna and me."

"Come on, Luke. You've been dating her, or you were, for three years. It's not like you've been hiding that fact." Phil looked at Luke with such disgust his stomach dropped to his feet. *This isn't good.*

"I know it appeared that way, but I promise you, it was all just for the press. We never had a romantic relationship. In fact, she'll speak first at tomorrow's press conference and admit everything publically. I would never disrespect Abbey like that. In fact, I asked your little girl to marry me earlier and she accepted. I wanted to get your and Monica's blessing first, but this weekend didn't go as planned. I hope you can find it in yourselves to give us your blessing now?" Luke held out Abbey's left hand, allowing everyone to see the shimmery engagement ring.

"Wow! That's some rock," Grandma Ruth exclaimed.

"What is that, ten carats or something?" Grandma Beverly asked excitedly.

"I had originally wanted a ten-carat center stone, but I knew Abbey would feel uncomfortable with something that big. It's seven carats." Luke kissed the knuckles on Abbey's left hand.

"It's plenty big, too big actually, but I know Luke too. He would never settle for something small."

Leah clapped her hands. "Congratulations! This is great news."

"Good going, little brother," Heath added.

"Welcome to the family, right, Dad?" Cassie asked cautiously.

Phil didn't look convinced or happy. Monica nudged him with her elbow, but he didn't budge.

"Dad, Luke's telling the truth about Brenna. I spoke to her earlier. She admitted everything and I believe her *and* Luke. She's a nice person. She's thrilled Luke and I are together. It's all going to *come out* at tomorrow's press conference."

"See Phil, Brenna's going to tell everyone she's a lesbian tomorrow. Don't be an ass and give Luke your blessing." Grandma Ruth glared at her son and waited.

"Mom! Fine. If Abbey believes Luke and Brenna, then I believe them too. You have my blessing, but treat my girl right." Phil stood and walked toward him and Abbey. Luke and Abbey stood and held hands, presenting a united front.

Phil extended a hand and Luke sighed in relief. He shook Phil's hand and then his future father-in-law brought him in for a hug. He clapped Luke's sore shoulder a little too hard, but Luke didn't mind. Phil wasn't angry at him. He considered it a win. The room erupted in applause.

"I'll do right by your girl, Phil. She won't want for anything," Luke whispered as they broke apart.

"That's all I ask. Welcome to the family, Luke." Phil hugged his daughter and inspected the rock Luke put on Abbey's finger. *That's right, Phil, a ring fit for a princess.* My *princess.*

Suddenly he and Abbey were surrounded by the rest of their family. Everyone offered their congratulations and hugs. So many hugs. Luke would have to apply more emu oil cream and take more pain reliever once he and Abbey returned to his suite. The ladies oohed and aahed over Abbey's ring and his woman beamed with pride.

Jake and Cassie's secret reveal received the attention it deserved too as everyone turned their attention to the newlyweds and expectant parents. The ladies all wanted to touch Cassie's still-flat stomach. *Pretty soon they'll be touching Abbey's pregnant belly too.* The thought had Luke stiffening in his jeans. Unfortunately, fucking Abbey again would have to wait as he saw Jake regroup. Their family conference wasn't over yet.

"All right, I don't think our meeting is over just yet. Does anyone else want to share anything?" Jake looked directly at his sister Leah and Heath.

Heath blushed and looked at his shoes. Leah, not surprisingly, took the lead. "Heath and I want to see if we can make a relationship work, right?" Leah turned to Heath, encouraging him with a bright smile.

Heath looked at a confused Dan Tyler, Jake and Leah's father. "Yes, it's true. Dan, I hope you're not angry with me. You've known me for a long, long time…"

"Since when have you two been dating? I don't

understand." Dan scratched his head, as though he was unsure of whether to be angry or accepting.

"Dad, I've loved Heath all my life. He's always put me off because he didn't want to betray Jake or our family."

"But I knew Heath's had feelings for Leah for a while now. I told him that as long as he made an honest effort with Leah, regardless of the outcome, he wouldn't have an issue from me. I think the two of them should give it a try," Jake told his father.

Jake and Leah's mother Sara nodded and smiled. "I can actually see the two of you together. It's really up to the two of you though. You both know what's best." She looked at her husband.

Dan shrugged. "You're both adults. It's not my place to dictate who you date. We've been friends or rather family for a long time. Let's agree to not let whatever happens between the two of you affect our relationship."

Both Heath and Leah smiled. "Agreed," they both said to Dan.

"All right, anyone else have something they need to come clean about?" Jake asked everyone standing around each other.

Luke looked to his uncle, hoping he would speak up. He saw the hesitation in his eyes. *Come on, Dad.* Obviously, he wasn't ready. Luke assumed there would be an aggressive treatment regime that would begin next week. Darren needed to say something *now*. Luke would have to ease his father into sharing his devastating news.

"Abbey and I have been having unprotected sex all weekend, trying to get pregnant," Luke blurted out.

"Luke!" Abbey's face bloomed with the prettiest blush.

"Can't you wait? You just got engaged," Phil

asked.

"First, Cassie got pregnant before *she* got married. Second, I'm planning on marrying your little girl as soon as possible, so you won't be walking her down the aisle with a visible baby bump. Third, I want Abbey pregnant with our first little Viking as soon as possible, giving Darren as much time as he can to be a grandpa." Luke didn't want to force the issue, but Darren couldn't sit on the information any longer.

Darren's eyes went wide and Maureen began to cry. "I'll be an amazing grandpa," he whispered.

Abbey started crying and Luke's eyes stung. "I know you will, Dad. I know you will."

Jake's brows furrowed and he shook his head. "Why the fuck are Maureen and Abbey crying? And what the hell did you mean about Darren being a grandpa as long as he can?"

Come on, Dad. Now's the time to speak up.

Jake looked between Darren and Luke, his eyes narrowed. The attorney was not missing a thing. "With all due respect, seeing that you're my boss. But we're on family time now, so Darren, what the hell is going on? Does this have something to do with the press conference tomorrow? And I don't mean the crap about Brenna."

Maureen wiped her eyes with her hands and put an arm around Darren's waist. "Go on, Darren. They should be told before tomorrow's press conference. They're family."

When Darren looked at him, Luke nodded his head. "Go on, Dad. It'll be all right."

Darren nodded in agreement. "Yes, you're right, Jake. Why don't we all pull our chairs closer together and we'll talk about what's going on?"

When everyone were seated closer together, Luke's heart raced. In a few minutes, everything would be out in the open to the people who mattered the most. Everything would be *real*. Abbey's tight grip of his hand gave Luke the strength he needed. She'd always been his strength, his love, his everything.

Darren took a deep breath and exhaled slowly. "Tomorrow after Brenna speaks, I'll be announcing that effective immediately, ownership of the Chicago Cobras, the Windy City Rattlers, the children's foundation, and Stryker Real Estate Holdings will be transferred to Luke and I'll be stepping down."

Jake raised a skeptical brow. "Because Luke hurt his shoulder? Bullshit. I don't buy it. It isn't even anything serious. He'll be back on the field in no time."

Darren shook his head sadly. "It was always the plan for Luke to take over, you all know that. We're transitioning now because I've been diagnosed with stage 1B exocrine pancreatic cancer."

The room was stunned silent. Aside from the sound of some women in the room crying, no one said a word. Luke didn't hold back his own tears. Not this time. Now that the news was out, Luke felt like a burden had been lifted off his shoulders. It was bad news. Really bad. But they'd deal with it together, as a family.

Jake collected himself and wiped a few of his own tears away. Everyone in the room waited for Jake to ask the next few inevitable questions. He blew out a breath. "Well, fuck me. What exactly does that mean? What are the treatment options and typical survival rates?"

Everyone in the room sat quietly as Darren Stryker calmly explained the shit hand his life had dealt him. He had developed a cancerous tumor nearly three centimeters large in his pancreas. The tumor was located at the head of his pancreas. Surgery to remove the tumor or as much of it that could be removed, was scheduled for Tuesday morning. Depending on the outcome from surgery, chemotherapy or a combination of chemotherapy and radiation treatments would follow. Unfortunately, the five-year survival rate for Darren's cancer was about twelve percent. And that sucked.

Grandma Ruth blew her nose and cleared her throat. "Well, if anyone can beat this bitch, it's Darren Stryker. Whatever I can do to help you through this, you can count on me."

Grandma Beverly nodded in agreement. "Me too. Whatever you need, I'm there."

Jake put a hand up before anyone else could offer their assistance. "Look Darren, before you tell all of us not to worry, and that you don't need our help—let me stop you. You're going to let us help you through this because that's what this family does. I know you and Luke are used to taking care of everything and everyone, but *this* time, you're going to let *us* do the helping. Understood?"

Luke was thankful as hell for his family and for Jake's support and levelheadedness at such an emotional moment. He was the luckiest man in the world.

Darren choked up, shed a few tears, and nodded.

Jake nodded back in affirmation. "I almost hate to ask, but is anyone else keeping any secrets? Now is the time to lay it all out there."

Both grandmothers looked at each other, silently communicating. If one or both of them was sick too, Luke would lose it.

****

Abbey's stomach roiled and her heart raced, waiting for the grandmothers to say something. They were hiding something. If either one of them was sick, she didn't know what she'd do. Darren's diagnosis was bad enough.

She was grateful that with Luke's encouragement, Darren had admitted how sick he was. Although his prognosis wasn't good, Abbey could sense both Darren and Luke were relieved the news was out in the open. She knew Darren would put up a good fight. He could very well be part of the lucky twelve percent that survived after five years. That was what Abbey and the rest of their family would pray for.

It turned out the grandmothers weren't sick, but had booked themselves on a senior's cruise with some of their friends. It departed from Miami a week after Jake and Cassie returned from their honeymoon. After some heated discussion and objections regarding the ladies' health and safety from Abbey's and Jake's fathers, Darren got everyone to agree he would hire a competent doctor and nurse to accompany the feisty women on their cruise as a safeguard, *not* to babysit them.

When a few stomachs growled, it was decided rather than risk another scene in one of the hotel restaurants, they would order room service.

Everyone was somber as they ate, Darren's condition likely weighing on everybody's mind. "Luke, you and Abbey need to start making wedding plans. You said you wanted to get married as soon as possible, didn't you?" Darren asked.

Abbey wasn't so sure how fast they should move now. With Darren's surgery coming up and his treatments following, maybe they needed to reconsider their timeline. She wanted Darren to be able to enjoy the day with her and Luke.

"No, Abbey, don't second-guess your plans. Move forward. I'll do my best to be there with you both in person, but if I can't be, with your technical know-how, we can live stream the entire day so I won't miss anything," Darren insisted and then took a bite of grilled chicken.

Luke picked up his cell phone and scrolled through his contact list until he found what he was looking for. "You good with having our reception at Cucina Antonetti's, too, but at their Barrington location?"

Jake and Cassie's reception had been so wonderful. Antonetti's Barrington location was newer and fancier than their Elmhurst restaurant. Abbey didn't want to step on Jake's and Cassie's toes. She didn't want them to think she and Luke were copying them.

"We're fine with it, Abbey. They do a great job with weddings and banquets," Cassie said around a mouthful of steak stir fry.

Luke pressed the call button and put his phone on speaker. After two rings, Carlo Antonetti's voice came on the line. "Cucina Antonetti's, this is Carlo."

"Carlo, it's Luke Stryker. You're on speaker with Abbey and our family. I need your help. When's the soonest you can host our wedding reception at your Barrington restaurant with the large combined room?"

"Congratulations! Let me see what we have. One second." They heard the click of the keyboard as Carlo must have looked up the restaurant's event calendar.

Abbey heard Carlo sigh. That didn't sound good. "Luke, it's party and wedding season, and the rooms get reserved far in advance." Abbey's heart sank. This was going to be a problem. Carlo was right about booking. Jake and Cassie booked their own reception a year in advance.

"Wait, I think I might have something. Does the day of the week matter?" Carlo asked.

Abbey and Luke looked at each other and shrugged. "No, not really. What do you have for us?" Luke asked and took a hold of Abbey's hand.

"I have the large combination room for you on Wednesday, September sixth. It'll hold four hundred guests. There's a small business dinner in one of the smaller rooms. I can block out the other rooms like we did for Jake and Cassie."

Luke cupped her cheek with his strong, warm hand and looked at her tenderly. "Do we have ourselves a wedding date, princess?"

Abbey felt a tear slide down her cheek. She nodded and smiled at her amazing Viking fiancé. "Yes, we have ourselves a wedding date." The room cheered and Abbey cried.

"All right, Carlo, mark the groom's name down as Lucas Morrison."

Lucas was Luke's legal first name. Abbey knew Morrison to be his mother's maiden name. To avoid another fiasco, they would have to be careful. Different names were a must. She didn't want to think about what kind of extensive security detail they would need.

"Mark the bride's name down as Leann Reynolds," Abbey's mother called out. Leann was her mother's middle name and Reynolds her maiden name. Abbey saw Cassie immediately make a call and speak in hushed tones.

"All right, we're set."

"One other thing, and don't argue because you know I'm right, Carlo," Luke began. Abbey had no idea what he meant. "We'll pay you to close the restaurant for the day. We have no choice and you know it."

Carlo sighed over the line. "Fine. If you're not able to find a church, we can remove the tables from the main dining room, set up chairs, an altar, and make due. Call me when you're ready and we'll work out the details."

"Thanks, Carlo. I'll call you by the end of the

week."

Cassie disconnected her call and clapped her hands. "I spoke to Pastor Jenkins at Grace of God. The church is available for Leann and Lucas on Wednesday September sixth. You can have the rehearsal on Monday September fourth! That's Labor Day. You should have your rehearsal dinner at Golden Horns."

Their wedding day was taking shape. Abbey couldn't believe it. But what about a dress? It took Cassie months to receive hers. "Luke, I won't be able to get a dress in time." Abbey felt tears pricking her eyes.

Luke kissed her cheek and flashed her a cocky grin. "No worries, princess." Luke scrolled through his phone contacts again and pressed the call button.

After the first ring, a southern man's voice Abbey didn't recognize spoke. "Asher."

Kyle Asher? From Golden Horns? The Dom who owned Club Envidious and that Twisted Tea Society ladies social group?

"Kyle, it's Luke Stryker. I need your help."

"Hey, Luke. If I can help, I will. What do you need?"

"First, do you have a room on Monday September fourth for my wedding rehearsal dinner? The names are Lucas Morrison and Leann Reynolds. And second, my bride needs a Bellatoni wedding gown. The wedding date is Wednesday September sixth."

Abbey widened her eyes in surprise. How did Luke know she'd dreamed of wearing a Bellatoni at her wedding? Abbey heard Kyle Asher clicking away on a keyboard.

"I might have accidentally found your wedding folder back in the day, princess. You had magazine pictures of Bellatoni wedding gowns. I vowed to myself that day that you'd wear the Bellatoni gown of your dreams at our wedding."

Abbey hugged Luke so hard her arms ached. How could this man, *her* man be so sweet? So accommodating, so considerate?

"All right, I moved a couple things around. I have a room you can use. It can hold up to forty people. I can squeeze in a few more if you need them. For the gown, I'll give Heather Bellatoni a call. I don't think getting a nice selection of gowns for your bride to choose from will be a problem. Don't forget the bridesmaids. Text me everyone's measurements and an idea of what the bride is looking for in the next couple of days and I'll pass that along to Heather. I'm assuming we're talking about that beautiful blonde I saw you with on Facebook yesterday?

Luke kissed Abbey softly, his warm lips heating her blood. "Yes, that would be my princess. I'll call you in a few days to work out the details for our rehearsal dinner. I'll text you measurements and preferences as soon as I can. Thanks, Kyle. We appreciate it."

"You're welcome, and congratulations."

Darren texted furiously and then looked up. "Hannah Hailey's available and on board for us. I've texted her the details we have so far."

"Great. Thanks, Dad. See? This is all coming together. You don't have to worry, princess."

Abbey felt hot tears slide down her cheeks. Her heart was full. She was overwhelmed. Luke gathered her in his arms and drew her onto his lap. His body heat and strong loving arms wrapped around her made her feel loved, cherished, and protected. Everyone around them chatted happily about their upcoming wedding and continued eating.

Luke kissed her tenderly, just a soft brush of his lips. It was still enough for her body to respond. She couldn't wait until they were alone again. Baby making or not.

"It's all going to be all right. I know it seems overwhelming, but with Hannah's help and the rest of the family, it's all going to come together just the way we want it. I'm going to splurge and spoil you, just so you know. And unlike Jake, you will not give me any shit about it, right? You're going to let me loose without an argument?" He arched a brow, waiting for her reply.

Abbey rested her head on Luke's shoulder, revelling in the feel of him wrapped around her. She was right where she'd always wanted to be. Although there was still so much to do and the future was uncertain, she knew with Luke and everyone else in the room, they'd make it through.

"No arguments from me, Luke. Consider yourself let loose."

Epilogue

The next day, Monday—1:00 PM at Chicago Cobras HQ

Abbey stood in the lobby of the Chicago Cobras' headquarters, holding on to Luke's hand for dear life. Although the press turnout from television, print, and the Internet was a much more organized and civilized affair than the onslaught at the Fairchild Hotel the previous afternoon, her stomach still fluttered and her heart raced. *Will I ever get used to this?*

Brenna Sinclair stood at the podium, poised and graceful. A star who had just admitted to lying about her relationship to Luke for the last three years and lying about her sexual orientation. The press ate the news up, but to Abbey, they didn't seem all that shaken up or scandalized. For that, she was grateful.

"So in conclusion, I'd like apologize from the bottom of my heart to my fans for not being truthful with you and with myself. I've always tried my best to be a good role model and in this instance, I've failed. I'll work hard to regain your trust and I assure you I will not betray your trust again."

Brenna turned to her and Luke and gestured for them to join her at the podium. "I'd also like to publically apologize to Luke and Abbey for the stress and embarrassment I've caused. Yesterday's fiasco at the Fairchild Hotel just proves that sometimes I really *need* a script." Many in the audience laughed.

"Luke, I can't apologize enough. You've been an incredible friend and I didn't treat you like I should have. Our friendship means the world to me and you have my word moving forward I'll do my best to be as good of a friend to you as you've been to me. I hope you can forgive me."

Brenna and Luke hugged while the press's cameras went into overdrive. It was Abbey's turn next. She hoped she didn't embarrass herself. She took a couple deep breaths to steady herself.

"Abbey, I hope that after all of this, you and I can find a way forward as friends. From what I've gotten to know about you so far, Luke is a lucky man. Congratulations on your engagement. I hope you can find it in your heart to invite me to the wedding. I would be honored to be there to support the both of you when you become man and wife."

Brenna opened her arms and Abbey hugged her tight, shaking. "You're doing fine, Abbey," Brenna whispered.

When Abbey and Brenna ended their hug, they were barraged with questions about their upcoming wedding. Abbey had memorized everything Luke had told her they would tell the press. Most of it lies to maintain their privacy.

Luke smiled his million-dollar dimpled smile as camera flashes nearly blinded them. He held out her left hand so pictures could be taken of Abbey's engagement ring. "Only the best for my, princess. Flawless and colorless, everyone. Flawless just like my girl." Luke kissed her as the cameras continued to click.

"We're thinking a destination wedding, next spring," Abbey announced. "Somewhere tropical, most likely." She hoped she didn't sound nervous.

"My fiancée and I want to enjoy our engagement a little while before we get busy making wedding plans," Luke added and waggled his eyebrows. The press laughed, shaking their heads. Abbey's cheeks heated.

"In all seriousness though, I want to bring my

uncle Darren Stryker, or rather my second dad and owner of the Chicago Cobras organization, including Stryker Field, up to the podium so we can get on with the important Cobras business we called this press conference to discuss."

Luke and Abbey moved aside as Darren stepped up to the podium's microphone. "Thank you, son," Darren began. "As you all know, the Chicago Cobras organization was started by my father Bradford in 1927. His love of baseball and the city of Chicago, as far as he was concerned, went hand in hand. He passed the love of the sport down to me and my late brother James who was an Army veteran and a member of the All Army Sports Program for softball."

Luke squeezed Abbey's hand. It had been twenty years since Luke's folks had passed away, but talking about them still wasn't easy for him.

"When my brother James and sister-in-law Marianne were taken from us twenty years ago, it was my honor to assume guardianship of their only child and my ten-year-old nephew Luke. I can honestly say I do not consider Luke my nephew, but my son. It has been a privilege to watch Luke grow from a devastated little boy to the amazing young man he is now. My boy has taken his love of the game and helped bring Chicago four World Series Championships in the last ten years and has won three Cy Young awards. In addition to that, he's earned his degree in Business Management and his MBA, in preparation of continuing the Stryker legacy and inheriting the Cobras organization as I did."

Luke put his arm around Abbey's waist for support. This was it. The paperwork had already been signed and executed. This announcement was a public courtesy.

"Effective immediately, the Stryker legacy has

been passed on to Luke. The ownership of the Cobras organization, including Stryker Field and the children's foundation, as well as Stryker Real Estate Holdings, has been transferred to Luke. I have full faith and confidence in Luke's ability to lead the organization moving forward. Luke's number, twelve, will be retired."

The press hurled question after question at Darren. They waited patiently for the commotion to die down. "Are you all right, Luke?" Abbey asked.

"I'm fine. It's a relief in an odd kind of way." Luke kissed her and they waited for Darren to continue the press conference.

****

Later in the day Monday—6:00 PM at Office Supply Galaxy HQ

Luke followed closely behind Abbey as they were let into the Office Supply Galaxy headquarters lobby. He carried the box she'd put her personal belongings in. He fumed over how OSG was treating his princess. Like she was a criminal. She'd worked her fucking ass off for ten long years and deserved better than this. *It doesn't matter, she'll be working for the Cobras from now on.*

Luke wanted to get this ordeal over with so he and Abbey could join the rest of their family and spend time with Darren before his surgery the following morning. Darren had insisted they all carry on with their plans and let his surgeons and doctors take care of his him. The rest of the week would be busy with truck shopping for Rocco, wedding plans, and Darren's immediate recovery from surgery.

OSG's HR rep, a dark-haired woman Luke guessed to be in her late twenties, wearing a black pencil skirt and white blouse, widened her eyes in surprise when she recognized him. The fit middle-aged black security guard grinned and extended his hand.

"It's an honor to meet you, Mr. Stryker. I'm so sorry to hear about your uncle's condition. I'll be praying over his surgery tomorrow," the security guard, Calvin Hudson, according to his name badge, said after shaking Luke's hand.

Luke's stomach knotted. He was anxious for Darren's surgery to be over so his recovery could begin. He was grateful for all the well wishes and prayers. They'd come pouring in since the press conference ended earlier that afternoon. He and Darren heard from the mayor of Chicago, the governor of Illinois, as well as the entire Cobras' organization, many other MLB and MILB teams, and most of the sports channels. Even Brenna Sinclair had changed her schedule so she could join everyone at the hospital in the morning.

"Thank you, we'll take all the prayers we can get," Luke replied.

"Oh, congratulations on your engagement," the HR rep exclaimed. "Do you mind if I see your ring? It looked pretty on TV but…"

"Of course, Pam." Abbey proudly extended her left hand and showed off her ring. Pam gazed at it in awe and Calvin nodded his head and whistled.

"Very nice Mr. Stryker. You know, I played ball back in the day. Earned myself a full scholarship to Northwestern. I was good too. Not quite good enough to go pro, but I earned myself a degree in finance and accounting. With honors. My boys got the numbers bug too, they're both in college earning their degrees."

"Yes, that's right," Pam added. "Calvin's working here several nights a week to help with those high college costs. You're a great dad, Calvin. I hope your sons appreciate you. I didn't get any support from *my* parents. Barely any encouragement at all. But I did what I had to and didn't incur too much debt since

OSG's tuition reimbursement program paid for my last several semesters."

Luke knew Abbey's entire college education, including her MBA, had been paid for by OSG's tuition reimbursement program. Calvin and Pam weren't the asshole corporate heads that treated Abbey like shit. They were just dedicated employees like Abbey had been. Working hard, doing their best. The Cobras organization had a similar policy, if not even more generous. They encouraged their employees to seek higher education.

Abbey looked at him, a gleam in her eyes. "When you went over the organization particulars with Darren, weren't there openings in accounting and HR?"

Shrewd, princess. Abbey was right, there were. The Cobras organization was rated one of the best places to work in Chicago every year. They had an abundance of applicants for every open position, even custodial and Stryker Field maintenance jobs. They paid well, offered outstanding benefits, and expected the very best from their employees. And they got it.

"Abbey's right. If you're interested, email Abbey your résumés." From the excited looks on Pam and Calvin's faces, Luke had no doubt they'd email Abbey.

"Oh my God, thank you," Pam cried. "That would be amazing!"

"Thank you, Mr. Stryker!" Calvin enthusiastically shook Luke's hand, smiling from ear to ear.

The three of them rode the elevator to the fifth floor where Abbey's cubicle was located, as well as the support desk analysts. Pam and Calvin eagerly saved Abbey's email address on their cell phones. Luke hoped that asshole Tom Murphy wasn't lurking around and waiting on Abbey's arrival.

Luke followed as Abbey made her way through

the cubicle rat maze until they reached her space. He much preferred the Cobras' open concept to OSG's cubicle wall prison. He'd expected better from the office supply giant. OSG created modern, ergonomic office space for large companies but kept their own employees housed like rats. Luke was grateful that after tonight, Abbey wouldn't ever have to come back.

Calvin and Pam stood back along a hallway several yards away. "We don't need to hover and watch your every move, Ms. Jayne. Take your time packing up. It's company policy that we have to be present." Calvin frowned and shook his head.

Abbey's cubicle had been stripped of her company laptop. Luke placed Abbey's box on the cheap desktop surface while she went through her files, deciding what to take.

Luke smiled when he saw a couple of framed pictures on her desk. One was from Christmas and featured a large group shot of the Jayne family happily smiling in front of a brightly decorated tree. The other was of Abbey's graduation from graduate school.

Abbey stood in her cap and gown with her good friend and third bridesmaid, Karla Collins. Six months ago, Karla had opened her own coffee shop, Karla's Koffee Klatch and from what Abbey had told him, served coffee so delicious, it was nearly a religion.

Abbey had just finished putting all of her things into her box when that asshole Tom Murphy skulked into her cubicle. *Oh, hell no.*

Luke walked right up to Tom, stopping inches away from the dickhead's face and clenched his hands. "What the fuck do *you* want?"

"Is everything all right, Ms. Jayne? Mr. Stryker?" Calvin called out.

"Yes, everything's fine. I'm just finishing up,

thank you," Abbey replied, glaring at Luke.

Tom held his hands up and stepped back. "I know you're pissed. I just want to apologize, all right? Abbey, your hard work hasn't gone unnoticed. The CIO was really pissed that Tim let you go. I wouldn't be surprised if they ask you to come back."

That wasn't going to happen. No way in hell. "Abbey works for me or rather *with* me now, so OSG can go fuck themselves." Luke nodded and crossed his arms in front of his chest.

Abbey nudged him with her elbow. "Stop being such a caveman for a minute, will you?"

Tom frowned and shook his head. "Looks like the rumors are true, Abbey. Walmart's looking to acquire us. With OSG's extensive retail footprint, the lucrative business accounts, and government contracts—they see a lucrative opportunity."

Luke had no idea OSG had been in play. He supposed from Walmart's perspective an acquisition made sense.

Abbey nodded. "So that means this layoff is most likely just the first with more to follow. Update your résumé and email it to me, okay?"

What? What was Abbey doing? She expected him to hire this jerk? Luke had news for his princess. Luke scoffed.

"Stop it, Luke. We'd be lucky to have Tom. You need to trust me on this one. He and I make a pretty good team, *professionally*, that is. So put your personal issues aside and do what's best for the organization." Abbey went on her tiptoes and kissed him lightly on the lips, smiling sweetly up at him.

Damn it. Luke didn't want to disappoint her, but Tom? Really? Luke trusted her. Completely. He grunted and shrugged. Fine, he'd consider Tom Murphy for his princess.

Tom had the decency to look surprised and grateful at least. "You won't regret it. I promise. I know my reputation isn't the greatest when it comes to women. That's why I was trying to so hard to win you over. I'm looking to settle down. Looking for more stability. A family too. I thought since you and I worked together so well professionally, maybe we'd work personally too."

Luke growled and Abbey elbowed him again. Abbey was *his* and no one else's. *Ever.*

"That's flattering, but I never had romantic feelings for you, Tom. I'm with the only man I've ever loved. The *right* man for me." Abbey affectionately shoved at Luke and he immediately wrapped his arms around her.

That's right, Tommy boy. She's mine.
****

September 6th—Wedding Day

Abbey stood in the en suite bathroom of the Fairchild Hotel's honeymoon suite. It was her and Luke's turn to stay here. She read the results of the pregnancy test Luke insisted she take and tossed it in the garbage.

"Abbey, come on, it's time to get dressed," Cassie called out from the bedroom. There was no time to react to the test results. She needed to get moving.

Dressed in her white silk and lace wedding lingerie, made especially for her by the Bellatonis, Abbey walked into the bedroom.

She proceeded through the bedroom to the large living room area everyone was getting ready in. They'd gotten the band back together. Angel, Vanessa, Madison, and Roxanna were busy putting the finishing touches on Cassie's, Leah's, and Karla's hair and makeup.

"Have you ladies decided what you're going to do with the diamonds in your pretty hair combs?" Luke had replaced the crystals in the bridesmaid's hair combs with genuine diamonds and had offered to reset the stones into jewelry for them. Their custom Bellatoni wine-colored strapless dresses had a beautifully sequenced lace bodice, similar to Abbey's gown.

Since Abbey had given Luke the green light at being set loose, all the crystals that had been an original part of her Bellatoni couture sleeveless gown had been replaced with diamonds as well. Since the back of Abbey's gown was open and draped in sixteen strands of diamonds from just below her neck down to her waist, she was literally dripping in diamonds.

The crystals in the entire form-fitting bodice of her gown that reached to mid-thigh were also replaced with genuine diamonds. The fluffy tulle skirt began at mid-thigh and extended to more than a chapel-length train. Her princess look was complete with a low-height diamond tiara. Abbey truly felt like a princess today.

Karla sighed. "I don't know. I can't believe Luke did this for us. I'm never taking this dress off! But I think maybe a tennis bracelet?"

"I think I might go with earrings and a pendant," Leah contemplated.

Cassie rubbed her nearly five-month pregnancy belly. Abbey thought she looked absolutely adorable. "I'm not sure, I've been looking online for settings. I do like Karla's tennis bracelet idea though."

Abbey's cell phone rang from one of the living room tables. Karla leaned over to see who it was and blushed. *It must be Tom Murphy.* Whatever was going on between the two of them, they were keeping it close to the vest.

"Put it on speaker. Roxanna, you're going to help me get into my dress," Abbey asked, ready to head to the church and Luke.

Roxanna nodded enthusiastically and held up her hands. "Just washed my hands. I'm ready."

"Hey Abbey," Tom Murphy called out from her cell phone speaker.

Abbey carefully stepped into her dress while Roxanna held it open for her. "Tom, tell me everything's set up and ready to go."

"We're all set. Everything's been tested. We can stream from the church and from Antonetti's in Barrington. Darren's at the church already. He's feeling pretty well, considering. We have his cane and his wheelchair in case he needs them."

What a relief. Darren's treatment post-surgery had been progressing well. They were all pleased with his progress to date and thrilled he felt well enough to attend the wedding. So far so good.

"Thanks so much, Tom. Luke and I really appreciate it. We'll be heading to the church soon."

"Happy to help. I'll see you soon. Looking forward to seeing you your designer gown, Karla," Tom said before ending the call.

Karla turned a deeper shade of red and everyone laughed. Roxanna hooked all the diamond strands in place and stood back.

"Wow," all the women in the room said in awe.

"Abbey, the champagne-colored bottom half of your gown really sets off the diamonds. I've never seen anything so beautiful," Cassie observed.

From what Abbey could see herself, Cassie was right. Roxanna carefully placed Abbey's diamond tiara on her head, her hands shaking slightly. Abbey knew better than to tell anyone how much what she was wearing was worth. Luke had been smart and had her dress, tiara, and engagement ring with matching wedding band insured.

Abbey stood with a smile on her face as all the women in the room snapped pictures with their cell phones. She couldn't wait to see what the professional photographer's pictures would look like.

About thirty minutes later Abbey, her bridesmaids, little Amy dressed in a matching flower girl's dress, and her father stood in front of the closed vestibule doors at Grace of God Lutheran Church. The ceremony was due to begin soon.

Her father leaned in close. "So tell me again about this resort Luke bought you?"

"What's a resort?" Amy asked.

Just then, Hannah and her assistant approached. Hannah was dressed in a lovely form-fitting, Kelly-green lace, off-the-shoulder, tea-length cocktail dress. Hannah had not only helped to organize Abbey and Luke's wedding, but she was also attending as Rocco's date. Abbey had high hopes for the Marine and event planner.

"We'll be starting in just a few minutes. Rocco mentioned something about a swanky resort Luke bought you," Hannah added.

Abbey's cheeks heated. Luke had taken being let loose to a new level. "Actually Stryker Real Estate Holdings bought it. It's called Providence St. Lucia. It's an exclusive, private, luxury boutique resort. It's so expensive to stay there that only celebrities, professional athletes, and the rich and famous can afford it. Five of its VIP suites have been permanently reserved for our families' use only. Our family and any guests we bring will get their entire stay comped, including food, alcohol, spa treatments, and excursions."

"Holy shit. Sorry, Amy. I said a bad word. Don't repeat that, all right?" Leah said, shaking her head at Amy.

"I won't, but Daddy says it sometimes," Amy

said and shrugged.

Abbey's father looked at her, uncertain. "So after you and Luke return from your two-week honeymoon, would it be all right if I brought your mother there? A second honeymoon for us?"

"There are five luxury suites. You can go whenever you want. But yes, I think it would be great if you and Mom went. Any of you. That's why Luke had the holding company buy it. We just finalized the reservation process that our family will need to use. I'll forward it to everyone when we get back." Abbey was delighted by everyone's happy expressions.

Yes, purchasing the resort had been way over the top, but it was an opportunity Abbey and her family would have never had otherwise. It would also bring in a substantial income.

Pachabel's Canon in D began to play and Hannah and her assistant opened the vestibule doors. Karla started down the aisle and Abbey felt a sense of peace and calm wash over her. There was nothing to be nervous about. She'd been waiting for this day for what felt like her entire life.

Before she knew it, the bridal march began to play and everyone inside the church stood. Her father, beaming with pride, led her slowly down the aisle to the man her heart and soul knew to be hers.

In addition to family and friends, those in attendance included Cobras team members, other professional athletes, A-list celebrities—including Brenna Sinclair—and even the handsome big bad southern Dom Kyle Asher. Abbey tried not to be intimidated by their extraordinary guest list.

Abbey's attention was fully on her big, sexy Viking groom dressed to the nines in his charcoal gray tails. She noticed joyous tears streaming down Luke's cheeks. She laughed when she saw Jake's top hat had made an encore and was currently on Rocco's head.

A teary, speechless Luke shook her father's hand and hooked their arms, leading her to Pastor Jenkins. "The men in this family sure are emotional, aren't they?" Pastor Jenkins chuckled along with the ceremony attendees. "Who gives this sparkling young women to this emotional young man?"

"My wife and I do," Abbey's father proudly called out behind her.

Abbey smiled at her emotional hunk of a Viking groom. Her heart swelled with love and joy. She took Luke's hand, lacing their fingers together, and placed their joined hands on her stomach. Luke's eye grew wide with acknowledgement.

In front of God and Luke, Abbey could now rejoice in the fact that a little life was growing inside of her. A piece of each of them, only but a tiny speck at the moment, would grow to become what Abbey knew would be an amazing person. She didn't know if Luke's conversation with their *baby makers* would end up making any difference as to the gender of their first child, but to her, that didn't matter.

The beginning of their family and their lives together started today. Abbey wasn't sure what to expect, but she couldn't wait to see what their future held. Knowing Luke, it would be one hell of an adventure.

****

Five years later—Darren's Dugout Bar and Grille ribbon cutting ceremony

Luke and Abbey's one-year-old, Evan, held on to him for dear life, facing away from the photographers trying to get that elusive shot of the youngest Stryker boy. From the start, Evan had not been a fan of getting his picture taken unless it was taken by a family member. Their youngest was shy, like Abbey had been in the beginning.

Ethan, their four-year-old, was standing a few feet away next to his Grandpa Phil hamming it up for the crowd. He happily waved and flashed the famous dimpled Stryker smile much to the delight of the press. Rocco and Hannah's dark-haired three-year-old, Rocco Junior, or RJ as the family called him, waved and smiled along with Ethan. It was cute as shit.

They couldn't have asked for a nicer day in Chicago in early September. It was an unseasonably warm eighty-two degrees and mostly sunny. The perfect day for the ribbon cutting of Darren's Dugout Bar and Grille.

Everyone around him was in a festive mood, but Luke's heart ached. Having his Uncle Darren by his side during the ribbon cutting ceremony would have made the day truly perfect. Unfortunately it wasn't mean to be.

Darren had passed away six month ago. His cancer had returned and spread quickly, ultimately taking his life. He'd survived four and a half years after his initial cancer diagnosis. At least he'd had the chance to be a grandfather to Ethan and Evan for a little while. Luke had plenty of pictures to look back on.

Sadly, Darren would never have the chance to meet his third grandchild. Abbey was due any minute from a rescheduled OB/GYN appointment. They would find out the sex of their third child today. Luke already knew it would be a girl. His little Shieldmaiden. Two boys *then* a girl. That had been the plan. They had their two little Vikings already. They were two thirds of the way there. Luke had asked Rocco to take Abbey to her appointment as a precaution.

Luke was comforted by the family, friends, and

Cobras colleagues who surrounded him as they waited to begin. Darren's Dugout Bar and Grille was a tribute to its namesake, Darren Stryker. A friendly and inviting sports bar and grill where people could come and shoot the shit about sports, preferably baseball, enjoy a drink or five, and eat delicious food from standards like burgers, wings, sandwiches, and wraps, to comfort food favorites like baked potato soup, meatloaf, and macaroni and cheese. Luke's stomach growled.

What was taking Abbey so long? What if something happened to her? Or the baby? Did Rocco get into a car accident? Luke's stomach roiled, and he shook. If something happened to Abbey or their little girl, he'd fucking lose it. His baby boy seemed to sense his unease and whimpered in his arms. He held him tighter.

Luke was about to hand Evan over to Jake, who was standing next him with Cassie, when he saw his princess's golden mane in the crowd, along with Rocco making room for her to pass. Thank God. *She's all right, calm down.*

Luke rubbed Evan's back in small circles, hoping to calm the boy down. "Look Evan, Mommy's coming."

Evan immediately stopped fussing and turned is head slightly to take a peek. "Come on, Evan, smile for us. Just once!" The press gave it a shot but his little boy wasn't giving an inch. Not yet. He'd bet all the money the restaurant earned on their opening day Abbey could coax a little smile out of Evan for the cameras.

Yeah, Evan was a bit of a mamma's boy. So what? Luke and Ethan adored her too. They were a close little family unit. Just like Luke had envisioned.

"Sorry we're late. There was an accident on the way," Rocco apologized.

"Daddy!"

Rocco smiled over at his son and went to join him and Hannah.

Evan, keeping his head turned away from the cameras, stretched out his little arms to Abbey. Abbey happily took him from Luke and held him tight. Luke kissed her as the cameras continued to shutter.

"I'm so glad you're here, baby. So, tell me what I already know. Is our little Sheildmaiden on the way?" Luke asked as he was given an oversized pair of scissors for the ribbon cutting.

Abbey said nothing for a minute then finally shrugged and nodded. "Yes, she is."

"I knew it! Hey everyone, we're having a girl," Luke shouted to the crowd. "Two boys then a girl, just like I planned it!"

The crowd cheered. He and Abbey laughed as they got ready to cut the yellow ribbon and officially open Darren's Dugout.

"Abbey can you make Evan give us a little smile this afternoon?"

"Let me see," Abbey told the press. "Sweetie, can you give everyone a cute little smile?" Evan whimpered, keeping his head turned away from the photogs. "For Mommy? One little smile? We'll smile together, how about that? Please?" Abbey kissed Evan's cheek and he sighed, about to give in.

Evan turned to the photographers with a frown on his face. "Will you smile with Mommy, Evan?" Abbey smiled brightly for the cameras and Evan, being the little stinker he was, flashed the hungry press a cocky little grin for just a few seconds and then turned away again.

Phil brought Ethan over to join their little family group. Luke laughed at his youngest, hugged Abbey tight, and held on to Ethan's hand. *This is my family. I'm so fucking lucky.*

Luke positioned the large scissor blades over the yellow ribbon being held for him. "Thank you for joining us today. I'm going to keep this short, since so much has already been said about my Uncle Darren, my second father, these last six months since his passing. I would like to dedicate Darren's Dugout not only to Darren Stryker, but to my folks and the entire Stryker family. May you all find good conversation, a delicious meal, and a great time whenever you stop by." Luke cut the ribbon to enthusiastic applause, flashing cameras, surrounded by everyone who meant the most to him.

Just then, the sun peeked through some slow passing clouds. Luke couldn't explain how he knew, but he felt and recognized the presence of his family members who were no longer with him. Tears sprang to his eyes as they communicated their love to his heart and soul. He felt the words they said that no one else could hear.

We're proud of you, Luke. We love you.

Luke closed his eyes and looked up, feeling the warmth of the sun on his face, basking in his family's love and praise. His heart and soul spoke back. *I love you, too.*

The End

www.daniavoss.com

DANIA VOSS

EVERNIGHT PUBLISHING ®

www.evernightpublishing.com

Made in the USA
Monee, IL
03 November 2021